Florence Arnold-Forster

Francis Deák - Hungarian Statesman

A Memoir

Florence Arnold-Forster

Francis Deák - Hungarian Statesman
A Memoir

ISBN/EAN: 9783337129507

Printed in Europe, USA, Canada, Australia, Japan

Cover: Foto ©Raphael Reischuk / pixelio.de

More available books at **www.hansebooks.com**

Deák Ferencz

FRANCIS DEÁK

HUNGARIAN STATESMAN

A MEMOIR

WITH A PREFACE BY

MOUNTSTUART E. GRANT DUFF, M.P.

MARCIUS. "I have done,
As you have done: that's what I can; indue'd
As you have been; that's for my country. . . ."

COMINIUS. "You shall not be
The grave of your deserving."

COR. Act i. sc. 9.

London
MACMILLAN AND CO.
1880

NOTE.

THE defects and shortcomings of the following memoir, whether regarded as an attempt to portray the character of a great man, or to describe the far-reaching historical events of the time in which he lived, are so patent as to require an apology for thus laying it before the public. Nevertheless it is hoped that, in the absence for the time of a more satisfactory biography, this memoir, superficial though it be, may serve some purpose in bringing the character and work of Francis Deák more clearly before the minds of those English readers to whom he has hitherto been little more than a name.

In M. de Mazade, France has furnished a worthy biographer of Cavour, the principal hero in the drama of Italian Unity. Would it not seem in all ways fitting, that an Englishman, equally well qualified for the task by wide knowledge and genuine sympathy with his subject, should one day present his countrymen with a complete and living portrait of the law-loving Hungarian citizen, who played so noble a part in the political regeneration,

b

not only of his own country, but of the Austro-Hungarian Monarchy ?

For most of the extracts quoted from Deák's earlier speeches, as well as for many personal incidents recorded, the writer is indebted to the interesting Memorial Address delivered by M. Csengery in 1877, translated into German by Professor Heinrich of the University of Pesth ; to the biographical sketch by Herr Rogge in the volume of ' Unsere Zeit' for 1876 ; and to the chapter on Francis Deák, in ' L'Autriche et la Prusse depuis Sadowa,' by M. de Laveleye.

PREFACE.

When I was asked to put a preface to this book, which I had read through in manuscript, my first thought was, "Why does it need a preface? It will soon find a public for itself without a recommendation from any one." On reflection, however, I came to the conclusion that authors, like other people, usually understand their own affairs best, and that it was not for me to set up my own judgment against a deliberate opinion. Nor will I attempt to deny that it gives me pleasure to connect my name with what, although it is the first work of a new writer, would, if I am not strangely misled, do great credit to many mature politicians.

The subject, too, has long had the greatest interest for me, and I have often wondered that no Englishman had ever produced for the benefit of his countrymen a biography of a man who united so many of the qualities which we most admire. It is interesting to pass in review some of the statesmen who were Deák's contemporaries, and who have also gone to their rest.

Guizot was at best a stately failure. The ultimate success of Thiers must not blind us to the fact that his career taken as a whole was an evil to his country and to mankind. Palmerston will be remembered for some time with kindness, on account of his sympathy with constitutional government upon the continent of Europe, but his name, a generation hence, will be rarely mentioned. Peel had the terrible misfortune of being born in the wrong camp, and of necessarily incurring the hatred of those amongst whom he lived by all his best deeds. Cavour had to act under circumstances which obliged him to be unscrupulous, and lived only to see the beginning of the end. Louis Napoleon verified alike in his obscurity, in his triumph, and in his fall, the words of M. de Falloux : " Il ne sait pas là différence entre rêver et penser." Thorbecke, a great capacity far too little known beyond the limits of Holland, had no striking or dramatic, though much useful work, to do. Cobden would have been in all probability one of the greatest statesmen of his time, if he had been born in the year in which he died, for he was emphatically one of the singular few of whom it may be said "that they are worthy of a better age," while his friends may comfort themselves with the reflection that "if this was not his century, at least a great many others will be."

All of these had far wider fields of action : most of them had more brilliant abilities and wider knowledge, several of them as strong a character ; but of which of them can we say that his life was so grandly and absolutely victorious ? " Qu'est-ce qu'une grande vie ? " asked Alfred de Vigny. " Une pensée de la jeunesse réalisée par l'âge mûr."

Even in these days in which our lot has been cast, so full of picturesque and striking historical scenes, it would be difficult to mention many as picturesque and striking as that which was witnessed when the Empress of Austria went to lay her wreath on the bier of the man who had fought the battle of his country against the whole might of the Hapsburgs, so steadfastly, so wisely, and with such utter success.

Of all Englishmen, he whom Deák most resembled was probably the great Buckinghamshire squire who received his death-wound upon Chalgrove Field. We may be perfectly certain that in the correspondence of the Austrian Court party, all through the years of struggle, he was again and again described almost in the very words which Clarendon applied to Hampden : " He was indeed a very wise man and of great parts, and possessed with the most absolute spirit of popularity, and the most absolute faculties to govern the people, of any man I ever knew. For the first year of the Parliament he seemed rather to moderate and soften the violent and distempered humours than to inflame them. But wise and dispassioned men plainly discerned that that moderation proceeded from prudence, and observation that the season was not ripe, rather than that he approved of the moderation." In a word, what was said of Cinna might well be applied to him: "He had a head to contrive and a tongue to persuade, and a hand to execute any mischief."

But Deák was a Hampden, born in a happier hour, in an hour when knots could be unravelled which in the seventeenth century could only be cut. "Felix opportunitate mortis," Hampden is probably a greater and more generally revered name to his countrymen than he could possibly have been if he had lived through the war. Lammenais once said: "There is something wanting to the noblest life that does not end either on the battle-field, in the dungeon, or on the scaffold." That of course was an extravagant phrase, and was used indeed under circumstances of great excitement; still there can be no doubt that martyrdom gilds all greatness.

> " Heaven must be hung with pictures of the dead !
>   The shroud must robe the saint !
> Never one halo round a living head
>   Did Raphael dare to paint."

Rare, very rare is it in human history for purely civic and perfectly prosperous greatness to attain the aureole of romance which surrounds, in the memory and imagination of his countrymen, the name of the man who forms the subject of this book. The mere fact that a private citizen who never possessed rank or title of any sort, and who died quietly in his bed, should have been buried in a grave dug out of earth brought from each of the fifty-two counties into which his native land is divided, is almost enough to put him in a class by himself. And yet, although their ends were so different, the reader of these pages will be again and again reminded of the stately inscription put up a few years ago upon the cross which marks the Ship Money field, amongst the beech-woods of the Chilterns :—

> " For these lands in Stoke Mandeville
> John Hampden
> was assessed in Twenty shillings
> Ship Money
> Levied by command of the King,
> without authority of Law,
> The 4th of August 1635.
> By resisting this claim of the King
> in Legal Strife,
> He upheld the right of the People
> Under the Law :
> And became entitled
> To grateful remembrance.
> His work on earth ended
> After the conflict on Chalgrove Field
> The 18th of June 1643
> And he rests in Great Hampden Church."

It is good to read the history of such men at all times, but never perhaps more than now, when

a school has arisen and attained to no small measure of political power which pooh-poohs the idea
that morality has anything to do with politics, or
that there is any other test of statesmanship than
obvious and immediate success.

M. E. GRANT DUFF.

YORK HOUSE, TWICKENHAM,
January 1880.

CONTENTS.

PART II.—REVOLUTION.

CHAPTER X.

CHAPTER XI.

CHAPTER XII.

PART III.—REACTION.

CHAPTER XV.

CHAPTER XVI.

PART IV.—REVIVAL.

CHAPTER XVII.

CHAPTER XVIII.

CHAPTER XIX.

CHAPTER XX.

CHAPTER XXIII.

CHAPTER XXIV.

CHAPTER XXV.

CHAPTER XXVI.

CHAPTER XXVII.

PART IV.—RESTORATION.

CHAPTER XXX.

CHAPTER XXXI.

CHAPTER XXXII.

CHAPTER XXXIII.

CHAPTER XXXIV.

CHAPTER XXXV.

FRANCIS DEÁK.

PART I.—REFORMATION.

CHAPTER I.

Deák's claim on the interest and respect of his own countrymen and
of foreigners—Entry on public life—State of Hungary since the
Peace of 1815—Széchényi.

In the month of January 1876 a thrill of passing
interest was excited in the news-reading public of
Europe by the announcement of the death of
Francis Deák, a Hungarian, whose name, though
perhaps less widely known abroad than that of his
famous compatriot Louis Kossuth, yet seemed to
evoke in his own country the strongest feelings of
gratitude and veneration. The funeral of this simple
citizen of Pesth was like that of some European
sovereign. In the long procession that followed
the body to its last resting-place, in the dense crowds
that lined the streets of the Hungarian capital, were
representatives of every rank, every opinion, every
nationality in the monarchy, from the ancient dynasty
of the Hapsburgs to the most advanced Radical
constituency in Hungary, from the fiercely Magyar

watched with genuine sorrow, and the names of the
Hungarian patriots who fought and suffered in the
cause of national liberty were household words in
this country.

But the war of 1849 had been preceded by the
bloodless revolution culminating in 1847–48; a fact
less noteworthy in the eyes of foreign nations, but
of equal and indeed of more lasting importance in
the history of Hungary, as was shown by subsequent
events. Amongst the men whose labours contributed in the first place to make that revolution
possible, and in later years to make it bear good
fruit, none deserves more heartfelt gratitude from
his compatriots, a more cordial tribute of respect
from foreign observers, than Francis Deák.

Born at Kehida, in the county of Zala, in
October 1803, Deák belonged to an old Hungarian
family which could reckon amongst its ancestors
Verboczy, the celebrated jurist of the 16th century,
and author of the Corpus Juris of Hungary.

Young Francis Deák was educated at Comorn,
and at the University of Raab, where he graduated
in law and jurisprudence, and made his first essay
as an advocate ; but as with many of his compatriots
at that time, the fascination of politics soon over-
powered all other interests, and the keen intellect
and lucid, convincing speech of the young lawyer
were more frequently exercised in the debates of the
Congregations in the County Assembly of Zala

than in the courts of justice.   In 1833 Anton, Deák's elder brother, was forced by ill-health to resign the office of deputy for his native county.   On bidding farewell to his friends at Presburg, he assured them that he would send in his stead a young man 'who has more stuff in his little finger than I have in my whole body.'

In the same year Francis Deák was returned for the county of Zala, and took his seat in the Diet of Presburg, where he soon began to take a prominent part in the debates of the Lower House.

Any one who were to form a conception of the National Assembly of constitutional Hungary in 1833 from an acquaintance with the Parliament of constitutional England, would have a very erroneous idea of the appearance of the Diet at Presburg in the days when Deák made his first entry on political life ; for the scene presented by the meeting of the national representatives of Hungary was far enough removed in outward appearance from the grave, influential, and decorous assemblage, where in England, at the same date, two well-organised parliamentary parties were soberly discussing the political and social questions of the day.

In considering that latest and most elaborate development of parliamentary government which under the name of the ' Ausgleich ' (Compromise) is now principally associated with Deák's name, it is difficult to realise the quaint and almost archaic character of the institutions and customs prevailing in Hungary when the young deputy first took his seat amongst the legislators of his country.

And yet even at this time, even in the Diet of 1832–36, with its apparent aimlessness, its absence of all party organisation, its shrinking from reform, its sudden panic excited by the French revolution of July, its limpet-like adhesion to the ancient forms of the Corpus Juris, there was not wanting the germ of that healthy political vitality which was destined in after-years to shoot up into a plant worthy of the soil that produced it.

During the Napoleonic wars, the Hungarians had been fully occupied in fighting the battles of the Empire; for their loyal co-operation they had more than once received imperial thanks, and the tribute had been paid to their Constitution of summoning the Diet whenever fresh supplies of men and money were urgently needed by Francis II. and his allies. Should the deputies be so ill-judging as to take advantage of these occasions for demanding the redress of national grievances and the fulfilment of royal promises, they were speedily dismissed with reprimands or blandishments as seemed most advisable, and care was taken that no specially pertinacious deputy should be returned a second time to impede the Diet in the exercise of its true function,—that of providing supplies to meet the requirements of the imperial policy. The faint

glowworm light of modern ideas which had been
visible in Hungary at the close of the eighteenth
century seemed to have died out during the long
struggle which absorbed into a military channel all
the ardour of the Magyar nation. The Peace of
Vienna left Hungary bankrupt and exhausted, and
with her freedom more closely curtailed than before
the outbreak of that last campaign, which had been
fought,—according to the generous declaration of the
allied princes,—' to assert the liberties of the people.'

But the sturdy refusal of the County Assemblies
of Hungary to carry out the arbitrary ordinances
of the Austrian emperor, the unwearied efforts of
Magyar poets and writers to preserve the national
language, had succeeded in keeping alive those
ideas of freedom and independence which had lain
so long dormant.

In 1825, Francis I. once more summoned the
Hungarian Diet, disavowed the unconstitutional
acts of his officials, and assured the Estates of his
earnest desire to rule henceforth according to law
and usage. The Diet only sat for two years, and
few practical measures were enacted in it ; but none
the less it marked the opening of a new era of
internal activity in Hungary, and showed the intention of the Magyars to assume once again their
distinct national existence.

If for no other reason, moreover, the Diet of
1825 deserves to be remembered as being the

occasion of the first appearance upon the political stage of Count Stephen Széchényi, the great Radical magnate, who boldly carried the cry of reform into the camp of the Hungarian aristocracy, and dared to challenge the Conservative nobles of his country, not only to reform the Government, but actually to reform themselves, the hereditary champions of the Constitution.

Count Széchényi was rather a social than a political reformer, and his vigorous writings, which created such a flutter of excitement amongst the landowners of Hungary, were concerned chiefly with the abuses which, in his eyes, hindered the material prosperity of his country. With all his fiery energy of demolition, Széchényi, a thorough aristocrat of the old school, had in him a strain of the benevolent despot, and was somewhat disposed to force improvement and progress upon his countrymen at the point of the bayonet; it was perhaps this belief in the salutary influence of unquestioned authority which inclined him, under all circumstances, to keep on good terms with the Vienna Government, and endeavour to carry out his reforming projects for the people, but not through the people; indeed, he was at no pains to conceal that, ardently as he loved his country, he had the meanest opinion of the intellectual capacity of the mass of his countrymen to decide upon national questions of 'high politics.'   It was this

tendency which in late years led to an estrangement
between the modern Liberals of the type of Deák
and Baron Joseph Eötvös, and the brilliant magnate,
the 'great Hungarian' par excellence, whose self-
sacrificing patriotism and noble character have
justly endeared him to all parties amongst his
countrymen.

With the reassembling of the Diet in 1825 a ray
of light had seemed to shine upon the gloom and
stagnation in which Hungary had been lying for
the past ten years ; but at the same time, the light
revealed a state of things social and political which
might well make the most stout-hearted patriot
despondent. The anxious desires awakened for
the introduction of a new and freer order of things,
for a more clearly realised national life, only served
to bring clearly home to the minds of some, the de-
pressing and backward condition of their country.
The combined weight of absolute power abroad
and feudal institutions at home, seemed as though
it must crush all life out of the newly apparent
aspirations after freedom and progress.

Kölcsey, the favourite poet and author of this
period, after exhorting his countrymen to achieve
what their ancestors had left undone, and reminding
them that 'not in vain did the brave nations of
the world cling to their traditions, and hold in deep
reverence the histories of their past,' had withdrawn
from the Diet of 1832 in profound despondency.

Deák himself was not of a sanguine temperament, and he felt painfully the backward and chaotic state into which his country had fallen—the country that at one time had held a foremost place amongst European states.

Some of his speeches in the Diet at this period are as melancholy as Hungarian music. 'The feeling of patriotism is not kept alive in a Hungarian to the same degree as it is in the men of other nations, either by the inspiring memories of the past, or by a sentiment of vanity and self-esteem. The free citizens of powerful Rome or of free Greece, could draw inspiration from the annals of their native country; they were proud in the consciousness of the greatness and glory of their nation, and each felt his own country to be of all others the best and the most favoured. In like manner, Frenchmen and Englishmen can look back with enthusiasm to their past history, and they too can feel that no country in Europe can boast such stability as theirs. Amidst the ruins of his shattered freedom, the ardent spirit of the Italian still kindles with the glowing memories of a famous antiquity; the Russian finds something sublime at least in the physical greatness of his country. But the Hungarian cannot share in such feelings as these.

'Our history can look back to nothing but disastrous civil wars, and bloody struggles for the preservation of our very existence; it can offer but few examples of the pure-minded noble citizen, few brilliant pages which can make our hearts swell with a glow of proud self-consciousness.

'Nor have we the consolations of vanity. Europe is hardly aware of our existence, and there are, it may be, many colonies in Africa better known to other nations than is our Fatherland, which is looked upon abroad as a fertile but un-cultivated province of Austria. Our present con-dition is not brilliant, nor even of such material prosperity as to enable us on this ground to rival other nations. Our future is in God's hands; but to say the truth, he must be a determined optimist who can believe that it has any very bright prospect in store, though we must needs hope for some improvement on the present.'

Desponding Deák certainly was, but not weakly despairing. In the course of the same speech he adds: 'There exists in the heart of every man a pure and ardent feeling which, quite independent of all these outward helps, binds him closely to his Fatherland, and I hold him for no brave man, no true Magyar, to whom this poor suffering country is not dearer than the most brilliant empire in Europe.'

In this spirit Deák plunged vigorously into the complex politics of the time, determined to do all that in him lay towards re-building and establishing the fabric of national life upon a broad and lasting foundation.

CHAPTER II.

SELDOM has a country set to work more zealously to reform itself than did Hungary, as represented by the Opposition party in the national legislature and in the country.

At this time parties might be described broadly as consisting not so much of Liberals and Conservatives as of Government and Opposition. The object of the former was to keep the country in as good humour as was compatible with the scrupulous maintenance of the state of things social and political, sanctioned by royal and diplomatic authority at the Peace of Vienna.

The object of the latter party—which included men who developed subsequently all shades of political opinion—was to resist the encroachments and unconstitutional practices of the Government, and to carry their country a step farther along the path of civilisation and progress, in which England, France, and even Germany, had outstripped them.

In thus entering on a campaign at once defensive

and offensive, the Hungarian Opposition were undertaking a task that required no small amount of courage, patience, and tactical ability.

The course of a contested bill through the English Houses of Parliament is plain sailing indeed compared with the stormy passage that awaited a reform measure in Hungary between its first incorporation in the 'Mandate' delivered by the County Assemblies to their deputies, and its final appearance in the tranquil haven of the Statute Book—that august volume a copy of which was always to be found on a table in the magnates' club at Pesth, open to the daily perusal of the law-loving Hungarian citizens, who felt for the Corpus Juris something of the same veneration as for the mystic circlet of the Crown of St. Stephen itself.

The usual form in which a measure came before the Diet was either as a Royal Proposition presented 'with becoming pomp' to the assembled Estates for discussion in the two Houses, or as one of the 'Gravamina,' brought forward by the Estates in opposition to the royal demands.

Having decided on the subject of their first consideration—and this in itself was a matter for grave deliberation—the two Houses, or 'Tables,' began the debate in good earnest.

In the Diet of 1833 the Lower House, consisting of the deputies from the fifty-five counties, some of the lower clergy, and the town deputies (who, however, had no vote), was, if not quite unanimous in its advocacy of reform, at least quite unanimous in its opposition to the Government.

But even supposing a measure to have succeeded in uniting in its support the various fractions of the Opposition, and to have passed triumphantly through the Lower House, it had to encounter more stubborn resistance in the Upper, where the magnates, acting on the principle that a state of society which was satisfactory to them could be in no need of reform, preferred to support a Government that, whatever might be its shortcomings from a national point of view, had at least the merit of being identified with the existing *régime*, and of showing small inclination to launch out into so-called 'reforms,' founded on mere sentiment and theoretical notions of justice.

Even if a majority of the magnates were won over to the popular side—and thanks to the brilliant eloquence of the great Count Széchényi this was sometimes the case—the king could still exercise the royal veto and refuse his assent to the proposal accepted by the two Houses ; a drag quite sufficiently powerful to prevent the wheels of the car of Progress from running too fast.   On this would follow resolutions, representations, negotiations innumerable, interspersed with more debates and sessions, 'mixed' or 'separate,' of the two Houses ; but in the end, the proposed reform usually found itself relegated for further discussion to the next Diet, or so greatly modified as to make but slight improvement in the actual condition of the people. This was the fate of the Urbarial Law, the first grand attempt that had been made since the time of Leopold II. to raise the non-noble class of the community from that state of social and political degradation in which they had been allowed to remain ever since the days when serfdom appeared the natural position for all who were not warriors and therefore 'nobles' in the old feudal sense of the term. 'In Hungary the nobility = 1000; the people = 0,' writes an impartial but by no means unfriendly German observer passing through Hungary five-and-thirty years ago.[1] Ask the ordinary English traveller in the country during the first quarter of this century his impression of Hungary and its people, he will speak not of ancient institutions and widespread political activity, but of the vast possessions and feudal state of the great magnates, the complete personal subjection, closely resembling serfage, of the mass of the peasantry.

It was not the fault of the nobles themselves that this stigma was not earlier removed from their country.

'It would be vain in me to attempt hiding my grief at our present discomfiture,' said Kölcsey; 'but it ministers on the other hand to my no small gratification to know that the reproach which hung

---

[1] Kohl.

for centuries on the nobles is from this day attached to the Government.   I will proclaim that in the year 1834 the Hungarian legislature tried to open a way for the emancipation of the people, and that this was opposed by the Government.'[1]

In the Diet and out of it, the subject excited eager interest, though there was wide divergence of opinion even amongst the Opposition as to the nature and extent of the reforms needed, and already the symptoms were visible of a split in the Opposition phalanx.

Both from national and from philanthropic motives, Deák threw himself heartily into the whole question of the Urbarium,[2] declaring that every minute that was allowed to pass without speaking out the salutary truth was so much time lost to the country, and that in asking that the protection of the law might be extended to the person and goods of the peasant, the reform party were not craving a boon or begging a favour, but simply demanding an act

---

[1] See Szabad, *Hungary Past and Present.*

[2] The 'Urbarium' was the name given to the Statute issued by Maria Theresa in 1764, for the mitigation of the feudal institutions of Hungary. It contained the following provisions : 1. The serf was allowed to leave his master if dissatisfied with his condition. 2. The labour to be done by the serfs was fixed with due regard to the extent of their tenures. 3. The children of peasants were declared competent to fill the public offices of teachers, etc. In the Diet of 1790, this Royal Statute was provisionally recognised as a law, and since that time all the laws of the Diet of 1832–36, bearing on the relations of landlord and peasant, were called 'urbarial' laws, and each separate enactment an 'urbarium.

of justice, which could not be withheld without a violation of the rights of humanity.

We have said that the general tendency at this time was in favour of progress and reform, but the Liberalism of many of the Opposition was of so very faint a tinge, and would have been content with the extension to the tax-paying (i.e. the non-noble) class of the community, of so small a modicum of political and even social enfranchisement, that Deák's eloquent attempt in the Diet to place the matter upon broader grounds, and prove that the safety of the Constitution did not depend on the limitation of its benefits to a privileged class, was by no means the forcing of an open door.

That the picture he drew of the peasantry in Hungary, who were excluded from all share in the possession of the soil and from the enjoyment of all civic rights, was not over-coloured, will be acknowledged on simple reference to the laws in force at that period. In allusion to the practice of billeting the troops upon the peasants, Deák declared, ' The wild beast has its den, and the bird its nest, from which they have the power to keep off all intruders ; but the Hungarian tax-payer is not even master over that which is most exclusively his own—he is not free to do as he likes in his own house ; for the State, whose whole burden falls on his shoulders, does not leave even the peace of his home undisturbed, but foists upon him guests whose presence he is compelled to tolerate, who are frequently aliens from foreign lands, and who are not even connected with him by the bond of a common tongue and the love of a common country.'

In speaking of the resistance offered to the proposal that the peasants should be allowed to possess land in their own right, he says, 'We have felt most deeply the injustice of this exclusion, and have said, " Let us grant to the people the right of property, and thereby draw them closer to us, and attach them with a bond of affection to that Father-land which has been in great measure both supported and defended by them ; let us allow the people to hold land of their own."   " No," answered the majority, "for—'omnis terrae proprietas ad dominum spectat'—property is sacred and inviolable." " True," we replied, " we are willing to grant that the people must obtain property from the lord of the soil, 'ad quem omnis terrae proprietas spectat,' by means of voluntary sale."   "Heaven forefend !" exclaimed our opponents ; "such an idea is contrary to the Constitution ! "

'Thus limited in our scope, we finally prayed that the people might at least be absolved from giving compulsory labour, and might employ for their own and the country's profit the time which is now wasted in bad work grudgingly rendered to their landlords. To this it was answered, " We will consider that question another time, for it also affects

the Constitution."   And now we have come to the
very last clause of our humble petition, so much of
which has been refused.   We have now but one
request to make, and that is, that the bodily sus-
tenance of the people may be cared for ; that they
who bear on their shoulders the burdens of the
whole nation should not have the very bread taken
out of their mouths.   This can hardly be refused ;
this surely is not "contrary to the Constitution."
That would indeed be a merciful Constitution which
should forbid us to take thought for the maintenance
of some millions of our most useful fellow-citizens !
That would indeed be an unhappy country whose
institutions should require us to deprive of the very
means of existence those to whom all rights have
already been denied ; to rob of their support those
whose sole privilege consists in the permission to
eke out a livelihood on the soil of their native
country, whose burdens they bear, though they are
forbidden to share in its possession !

' I wish to see the injustice which has gone on
during the eight hundred years of our constitutional
existence atoned for.   I wish it in the interest of our
country, for political welfare can never be universal,
the full development of the nation can never be
achieved, so long as personal security is only a
privilege—a privilege, moreover, enjoyed exclusively by the minority.'

On hearing it constantly asserted that in Hungary

all property in land belongs of right to the lord of the soil, Deák declared that the countless divinities of Greece displayed far greater modesty in their pretensions than the noble proprietors of Hungary, for the former claimed but a share in the ownership of wood, fields, and waters, whereas the Hungarian noble was absolute lord over all. The final result of the long debates over the Urbarial Laws was but small as regards the actual addition made to the Corpus Juris. The measure that at last received the royal sanction bore evident traces of that careful regard for the Constitution which had induced the Government and their allies in the Upper House to suppress any reform that looked like too serious an innovation upon the Constitutional rights of the privileged class.

The Robot, or forced labour, was modified, but not abolished; the nobles gave up their right of summary jurisdiction, and of inflicting corporal punishment; but the clauses establishing for the peasant absolute security of property and person, and the abolition of the 'Jus Avicitatis,'[1] were rejected. The non-noble class was relieved from the charge of defraying the expenses incidental to the meeting of the Diet, but most of their other burdens, feudal dues and ecclesiastical tithes,

---

[1] A law by which landed property belonging to a noble might be reclaimed by its original proprietor, even should it have passed by sale into other hands.

were left unlightened, and the great gulf between
the tax-paying people and the nobles was not
filled up.

There was, perhaps, no department of public life
in which Deák rendered better service to his
country at this time than in that of legal reform,
and there was none in which from natural disposition and ability he took a keener interest. His
great legal knowledge and acquainance with the
judicial systems of foreign nations found worthy
employment in the compilation of a civil code
drawn up by a parliamentary commission under his
supervision.   But it fared as ill with the legal
reforms proposed as with those concerning the
emancipation of the peasantry, religious liberty,
freedom of the press, and public instruction. With
reference to this last subject, when the Government
for the fifteenth time evaded the proposition of the
Diet for the complete reorganisation and reform of
public instruction throughout the country, Francis
Deák, usually pre-eminent for the moderation of his
language amongst his fiery colleagues, waxed
ominously indignant, and almost menacing, in his
condemnation of the Government policy.

'In more than one heart,' he exclaimed, 'will
spring up the bitter thought, that the Austrian
Government, dreading the prosperity of Hungary,
is striving henceforth to check its onward progress.

An ill-fated policy, a false and miserable calculation ! for could there possibly be a more false calculation than thus to inspire us with bitter sentiments at the moment when the Diet is about to dissolve, so that we may instil into our constituents these same sentiments which three years hence will again animate the representatives of the country.

'There is no need to be a prophet to foretell that the policy of the Government, far more than any Polytechnic Institutions, will encourage the development of our national faculties. I am of opinion that the representation to the King should be repeated, but I counsel the nation to trust only to itself.'[1]

After having promised much, and allowed copious discussion, the Government in the end, when the requisite supplies had been voted, refused to sanction the various reforms proposed, and dismissed the Diet.

'We should have liked to obtain more concessions, to extort more guarantees,' says Deák in his address to his electors, 'but the combined strength of many separate interests has prevented the success of our cause.' Yet it was no small triumph for the Liberal party in the Opposition of 1836 to have made this short step forward in an aristocratic country like Hungary, dominated by the over-

---

[1] 'De l'Esprit public en Hongrie,' De Gérando, p. 193.

shadowing influence of the most august despotism in Europe.

The people, who had so often maintained the doctrine of national independence by force of arms, were now prepared to carry on the struggle for constitutional freedom in a manner better suited to modern ideas, and the Imperial Government at Vienna soon discovered to its cost that the Hungarians were quite as well qualified to fight their country's battles in a political as in a military campaign.   The legal resistance of a Deák was in its way almost as inconvenient as the armed rebellion of a Bocksai or a Rákoczy.

CHAPTER III.

Deák's position in the party—A Conservative Reformer—Belief in law the keynote of his policy now and in the future—Spread of Liberal ideas through the country—Kossuth and Wesselényi—State prosecutions—Election of John Balogh.

THE unsatisfactory termination of the Diet in 1836 was succeeded by a ferment of discontent and agitation throughout the country, in the midst of which the gradual formation of political parties took a more definite shape. The experience of the past three years had fully justified the words of brotherly admiration with which Anton Deák had recommended the young deputy for Zala to his future colleagues at Presburg, and it was evident that in any new combination of parties Francis Deák would hold a prominent place.

In later years, in describing his first entrance into the Diet, Deák would draw a humorous picture of the embarrassing side to the reputation that had preceded him.

' I came to Presburg,' he would say, ' as a young man of nine-and-twenty, where I found that my late brother Anton, in his exceeding kindness and affection, had spread the most wonderful reports of my supposed intelligence amongst my fellow-deputies. The result was that members were perpetually tormenting me with the strangest and most miscellaneous questions, in order to hear my "wisdom." Even late at night, at the club and in the billiard-room, they pursued me with their questions. So I started the plan of putting them off with telling anecdotes instead ; and this is how,' Deák would explain, ' I have contracted the bad habit of telling anecdotes when I am not being asked questions.'

His way of living at this time was of the same simple, unostentatious character which he maintained to the day of his death. During the session of the Diet, he lodged at an hotel with his friends Edmond Beöthy and Gabriel Klauzal. He would rise at five, walk for three hours, and about nine o'clock go down to assist at the sittings of the Diet. The afternoon was devoted to reading and study, and in the evening he was accustomed to meet his friends and acquaintance over a game of billiards or cards at the Casino.

Such were the simple habits and surroundings of the young politician who was destined to become by the force of circumstance, and as it were in spite of himself, the leader and champion of his country, the chief representative of Hungary in the eyes of Europe.

The position deliberately taken up by Deák at the

outset of his political career, and consistently maintained throughout, was not an easy one.   Believing with Burke 'that a State without the means of some change is without the means of its conservation,' Deák was a 'conservative reformer';—a reformer as regards the internal social and political relations of his country; conservative as regards the connection of its present with its past history, and its relations with the Austrian Empire.   He formed in those days the nucleus of that party in Hungary which, according to modern parlance, might be described as the Left Centre, and which in the time of our own great parliamentary revolution was represented by statesmen of the type of Somers.

Fully as Deák acknowledged the value of Count Széchényi's services in the last Diet, he could not sympathise with the 'great Hungarian' in his desire to make a clean sweep of all the ancient institutions—including the Corpus Juris—and start the State upon an entirely new basis; for, with an Englishman's love of justice and independence, Deák had also an Englishman's regard for precedent, and fond clinging to all that was connected with an historic past.

He had perhaps still less in common with the old Hungarian Conservatives in the Opposition, who met every proposal for domestic reform with the cry of 'the Constitution in danger,' and by so doing played into the hands of the absolutist Government they opposed.

Royalist and patriot as he was, the watchword of Deák's life was neither king nor country, but law; *Law* in the sense used by the imperial philosopher when he affirms that 'nothing can harm the State which does not harm law, and that what does not harm law, does not harm either State or citizen.'

He believed that in demanding from high and low in the smallest matters of every-day life, as well as in great concerns of State politics, a strict observance of the law, he was most effectually serving both king and country. He recognised clearly that it was this principle, the real kernel of the Hungarian Constitution, which had caused it to remain for centuries a living reality, and had been the very salt of the nation, preserving it from the fate that had overtaken other States no less famous in their day than the Kingdom of Hungary.

From the beginning of his public career to the end, the motive of his actions was invariably to be found in this deeply rooted reverence for law,—using the word in its widest sense as expressing absolute justice, and as defining the right relations of man to man, and of class to class; law, as comprising the body of well-weighed opinion arrived at by the highest wisdom, ratified by the common acknow-ledgment of rulers and people, and equally binding upon all the constituent parts of the State.

In Deák's view no circumstance whatsoever
could absolve either king or people from the duty
of rendering strict obedience to the law.   The king
might be tempted by the consciousness of power
into arbitrary acts, the people might see itself
compelled by force, or incited by revolutionary
passion, into a violation of the original compact ;
but the duty incumbent upon both king and people
remained the same, and each party was entitled to
demand its due fulfilment by the other, not as a
boon, but as a right.   Deák believed that it was in
a faithful adherence to the Constitution thus understood that the strength of Hungary consisted, and
the events of later years showed that he had not
miscalculated.

It was in obedience to these principles that Deák
strove earnestly in 1834 to insure precedence for
the debate on the Gravamina, or national grievances,
before that on the Royal Propositions, however
satisfactory the new measures proposed in them ;
it was the same motive that prompted him in 1861
to refuse for his country the new Constitution
' octroyé ' at Vienna, as a compensation for the
unredressed wrongs of Hungary.

' Not only a violation of the rights of the nation
as a whole,' said Deák, ' but also any infringement
of the rights of individual citizens, magistrates, or
associations, is a matter of common concern, for
such an infringement is a violation of law and liberty,

and law and liberty are the common property of
the nation. Law imposes limits upon force, and
it is in the strength of law that the citizens of a
country seek protection against arbitrary power.
But law itself, with all the strength for resistance
which it bestows, is only secured against arbitrary
violence by the moral strength of the nation ; and
if a nation from lack of this moral strength is unable
to maintain unimpaired the inviolability of its laws,
and enforce respect for them, its independence is
at the mercy of any unforeseen event, and no
creation of new laws will ever avail to preserve
it from utter destruction. If a nation raises no
protest against the violation of its laws, but with
silent acquiescence creates each time a new provision in place of the one which has been set at
nought, it contributes of itself to impair the respect
due to its laws, for its silence seems to imply that
it approves of what has been done, or at least
condones it, on the ground of the ambiguity of the
law. If those in authority have been permitted
to transgress the law without any protest from the
nation, who will venture to remind the Government
of their past misdeeds, and invite them to return to
the path of justice, from which they have erred ?

' Moreover, a solemn and dignified protest raised
in vindication of a disregarded law honours the
sovereign more than a cowardly silence ; the one
shows a manly confidence in his sense of justice,

the other a timorous disbelief in it. The nation which submits in cowardly silence to the violation of its laws would be also capable of a cowardly desertion of its sovereign in the hour of danger. Princes themselves have no cause to delight in such a people, for never do fear and confidence, loyalty and cowardice, exist side by side in the same nation.'

Notwithstanding the small practical outcome of the Diet that closed in 1836, it was obvious that a powerful impetus had been given to the Liberalism of the country; that modern Hungary was beginning to feel ill at ease within the too narrow limits of the old Constitution; and that a spirit of insubordination was rising against the rule of the Vienna Government, even when administered through the medium of the docile Hungarian Ministry at Presburg.

No one recognised the danger more clearly than the imperial ministers themselves. They perceived that the influence of civil speeches and fair promises from royal and arch-ducal lips was beginning to wane before the growing might of that mysterious and unconstitutional power, 'public opinion'—the Democracy, as the dreaded spectre was usually designated in awe-struck terms by the frightened magnates.

The brilliant weekly reports written by Louis Kossuth,—ostensibly for the information of those absent magnates,[1] who in accordance with the prevailing custom had appointed the clever young advocate as their silent proxy and private reporter at the sittings of the Diet,—were secretly lithographed and circulated throughout the country, where they found thousands of eager readers.

The Government saw that the thin end of the wedge was thus being introduced which would lead finally to the admittance of the outside public into the sacred mysteries of legislation. The right of freedom of speech, too, was beginning to be understood in a more extended sense than the most tolerant of despotisms could endure, and it was felt that strong measures must be resorted to.

Louis Kossuth, Baron Wesselényi (the 'giant of Transylvania'), and several of the younger members of the Liberal party were accused of high treason, and condemned to various terms of imprisonment, on no other ground than their free expression of Liberal opinions, and the attempt on the part of Kossuth in Hungary, and Wesselényi in Transylvania, to publish lithographed reports of the discussions in the County Assemblies as they had done of those in the Diet. John Balogh, deputy for the county of Bar, who had indulged in too vigorous a remonstrance in the Lower House

---

[1] Kossuth's first appearance in the Diet at Presburg was as the deputy of a magnate's widow, entitled by her rank to be thus represented in the legislature.

against these illegal proceedings, was prosecuted by the Government, who, relying on their firm hold over the peasant nobles in the county, looked forward confidently to replacing the obnoxious deputy (now unseated in consequence of the prosecution) by the ministerial candidate. To make matters quite safe, the 'Comes,'[1] or lord lieutenant of the county, had received instructions to present the electors with five florins apiece beforehand, as a polite indication by the Government of what was expected of them. But the court party had not reckoned on the extent to which the new leaven had penetrated even to the lowest substratum of the Constitution.

The experience of the Comes, Count Keglevich, was as novel as it was disagreeable.

Urged by the Government, he had done all that man could do to insure the return of the desired candidate. The salt depôts had been thrown open, that the electors might help themselves to as much as they could carry away, and money had been lavished with unstinting liberality. But all proved

---

[1] The fifty-two provinces, or circles, into which Hungary has been from time immemorial divided, are called Comitates or Counties ; over each is placed a ' Comes '—a Magnate of the Empire, usually appointed by the Crown, like our lord lieutenant, but in some cases holding the office by hereditary right. The Comes is assisted in the administration of the county by two deputies or Vice Comes, under whom are many subordinate officers, elected by the ' nobles ' of the province at the triennial ' Restorations,' the exciting municipal elections of Hungary.

useless, or rather worse than useless. The re-
doubtable John Balogh was re-elected by a large
majority; and not content with displaying their
superabundant enthusiasm by carrying the favoured
candidate in triumph on their shoulders, the peasant
nobles swarmed into the Assembly Hall, their five-
florin notes stuck at the end of their staves, over-
whelmed the astonished 'Comes' with reproaches,
and compelled him by main force to remain in his
seat for four mortal hours, whilst the chief county
officials, judges, notaries, and, in short, the whole
body of electors, upbraided him in no measured
terms for his treacherous and unpatriotic conduct.

After this highly unsuccessful attempt at coercion,
the Government thought it prudent to drop the prosecution of John Balogh.

CHAPTER IV.

THE Government soon found that the close of the
Diet brought no cessation of activity on the part of
the Liberal leaders, the only difference being, that
the discussion of 'burning questions' was now
carried on with unabated energy in fifty small Diets
instead of in one.

Of all the venerable institutions of Hungary, none
is more interesting or more unique than this of the
County Assemblies or Congregations—with their
Comes and Vice-comes, their 'restorations,' their
exciting municipal and political elections, and
their animated public discussions ; miniature parliaments, exercising each in its own province a jurisdiction so complete as to render the counties virtually
independent, not only of an arbitrary Government,
but even of the National Legislature, whose decrees
were calmly ignored if they ran counter to local
opinion as represented in the County Assembly of
a province.

It was this local organisation which had from time immemorial played an important part in keeping alive the innate love of the Hungarians for political independence and self-government, under the most adverse circumstances.

The County Assembly in Hungary was no artificial organisation, laboriously devised by official authorities, and pressed upon an indifferent people for their good, like the elaborate system of local government which Catherine II. had in vain offered to the Russian nobles with the wise object of mitigating the evils of a centralised bureaucracy ; it was no 'caucus' of self-constituted officials, managing the political concerns of a population too careless or too ignorant to assert themselves, except on occasions of great national crisis ; but the effectual, if somewhat imperfect, system, which enabled the Hungarian gentry to bring their keen political faculties to bear upon the practical conduct of public affairs, and to render their meed of unpaid service to the State.

In this fact, perhaps, more than in any other, lies the secret of that peculiar affinity which has always been felt to exist between the social and political constitution of Hungary and that of England. A perfect constitution on the English pattern, and the most approved modern institutions, not even excluding county government, may be introduced with more or less success into any country in the universe,

from the Chinese Empire to the Argentine Republic;
but the disposition which induces a man to give
hard work and honest service to the State from
no other motive than keen hereditary interest
in the political welfare of his country, and with
no desire for a more tangible reward than the
prestige conferred by the approbation of his contemporaries, or, if this be withheld, of his own
conscience,—this is a peculiar growth not every-
where native to the soil, as it is in England and
in Hungary.[1]

The defects of the ancient county organisation,
and its tendency to weaken the strength and unity
of the State as an executive body, were plainly
recognised by Francis Deák; but with the instincts
of a true politician, he set himself to use to the best
advantage of his country the instruments at his
disposal, however imperfect, until the time when,
by means of these very instruments, the way

[1] No more touching instance of this public-spirited patriotism, 'the
ruling passion strong in death,' could be found than in the letter of
remonstrance addressed by the 'great Hungarian' in 1858, from his
then self-imposed prison within the sheltering walls of the Asylum at
Döbling, to a brother magnate who was proposing to withdraw from
some arduous public undertaking. 'The Hungarian,' wrote Count
Széchényi, 'who at the present time occupies a post that is not opposed
either to his honour or to his conscience, or to the good of his country,
ought not to abandon it voluntarily, whatever humiliations may be
heaped upon him. If they do not appoint you, or if they turn you out,
that is another affair ; the man who has lost his fortune may one day
recover it, but he who of his own free will gives up his treasure will
never find it again.'—St. René de Taillandier, *La Bohême et la
Hongrie*, 470.

should have been prepared for a better state of things.

It is with a sense of fitness that the citizens of Buda Pesth have placed their noble portrait of Francis Deák, not in the Parliament House, but in one of the stately halls of the Liberal Club; for in the days when the meetings of the National Legislature were few and far between—and at times sadly barren in results—a great part of Deák's best and most fruitful work was being carried on outside the walls of Parliament, in the clubs and county assemblies, at party conferences, and even in private conversation.

The following graphic description of a party meeting, held during the sitting of the Diet, is quoted by M. de Laveleye in his interesting sketch of the Hungarian leader, from one of Deák's personal friends.[1] After describing the appearance of the club-room, dense with clouds of tobacco smoke, in which the members of the Opposition are wont to assemble in the evenings during the session, the writer proceeds : ' The excitement is intense ; to-morrow there is to be an important sitting in the Diet, for an Imperial Rescript has come down from Vienna, and this has to be answered ; the national pride is wounded ; " they are threatening our independence !" is the cry from all sides ; " they are

---

[1] L. Tóth, quoted by Laveleye, '*La Prusse et l'Autriche depuis Sadowa*' (1870), vol. ii. pp. 170, 171.

trying to enslave the free Kingdom of St. Stephen; they are attempting by gentle means, and by slow degrees, to deprive us of those liberties which we have preserved against all attack for three centuries! but the blood of our fathers still flows in our veins, Rákoczy is not forgotten!"

'So speak the more excited members; others preach moderation, but fail to make themselves heard; the discussion is brilliant but without definite aim; there are as many different opinions as there are members present; to win a hearing is impossible. At this moment there enters the hall a man, still young, and of sturdy build; on the broad shoulders and somewhat short neck, is set a round head with a face full of "bonhomie" and humour; bushy eyebrows overshadow the grey eyes, twinkling with a mixture half fun, half kindliness. Nothing about him bespeaks the orator. His black clothes are neat, but somewhat old-fashioned; in his hand he carries a stout ivory-handled walking-stick; you might take him for some good citizen of Presburg, coming to take his daily glass of beer at the "cabaret." He walks to a sofa, settles himself comfortably in the corner, and lights a fresh cigar from the one he has just finished.

'At first he follows the discussion with grave attention; then, as all seem to be awaiting his opinion, he speaks in his turn, expressing himself simply, as though in conversation; in a few words

he lays down the object of the debate, shows the
points on which all are agreed, and the end they
have in view; points out exactly the means by
which success may be attained, the weak side on
which the enemy must be attacked, the concessions
that may be made, the rights that must be maintained at all costs.   He enlivens this exposition—as
closely reasoned as the demonstration of a theorem
—with homely humour, anecdotes, and illustrations.
Under this vivid and diffused light, sophisms are
exposed, excitement is allayed, the Magyar imagination sobers down.   Good sense has spoken, the party
has received its instructions ; the plan of campaign
is drawn out ; the members break up, and go home
to supper.   The " bon bourgeois " who thus rules
the majority of the sovereign assembly is Francis
Deák.'

CHAPTER V.

SOCIAL reforms, new enterprizes of all kinds, the founding of a national theatre, of an art exhibition, of literary and commercial associations, accompanied the political movement in the country during the years that elapsed before the opening of the next Diet.

In one County Assembly after another, the discussions ended in instructions being given to the deputies to press in the ensuing Diet for such important reforms as freedom of conscience, equality before the law, emancipation of the soil, and improvement of the penal code. Many of the great proprietors, forestalling legislation, of their own free will made over land to the peasant occupiers, to be held by them in perpetuity.[1]

The state of popular excitement on the meeting of the next Diet in 1840, was such that the Vienna

[1] See Horváth, *Kurzgefasste Geschichte Ungarns*, vol. ii. p. 309.

Cabinet deemed it advisable to propitiate national feeling, by replacing the Hungarian ministers who had incurred odium on the occasion of the late prosecutions, by men like the Counts George and Anton Mailáth, and Stephen Szerencsy, who might be able, if any one could, to present the arbitrary proceedings of the Government in a favourable light to the Hungarian Opposition.

But no precautions could avail to silence the indignant remonstrances that at once broke forth from the Opposition, respecting the violation of their national rights which had been committed in the manner and matter of the recent prosecutions.

Count Louis Batthyány who led the Opposition in the Upper House, and Francis Deák in the Lower, made it quite clear that no Royal propositions would be taken into consideration until the 'gravamina' of the nation had been redressed; above all, till the right of freedom of speech had been fully acknowledged, judicial purity re-established, and the political prisoners set at liberty. The struggle was a long one, for the magnates again sided with the Government, who endeavoured to meet the fierce attacks of the Opposition by identifying loyalty to the King's ministers with loyalty to the King, and denouncing hostile criticism upon their illegal acts as high treason.

In the end, however, the Opposition gained the victory; the political prisoners were released, the prosecutions still impending were given up ; above all the great principle was acknowledged of the distinction between the King and his Government, and the way thus paved for the later doctrine of ministerial responsibility to Parliament.

In the last Diet we have seen Deák chiefly in the character of the modern philanthropist, striving to enlighten and overcome the prejudices of his countrymen and improve the condition of the sorely burdened peasantry. In this long contest of 1840, we seem to be carried back to the England of the seventeenth century, and find the stout-hearted patriot standing up boldly to resist the injustice of a powerful despotism, and assert the constitutional rights of a free nation.

He refused to be tempted from his position of uncompromising hostility to the Government by the proposal of the magnates that the two Houses should sink their differences on the subject of freedom of speech, in a general session for the amicable consideration of new laws. 'To complete what is wanting, to improve what is imperfect,' replied Deák, 'is the first and most sacred duty of the Legislature. But so long as the magnates lay down such principles regarding the judicature, and the Government persists in its present system of violating our rights (our countrymen meantime suffering under its yoke), so long as circumstances like these continue, under which mutual confidence is proportionately shaken—so long it would be useless, nay, even dangerous, to attempt a task, which from its bearing on the security of our position as citizens, indeed on the whole future of our country, would be, even under the most favourable conditions, an important and difficult undertaking for the Legislature.

At times the sense of the difficulties in the path of progress, and even of justice, seemed to Deák almost overwhelming. 'There were moments,' he wrote in later years, 'when the growing force of adverse circumstances threatened to endanger not only our hopes of a brighter future, but even the present time; moments when the general discouragement could only be kept at bay by a sense of the justice of the cause, and the conviction that it was our duty to fight for a righteous cause, even though every hope of success had disappeared.'

Not only were the principles of public law successfully asserted, but the Diet of 1840 was also marked by the introduction of reforms touching more nearly the actual condition of the people.

Of these the most important was the law enabling the peasantry to become permanent proprietors of the soil, with power to redeem their property form the burden of the Urbarial dues. The royal sanction to this law was received with indescribable enthusiasm by the whole Liberal Party throughout the country, and it was hoped that as the rejection of the measure had destroyed the good understanding between the Government and the Diet four years previously, so now its concession might tend to promote still further the reconciliation which the good sense and moderation of Hungarian statesmen both in and out of office—of Count Mailáth as well as of Count Széchényi—had brought about. For this happy result, few were more distinctly responsible than Francis Deák. Feeling strongly as he did that it was the duty of the country to hold fast by its political birthright, he felt no less strongly the need of an efficient and trusted administration; consequently he used every effort to smooth away difficulties, and replace by some approach to confidence that spirit of blank opposition which had found its sturdiest representative in John Balogh,—the man of whom it had been admiringly said by his contemporaries 'that he would fight tooth and nail for nine-and-twenty days on behalf of a certain measure, and then, when on the thirtieth day the court party agreed to it, would turn round and advocate the exact contrary.'

'A brighter future will dawn upon Hungary,' said Deák, 'only when the nation and the Government unite their forces and follow together the path of law and justice, instead of allowing the two forces to paralyse each other in a doubtful contest that may easily prove dangerous both to prince and people.'

CHAPTER VI.

Deák's Penal Code—Opinion of foreign judges as to his legal abilities
—Deák as a parliamentary leader.

AFTER the close of the Diet of 1840, Deák, who was now living with his friend the late Bishop Horváth—well known as one of the chief historians of Hungary—found ample scope for his activity in the elaboration of a penal code for Hungary. The new code never came into use, owing to the opposition made to the proposed judicial changes both by the Vienna Government and the majority of the magnates in the Upper House. But Deák's labours on this subject were not without effect in enhancing his reputation beyond the limits of Hungary. As a piece of legal workmanship the rejected code met with high appreciation from competent judges on the Continent and even in England; Mittermaier, the eminent German jurist, declaring that he knew no legislative work which satisfied so completely the progress of the age, the requirements of justice, and the latest scientific opinions.

In addition to his acknowledged merits as a jurist, Deák possessed many of the special qualifications for a parliamentary leader.   Always scrupu-

lously truthful in stating the arguments of his
opponents, a thorough gentleman in manner and
feeling, never, even in the heat of debate, losing
his sense of fairplay, he was universally respected
by men of all sides, at a time when party feeling
ran very high.   The weight of his position and
authority in the House, combined with remarkable
tact, and insight into the character both of men and
of parties, enabled him to exert a strong personal
influence without giving offence.   Never was personal influence more kindly or wisely used.   Deák
was as conscious of a high and worthy aim, had
as clear a perception of the folly and ignorance of
many of those with whom he had to deal, as keen a
sense of humour, as the great German Chancellor
who exercises with impartiality on friend and foe his
formidable powers of sarcasm and ridicule ; but he
had also that rare charity which prevents a man
from acting as though in public matters the feelings
and sympathies of his contemporaries might be
trampled on and disregarded with impunity ; as
though an active politician were by the nature of his
position absolved from all observance of the deeper
courtesies of life.   ‘ Beware of hurting the feelings
of others with the two-edged weapons of ridicule
and wit ’ he writes to a young friend ; ‘ the laughter
roused by the witty sarcasm is soon silent, but the
bitterness does not cease to rankle in the mind of
the man whose sensibilities have been wounded, and

you have purchased the momentary triumph of vanity, at the cost of friendship estranged and suffering inflicted.'

M. Csengery has given us an interesting picture of Deák's relations with his party: 'As soon as Deák had definitely taken his place amongst us, he made it his practice to communicate his views, first to his own friends, and subsequently, if they were approved, to bring them forward at the Party Conference.

' His view once adopted, he readily ceded to others the honour of introducing it in a public session either as their own proposal, or as a resolution of the whole party. Having no feeling of personal vanity, he gladly left free scope for the play of other men's ambition.

' Except in certain cases, where from the peculiar importance of the matter at issue, he preferred to take the proposal and explanation of it on himself, the leader, having once sketched out the plan of campaign, retired into the background, only to come forward again when the controversy seemed to be taking a new direction, or when the question was ripe for immediate decision.   And whilst in cases of the first description, and especially during the earlier sessions of the Diet, when " rules of the House " were unknown, his powerful reasoning frequently brought

¹ *Franz Deák*, p. 57.

back the course of the discussion to its proper
channel, so his appearance on the scene at an
advanced stage of the debate seemed of itself,—in
suggesting new arguments, and the possibility of
taking up a new standpoint,—to shed such light
upon the question as cleared up all difficulties.'

CHAPTER VII.

THE effect of the recent surrender on the part of the
Ministry, and the relaxation of the press censorship,
was soon visible in the audacity with which Kossuth,
now released from his illegal imprisonment and
become editor of the *Pesti Hirláp* (Pesth Gazette),
poured broadside after broadside into the abuses and
anomalies of his time ; directing his attacks not only
against judicial corruption and economic evils, but
hinting at such methods for the amelioration of these
evils as would have affected the relations hitherto
subsisting between the country and the supreme
Government. The more conservative and aristocratic members of the Opposition grew somewhat
alarmed. Count Széchényi himself, irate at seeing
his favourite project of gradually reforming Hungary
from above, through the means of a purified and
improved national government, thus endangered by

E

the vehement anti-governmental tone of the new journal, plunged into a controversy with the popular agitator. By a sharp attack upon Deák for an innocent speech on agricultural topics made by him in the provinces, he tried to draw the Liberal leader into the quarrel. But Deák had the faculty, so valuable in this ink-and-paper age, of knowing how to keep silence with his pen as well as with his tongue. When in 1848 the two were together in the Ministry of Count Batthyány, Széchényi reproached his colleague for his persistent refusal to reply to the attack then made upon him, 'Why should I have replied?' said Deák. 'As we are both of us of a passionate temperament, who knows how far the controversy might have led us? What good would it have done our country if we had quarrelled? Is it not better that we have remained friends?'

The remonstrances of the great magnate were not unavailing in checking the dangerous vehemence of the *Pesti Hirláp;* but popular opinion was entirely on the side of the editor of the offending paper, who was able to convey in the sober guise of a leading article, and under cover of a matter-of-fact disquisition on some question of trade or finance, thrilling appeals to the passionate 'nationalism' of the people, and eloquent incitements to changes so profound as to amount well-nigh to revolution in the eyes of moderate Liberals. The *Pesti Hirláp* had

a marvellous success for that pre-journalistic epoch ;
Louis Kossuth was the hero of the day, and the
interchange of pamphlets and articles between him
and Count Széchényi, was followed with eager
interest by many who had formerly stood quite
outside the range of practical politics. Pesth was
like one vast club; the great topic that absorbed
all interest and occupied all conversation being
indicated by the flaming red-and-yellow placards
that at the corner of every street announced to an
expectant public : ' Reply of Louis Kossuth to Count
Stephen Széchényi.' In every corner of the kingdom at this time the first question on a subject
was, ' What does Kossuth say ? '

The chief matter of dispute in the fierce electioneering contests that preceded the Diet of 1843, was
that of general taxation.

The party of progress in the County Assemblies,
which had in many instances opened their doors to
members of the non-noble class, including at that
time some of the most intelligent and cultivated
members of the community,—were fully determined
that this important reform should have a place
in the instructions to be delivered to the new
deputies.

The question, however, was one which naturally
united against it that large body of electors of
all ranks who objected to voting away their
ancient privilege of exemption from taxation, on

the sole ground of justice to the non-noble tax-
payers.

The election contest in the county of Zala was
the occasion of one of the most difficult and painful
incidents of Deák's public life.

He was firmly resolved that as a Liberal, indeed
as the leader of the Liberal party, he would not
accept the mandate of deputy for his county unless
the principle of general taxation were included in
the instructions.

But he was also firmly resolved that he, personally
at least, would do nothing to countenance the great
evil of 'Korteskedés,'—the electioneering violence
and corruption which he felt to be indeed, as one of
his countrymen has described it, 'a cancer at the
very root of public life in Hungary.' His friends
assured him that nothing should be done during
the election that could discredit his fair fame ; but
when the contest came on, the force of evil custom,
the practical interest of the question at stake, the
excitement amongst the hot-tempered Hungarian
electors, proved too strong for the best intentions
of Deák's Liberal adherents. Bribery and intimida-
tion were freely resorted to by both parties, and in
the end the victory of the Liberals was only gained
after lives had been lost in a free fight between the
two contending factions. To the deep disgust of
his excited supporters, and to the regret of many
sincere Liberals throughout the country, Deák

refused to accept the mandate, even though it contained the all-important instructions with regard to reform. 'He should always see blood-stains upon the mandate,' he wrote in a private letter, 'and he should never venture in the Diet to give free expression to his feelings with respect to imposing some restraint upon electioneering abuses, because he should read in every face the reproach that he himself owed his return to the various arts of " Korteskedés."'

It must have been no small trial to Deák to withdraw from public life at a time when his party was in full career, and the tendency of events seemed to be moving in the direction he desired ; moreover, the scene in the County Assembly when, with tears in his eyes, he was forced to confront the entreaties, the remonstrances, and the bitter reproaches of his friends,—some of whom did not scruple to charge him with cowardice in refusing the honourable responsibility they had laid upon him,—must have been deeply painful to a man of Deák's warm-hearted, sensitive nature, who cared for many things besides even the advancement of his political views. But he believed that on the whole he was best serving his country by following the dictates of his own conscience rather than the wishes and entreaties even of his friends and supporters. He honestly believed that so far as he personally was concerned, he should be doing greater wrong in accepting the election which had been won by such disgraceful means than in depriving his country of the services he might be able to render by his presence in the Diet. He believed that he should do more harm to the cause of parliamentary government by seeming to sanction the evils of 'Korteskedés,' than he should do good by appearing in the House with a mandate acquired under such conditions as had signalised the recent election in the county of Zala.

To his intimate friends Deák wrote, entreating them not to condemn him for a course which he had taken only after a long struggle and grave reflection. 'You,' he added, 'love me just as I am, with all my peculiarities and foibles, and you know too that this resolve which I have taken is only of a piece with the rest of my character. No one who knew me as you do could have doubted but that, under the circumstances, I should have acted as I did, and in no other way.' Nevertheless, Deák's conduct on this occasion was blamed by some of the most distinguished of his countrymen, and his absence from the Diet of 1843 was cordially regretted by Liberals of all shades of opinion. His political adversaries too, both in the press and in the Diet, joined in the general chorus of lamentation, and in paying a generous tribute to the worth of the absent leader ; Zsedényi, one of his chief opponents, declaring that 'the purest character in Hungary was missing from the Chamber.' The seat of the 'great deputy' was left unfilled, and during the session of 1843 the county of Zala sent only one representative to the Diet.

CHAPTER VIII.

Legislation of 1843—Embittered debates—Compulsory introduction of
  the Magyar language into the Diet and public instruction—
  Opinion of Count Széchényi on the subject—Small result gained
  in the Diet of 1843—Estrangement between the Opposition and the
  Government—Metternich's attempt to check the too great independence in Hungary—Appointment of Administrators—Indignation at this proceeding fully shared by Deák—Speech on the
  illegal conduct of the Government—Deák a supporter of the
  small party in the Diet in favour of parliamentary government
  —Unpopularity of the 'doctrinaires.'

DURING the session of 1843–46 the Legislature was
chiefly occupied with embittered debates on the
subject of mixed marriages, on the introduction of
Hungarian as the official language throughout
the kingdom, on the extension of further rights
to the non-nobles, and on the vital question of
general taxation.

On this last matter the Opposition were defeated
in both Houses, and a similar failure attended the
measure for the improvement of the commercial
relations between Austria and Hungary. The principal triumph of the Liberal party was in the enactment of a law granting permission to the peasantry

to sell the usufruct of their land, and to purchase complete liberty, on payment of a sum equivalent to the value of their holding ; and in the compulsory introduction of the Magyar language in the debates of the Diet, in some branches of the administration, and in public instruction. The unfortunate results of this last victory gained by the ultra-Magyar party in the Lower House, which were clearly foreseen even at the time by such Hungarians as Széchényi, Eötvös, Apponyi, and Mailáth, were a few years later only too visible to those who had most eagerly hailed the triumph of their misguided patriotism. But it is to be feared that the plain-spoken words of Count Széchényi would make as little impression on the ultra-Magyar zeal of his countrymen now, as they did five-and-thirty years ago. 'To impose our language by force,' exclaimed the Count, 'is to provoke revolt ; it is only our intellectual superiority that can attach these races to the Hungarian nationality. . . . How does a nation come to possess the force and virtue necessary for its political action ? If the majority of the individuals composing it are to fulfil humanely and honourably their appointed task, they must acquire above all the art of pleasing, the faculty of attracting and absorbing the neighbouring elements. Is it likely that a people will possess this faculty who will not respect in others that which it insists on having respected in itself ? It is a great art to know how to win men's hearts. Can they be said to possess it in the remotest degree who, when they have to deal with a generous adversary—passionately devoted, like themselves, to the traditions of his race—instead of according him chivalrous treatment, are always ready to fling mud at him ?"[1]

On the whole, the results gained in the Diet of 1843 were far from commensurate with the hopes which had been raised in the country during the exciting period of the elections ; and the absence of Deák's wise and moderating influence was but too apparent in the confused and embittered character of the party conflicts in the Lower House.

In spite of the advance made in certain directions, it was clear that the prospect of harmonious action between the Government and the Legislature, which the reconciliation of 1840 had seemed to hold out, was not yet to be realised.

The Hungarian ministers might have wished in all sincerity to return to the path of legality and justice, and even have shown some disposition to follow the bent of national feeling in the matter of social, if not of political, reform. But nothing was further from the intention of the Imperial Government at Vienna than that Hungary should quietly transform itself into a constitutional country of the modern stamp, with a popular element,

---

[1] Quoted by St. René Taillandier, *La Bohême et la Hongrie.* p. 422.

influencing, and even controlling, the action of ministers.

The tactics of 'opportunism' are not peculiar to republican statesmen. The later Stuart sovereigns in England had suffered the English Parliament to pass laws most distasteful to royal ideas, whilst they were content for the time to 'regulate' the local organisation of the country, and keep a close watch over the elections of the borough members, and the nomination of lords lieutenant.

In the same way the Austrian Government, having tolerated a certain amount of freedom in the discussions of the Hungarian Diet, felt that the time had now come when it was expedient for a judicious Government to deal with the evil at its roots. In the appointment of paid officials by the Crown, in place of the lord lieutenant of the county and his lawfully elected coadjutors, a blow was struck at the whole system of constitutional liberty and self-government in Hungary, which provoked a storm of indigation throughout the country,—an indignation that was as fully shared by the moderate and enlightened Deák in his retirement at Kehida, as by the most fanatical devotee of the ancient constitutional system of the kingdom. For by this act a flagrant breach of the law was committed, and eagerly as Deák longed for progress and reform, it would have been contrary to the whole principles of his life, if he had been content to occupy himself with questions of social reform and progress, whilst the political constitution of the country was thus openly defied. No man was less wedded to old customs and old rights simply from a blind desire to 'keep things as they are'; but he could not but feel that there were times when the only chance for the eventual progress of Hungary, lay in a dogged refusal to stir an inch forward, until an unconstitutional Government had been forced to go back upon its steps, and acknowledge the binding and irrevocable character of the existing laws of the nation.

'A constitutional duty incumbent upon every citizen,' said Deák in March 1846, 'is to protest against the Government which violates the laws. Let it not be thought that we are seeking an occasion to do this; it is rather a cruel necessity for men who would be loyal to their country and to the Constitution; this necessity, painful as it always must be, is doubly so in the present state of things, when we see ourselves being outstripped by other nations, and feel the need of attaining an equality with them. With us, progress has been made only by one class of the community; the great mass of the population has not followed in their wake. Our duty is to urge on those who are behind; and it is when we are striving to widen our institutions, to establish more equitable relations between all citizens, then it is, that circumstances compel us to turn away our attention to the defence of our ancient liberties. Our efforts being thus dissipated, we weaken our forces, we are divided amongst ourselves, we abandon our sacred object, the development of the people. I do not wish to speak with passion—though my heart is filled with grief; I will obey the dictates of reason, I will persist in believing that the Government will never dare to lay a finger upon our constitutional existence. I will even grant that it is seeking to develop it. But "order" is only a means of governing, not the end of the State's existence. For a Government to succeed in enforcing order, it must be strong, that is, it must have moral strength as well as material. But a Government which would possess moral strength submits to the law and respects the limitations which it imposes, even though these limitations be sometimes onerous. Is this the conduct observed by the present Government?"[1]

Deák, though he had withdrawn at this time from public life, was still making his influence strongly felt in the guidance and tendency of events. During the last Diet a small party had formed itself in the midst of the Opposition ranks, including such men as Anton Csengery, Baron Joseph Eötvös, and Lladislas Szalay (then editor of the *Pesti Hirláp*), which received from Deák all the sympathy and support that he could give in his private capacity.

[1] De Gérando, p. 262.

Whilst Széchényi and the extreme Right, as the conservative members of the old Opposition might be called, aimed at reforming and renovating the country through means of a patriotic Hungarian element in the existing Government, whilst Kossuth and the bulk of the Liberals in the Diet desired to do everything through the counties, independently of the central administration,—Deák and those who thought with him looked forward to the introduction of true parliamentary government, with a responsible Ministry ; thus combining the popular representative character of the county organisation, with the force and unity to be found only in a strong central authority,—a far-sighted policy, involving its advocates at that day in no little unpopularity. 'Granting,' it was said, 'that the substitution of a responsible central Ministry for the present Hungarian Court in Buda, and Hungarian Chancery in Vienna, might on certain grounds be desirable, yet the scheme of the "Centralist" reformers contains this fatal flaw, that it proposes to set up a nominally independent and responsible Ministry, without requiring guarantees that the abolition in its favour of the old system of local autonomy would not lead to a still more flagrant disregard of the laws and liberties of the country.' The bare idea of voluntarily confiding fresh power to the hands of a Ministry in any way connected with the 'Camarilla' was received with distrust and aversion ;

former Ministers had been too often servile tools of
the Court, and it was Count Széchényi's project of
improving matters by himself joining the Ministry
(a project of which he had vainly sought Deák's
approval) that had alienated from the 'great
Hungarian' many of his admirers. On the other
hand, it was one of the chief tenets of the Liberal
party, both in and out of the Diet, that patriotism
and independence were to be found only in the
County Assemblies, where in bygone days the
cause of national freedom had so often been
preserved against the numbing influence of a
despotic Government.

Therefore the opinions of the so-called 'doctrinaires' who presumed to conceive of the possibility of a higher political idea for Hungary, were
regarded with suspicion, or at least considered inopportune,—a view which was confirmed by the
conduct of the Government in their appointment
of the detested 'administrators' for the counties.
Under such circumstances, all thought of modifying
the local institutions, or of yielding one inch to the
Ministerialists, was more than ever unpopular. 'The
nation wants agitators—bloodhounds to be always
hanging at the throat of the Government—not
reformers,' exclaimed Count Batthyány.

Deák however was not the man to be turned
away from his object by unpopularity at home,
any more than by the pressure of unjust authority

abroad. He believed parliamentary government to be the true form in which to continue the traditions of a free and constitutional Hungary, and to this idea—as to other ideas once unpopular in their day—he held fast; content to bide his time, and wait till the willing support of his countrymen should enable theory to be converted into practice.

Little by little the views of the new Centralist party gained wider acceptance. Already in 1846 the Pesth County Assembly, always foremost in the cause of progress, resolved, at the instance of Baron Eötvös, to support the principle of ministerial responsibility through their deputies at the ensuing Diet; and this example was followed in many other counties.

CHAPTER IX.

Gradual approximation of parties and classes throughout the country
—Spontaneous character of the Reform movement in Hungary—
Change effected silently since 1825—Compact and well-organised
Liberal Opposition in the Diet of 1847—Kossuth the prominent
figure ; but guarantee of moderation given in the acceptance by the
party of Deák's Manifesto of 1847—Principles laid down in the
manifesto the same as those asserted in the addresses of '61.

AT this time a strong tendency towards union, not
only between the different fractions of the Liberal
party, but still more between the various classes and
interests in the country, became gradually more
apparent; an evidence of this was to be found in
the prominence given in the discussions of the
County Assemblies to such questions as the political
enfranchisement of the towns, the complete emancipation of the peasantry, and general taxation.

Nothing shows more honourably the genuine and
spontaneous character of the reform movement in
Hungary than the manner in which the nobles
themselves came forward to carry out at their own
cost the measures they thought desirable for their
country. In the county of Zala alone, not only the
great proprietors, but two hundred of the lesser

F

nobles, agreed to submit themselves to taxation ; whilst the Counts Casimir and Gustavus Batthyány, and Count Karoli, following the example set by Stephen Bezeredy a year or two earlier, sold part of their estates in perpetuity to the peasants of the adjoining communes.[1]

Seldom has a country more nobly worked out its own regeneration. No startling change, no 'Jacquerie,' no dramatic stroke of benevolent legislation had occurred to draw the attention of Europe to this remote 'province of the Austrian Empire.' To all outward appearance the Hungary of 1847 was much the same as the Hungary of 1825 ; but the transformation that had passed over the country was none the less real. Those who have followed closely the gradual development that had been going on during those twenty years will understand how it was that when the time of trial came, neither the internal troubles of 1848 nor the disastrous war of 1849 could destroy that national independence and unity which was the result, not of the sudden wave of Liberal feeling that affected all the nations of Europe in those eventful years, but rather of the persistent, unwearied labours of a people with whom love of freedom was no mere rallying cry to be used against the sovereign in his hour of difficulty, but a motive power strong enough to provoke constant unostentatious self-sacrifice, from men of all ranks

<hr>

[1] Horváth, vol. ii. p. 339.

and parties.   Count Széchényi's[1] famous bridge had done more than span the Danube ; it had bridged over the gulf that for centuries had divided the Hungarian nation into two distinct halves.   In the statute which compelled the proudest magnate in Hungary, the blue-blooded Szekler from Transylvania, to forego his ancient privilege, and pay toll as he passed over the new bridge, like the common burgher of Pesth, or the white-shirted shepherd from the Puzsta, the principle of equality before the law was openly recognised ; and the broad line between noble and non-noble, the privileged and the tax-paying people of Hungary, was for ever obliterated.

When the time came for the meeting of the last and eventful Diet, to be held at Presburg in 1847, the Government and their Conservative supporters found themselves confronted by a compact and well-organised Liberal Opposition.   The most conspicuous figure in the ensuing debates was undoubtedly Louis Kossuth ; a somewhat alarming fact in the eyes of less advanced Liberals.   But as the Republican

---

[1] The fact of belonging to the ' privileged class ' had formerly entitled the Hungarian noble to exemption from the toll levied for passing over the old pontoon bridge, replaced in 1848 by the present magnificent structure, built at the instance of Count Széchényi, at a cost of £500,000. ' The said privilege ' (exemption from toll) ' is so intimately connected with that of passing free over all roads, bridges, and highways of the kingdom, and finding " I am a nobleman " accepted at all turnpikes instead of Kreuzers, that the privileged orders dread of all things an attack upon this right, as the first breach in their grand aristocratic circumvallation.'—Kohl's *Austria*, 1843.

party in France in 1877 were provided at a critical juncture with a guarantee of moderation and a common basis of action in the posthumous manifesto of M. Thiers,—so every section of the Hungarian Opposition could accept with confidence the Liberal Programme of 1847, drawn up by Francis Deák, the leader on whose wisdom and moderation all parties had firm reliance.

It is interesting to notice how the same fundamental principles on which the cause of Hungary has been fought successfully in recent years, are already clearly laid down in the Liberal Programme of 1847. The claims then put forward were the natural corollary of the movement of the past twenty years. Neither in the Diet nor in the country was there a thought of revolt, of breaking with old tradition, of severing the constitutional connection between Hungary and the Austrian Empire. The aim of the Opposition, it was declared, was threefold—I. To check and counteract the illegal proceedings of a Government which, far from being responsible to the country, was, on the contrary, subject wholly to the influence of a foreign and unconstitutional element. II. To secure guarantees against future violations of the law, in the shape of ministerial responsibility, the concession of the right of public meeting, and the consolidation of the interests of all classes of the community upon the basis of nationality and constitutionalism, with care-

ful regard for the special interests of the non-Magyar
populations. III. The attainment of the reforms
desired by the whole country ; amongst these were
again put forward—this time it was hoped with
every chance of success—the demand for equal
taxation of all classes, subject to the supervision of
a responsible Ministry ; representation of the people
in the legislative and municipal assemblies, further
improvements in the land system, and absolute
equality before the law.

Whilst duly mindful of the provisions of the
Pragmatic Sanction, the Opposition declared their
intention to abide firmly by the Fundamental
Law of 1790, in which the independence of the
Hungarian Government is clearly acknowledged.
Though carefully avoiding anything that should
bring the interests of Hungary into collision with
those of the monarchy as a whole, the Opposition,
it was stated, could not hold it consistent with right,
justice, or expediency, that the interests of Hungary,
in respect especially to questions of trade and commerce, should be illegally subjected to those of the
other provinces. Ever ready to assist in arriving
at a compromise between conflicting interests, they
could not consent to sacrifice the National Constitution to the idea so favoured at Vienna of 'administrative unity' ; this unity had been achieved in
the Hereditary States on the principles of absolutism, and the Opposition, so far from being disposed

to renounce the national independence of Hungary in favour of such a system of government, were convinced that if the Hereditary States were also to regain their ancient constitutional rights and liberties, the conflicting interests of Hungary and the other provinces could be more easily reconciled. 'A greater unity of interests and a greater degree of confidence being thus established,'—so concluded the manifesto,—'every part of the Empire would be invigorated and knit together by a common tie; and the united monarchy, a guarantee being thus afforded for its material and intellectual development, would be enabled to brave with impunity the storms and convulsions by which it might be hereafter assailed.'

It is not difficult to trace in this programme the hand of the author of the Addresses of 1861, and the chief promoter of the Compromise of 1867.

During the vehement contests between the now sharply defined Liberal and Conservative parties that occupied the Diet during the autumn of 1847, Deák was living in retirement on his estate at Kehida. The previous year had been spent at the baths in his own county, and in travelling abroad for the benefit of his health, which had lately given grave cause for anxiety; he had returned the better for his journey, but still unable to accept the candidature for his county in the election of 1847. The excitement of public life had in itself no attraction for him, and his natural love for the quiet of his country home was increased by the tendency to heart complaint, of which symptoms had already shown themselves. That he did not the less follow with incessant interest and attention the course of public events, was sufficiently attested by the fact that to him, in great measure, was owing the union of all parties of the Opposition in the conference held in June 1847, and the incorporation in the Liberal programme of those Centralist principles, which three years earlier had seemed likely to cause a fresh split in the Opposition ranks.

Deák was at Kehida in the early spring of 1848, when he received news of the formation of the first responsible parliamentary Government of Hungary. The aid and wise counsel of the ex-leader were sorely needed, and by letter and deputation from the newly appointed Minister President, and from both Houses of the Legislature, Deák was summoned to the help of his country. 'Owing to my bad health,' he answered, 'I am hardly equal to the work, but no one shall be able to accuse me of not having done for my country at least the best I could. I will come.'

CHAPTER X.

Success of the Liberal Opposition at the commencement of the Diet of 1847—Loyal and constitutional character of the proceedings—Formation of Batthyány Ministry—Deák Minister of Justice—Laws of March 1848—Difficulties of the Minister of Justice—Speech on the rights of property—Landlord and tenant—State recognition of religious denominations.

THE first act in the drama of the Hungarian revolution had opened propitiously. In the midst of popular uprisings and conflicts throughout Europe, which cost kings their thrones and were accompanied by anarchy and bloodshed, Hungary presented the spectacle of a country where, thanks to the patient preparation of years, thanks to the wise direction given to reforming energy by the national leaders, thanks above all to that innate respect for law and order which distinguishes the 'Englishmen of Eastern Europe,' the principles of 1789 bid fair to triumph by a bloodless revolution over the ancient tyranny of feudalism and absolutism.

It was not the fault of Hungary that the grand experiment failed, and that the sanguine hopes of

1848 were succeeded by the reaction of despair in 1849.

The proceedings of the Diet that met in the autumn of 1847, though animated, had been conducted in a perfectly legal and orderly manner. The newly elected Palatine, the young Archduke Stephen, to the rapturous delight of his audience, opened the Diet with a speech in the Magyar tongue.   Kossuth's speech on proposing an address to the throne, after news had been received of the revolution in Paris in February, was couched in the most loyal terms, and the political and social reforms which it demanded were in every respect the same as those advocated in the Liberal programme of the preceding June.   Meanwhile the Opposition had not failed to take advantage of their numerical strength in the Lower House, and of the distinct advance which Liberalism had made even amongst the magnates.   It was a significant proof of this, that the final abolition of that most glaring of abuses, the Jus Avicitatis, which not so long since had been upheld as the keystone of the Constitution, —was proposed by Paul Somssich, the leader of the Government party in the Lower House.   The real point at issue, however, underlying the debates between the two parties in the Diet, was felt to be the great question of ministerial responsibility, as opposed to arbitary government ; and it was this which gave such special importance to the long discussions and constant negotiations between the two Houses on the subject of the 'Administrators.' The Address, carried by acclamation in the Lower House, was refused by the magnates, and the work of reform seemed destined to remain but half accomplished.

The sittings of the Upper House were suspended, under pretext of awaiting the return of the Palatine from Vienna, and two of the chief officials of the Government left Presburg to avoid the pressure of public opinion in the capital.

But all such expedients were unavailing. When the Diet reassembled in March 1848, it was plain that events abroad had so combined to further the aims of the strong constitutional Opposition at home, that continued resistance might endanger the authority not only of the Ministry but of the Crown.

On the 14th of March the Address was carried unanimously; the Court, after hesitating for several days, at length deemed it prudent to yield to the wish of the nation whilst still expressed in peaceful and constitutional form, and Count Batthyány was entrusted with the formation of an independent and responsible Ministry.

A glance at the names of the new ministers is sufficient to show that the much-dreaded republican element had not yet come to the front in Hungary. The most devoted absolutist could hardly maintain that Prince Esterhazy and Count Széchényi would be likely to have much in common with the defenders of the barricades in Paris, or the leaders of the revolutionary mob in Berlin or Vienna ; and however hateful to the Court was the recent administrative revolution, it was obvious that, in its present development at least, it could not be put down with bayonets.

Whilst Kossuth was appointed to the Ministry of Finance, Deák took part in the new Government as Minister of Justice, an office in which he found ample scope for the employment of his peculiar powers, in the attempt to prevent the vigorous reform of abuses from degenerating into contempt for law and order. The celebrated Laws of March had added the finishing touch to the work of years, and swept away at one stroke many venerable abuses which the labours of the Opposition had hitherto been powerless wholly to uproot. An annual Diet was henceforth to be held at Pesth, elected not by the privileged nobles in the County Assemblies, but by every Hungarian in the kingdom owning property to the value of £30; general taxation was enforced for all classes ; feudal dues and tithes were abolished on payment of compensation by the State ; judges were to be appointed for life.

Besides these new fundamental laws, other provisions were enacted concerning liberty of the press with specified safeguards, the establishment of a National Guard, and other domestic matters.

But Deák was well aware that the best of laws will not in themselves insure good government, and that the cause of fairness and justice needs to be as jealously guarded under a parliamentary as under a despotic rule, and he strove as earnestly to protect individual and local freedom against the tyranny of a parliamentary majority as he had formerly done to defend the political liberties of the nation against the open or insidious attacks of absolutism.

With the same sense of proportion which always distinguished his political action, Deák, who had at one time dwelt strongly on the necessity for a powerful executive, now showed himself anxious that even the reformed Government of which he was himself a member should not assume wider powers than were consistent with the rights of the Legislature and the country. 'Do not let us extend the power of the Government at the expense of the House,' pleaded the minister, when it was proposed to transfer from Parliament to the Government the duty of inquiring into election abuses. On the same ground he objected to placing extraordinary judicial powers in the hands of the Government, even at a time when the southern districts of Hungary were being overrun by Croat hordes.

'Troops and artillery are wanted there,' he said, 'but not gallows.'

The office of Minister of Justice under the first reformed Government of Hungary was no sine-cure. Deák's quarters at his hotel, 'the Archduke Stephen,' were continually besieged by a crowd of peasants of all nationalities, who came to implore the aid of the Minister of Justice in securing to them the property which they believed had passed, in virtue of the recent legislation, from the hands of the late proprietors to their own. It required all the fatherly authority, the patient kindness, the convincing arguments of the honoured minister to satisfy the demands of the excited people, and dismiss the claimants not only with increased confidence in 'Deák Ferencz,'[1] but with heightened patriotism and clearer views of justice. But it was not only with the ignorance of the peasantry that the new Government had to contend. 'If stupidity is naturally Tory,' says a modern historian, 'Folly on the other hand is naturally Liberal.'[2] In his capacity of minister during the excited period that followed the establishment of the new Hungarian Government, Deák experienced to the full the truth of both these assertions. Not only had the Ministry to stand their ground against the general dis-

---

[1] According to Hungarian usage the Christian name is placed after the surname.

[2] Lecky, *History of England in the Eighteenth Century*, vol. i. p. 474.

couragement which lent strength to the complaints of the injured interests of Conservatism ; but they were compelled also to withstand the pressure of those ardent supporters who considered that the exigencies of ' high politics,' and the claims of those who had been too long debarred of their just rights, ought to override all minute questions of justice. M. Csengery relates that on one of the deputies exclaiming, ' Do not let us weigh out in this cold-blooded manner exactly what is in accordance with strict justice, but consider rather what will best suit the interests of the Fatherland,' Deák referred in reply to the example of a certain Vice-Comes who, when he felt disinclined to enter 'in a cold-blooded manner' into the administration of justice, used to say, ' Don't let us trouble our heads too much over this case ; it will be all one to the State whether the plaintiff wins or the defendant.' The zealous advocates of the cause of the peasants failed to see that the strong current which, as it hurries round the bend of a river, adds constantly a fresh deposit to the soil on the one side of its banks, is at the same time weakening and under-mining the land on the opposite side. There were some ardent Liberals who, not content with eman-cipating the peasants from the burdens and unjust obligations under which they had so long suffered, would have established the theory that a peasant or village community, as such, should be freed at the cost of the State from all obligations whatsoever connected with the possession of the land.　By some communes it was lamented, that in the midst of universal freedom they still remained in slavery, because the proprietors of the adjoining estate, whose fields they held on lease, declined to dispense them from paying their rent ; others demanded that the State indemnity should extend to allodial lands which the proprietors had leased to their former serfs by private contract.

No one believed more firmly than Deák in the duty of a complete and immediate emancipation of the peasantry, and their admittance to a full share in the benefits of the Constitution.　' In this matter the condition of Europe has decided the question. In France the throne has been shaken ; Germany is in a state of ferment ;　all this finds an echo in Austria, and even in our own country.　The Legislative Assembly has rightly judged that any delay here may prove dangerous.　In times of such excitement there is no choice left with either Government or Legislature but to crush the movement or to lead it.　The Chambers have very wisely placed themselves at the head of the movement ; very wisely, I say, for in providing a sacrifice, not at the cost of private individuals, but of the national revenue, they have so acted as to prevent the agitation in the country from degenerating into civil war.'　At the same time, Deák felt bound to assert as vigorously the rights of the landlords. At a time when liberty was understood by many to mean liberty to benefit one class at the expense of another, he had the courage to maintain that the arbitrary transference of property by the will of the majority from one class of the community to another, was not justice, but confiscation. 'Either let property be inviolable, or let it cease to exist; the first theory corresponds with existing practice; the latter, which is communism, may be supported by philosophic arguments, but in practice encounters difficulties that have hitherto proved insurmountable. Property, if its rights are violated, will sooner or later have its revenge, even though for the time such a violation may appear to bring its advantages. We are not acting in the interests of the poor by ceasing to respect the rights of property. The peasantry can become free and prosperous only through their own industry and energy, and not by receiving gifts.'

With all his wish to see in Hungary a free and prosperous peasantry, Deák could not be brought to regard the obligation to pay rent as the mark of slavery and class oppression.

After pointing out in one of his speeches the advantages of the landlord and tenant system in other countries, and referring to the respectable class of citizens which had been formed from amongst the tenant-farmers in the counties of

Weissenburg and Tolnau, he proceeded : 'Such a development would be an impossibility if the proprietor were in constant alarm lest the Legislature should deprive him of the land he has let on lease. For the improvement of trade we are in need of much foreign money. Who will give credit on uncertain tenure ? . . . Philanthropy is a sentiment which the Legislature should not leave out of consideration, but it should apply it cautiously, otherwise it may turn out to be a two-edged weapon, with which we injure one half of the community while we are striving to benefit the other. Generosity is a fine thing, but justice is more—it is a duty. The legislator who only takes into consideration one class, one set of interests, is fulfilling only half his duty; he is bound to keep in view the interests of the country as a whole ; it is no less his duty to guard the inviolability of property than to forward the interests of any one particular class.'

Deák was strongly averse to taking advantage of the perturbed and disorganised condition of the political world, to impose upon the country measures which were certain to arouse a deep feeling of indignant resentment amongst those who would perhaps be unable to give full expression to their dislike in Parliament. Thus he opposed strenuously the proposal of the Radical wing of the Liberal party to appropriate to the use of the State all denominational endowments, religious or educational. With all his keen logical intellect and complete freedom from sectarian prejudice, Deák had no wish to force upon the people a theory of which, considered in the abstract, an enlightened politician might acknowledge the advantages. He never lost sight of the fact that, whatever the moral strength and virtues of the people, the time had not yet come when it was safe to appeal to their reason without regard for their feelings and prejudices; he preferred to bring his knowledge and experience to bear in influencing and raising the aspirations of his countrymen, rather than in aiming over their heads at some political ideal with which they could have little sympathy.

To the assertion that the State ought not to recognise various denominations, Deák replied that were he all-powerful it should be his first care, in the interests of the sacred cause of religion, to moderate or even to do away with all those differences of opinion which have a tendency to lead to persecution. 'But who has the power to do this? Moreover, the best of methods is only effectual for the achievement of an object if applied at the right time. At a time when the country is in a state of feverish excitement, when the nation is surrounded with dangers, when we are dreading total shipwreck, and declare that only the all-powerful hand of God can avail to save us,—at such a time, can we say

that a slight irritation arising out of a question of
religious belief is of no consequence ? Will not even
the man who is no bigot have all his feelings roused
against the tyranny of a law in which he sees a
restraint upon liberty of conscience and opinion ?
Such feelings are natural in any man ; they are
still more so in the general populace, who, in proportion as they are less enlightened, cling the more
tenaciously to "religionism" and external forms.
With the people, any attack upon external forms
is an attack upon their religious sentiments ; to
wound these feelings, merely in the interests of
some fine theory, and when the cause of the State
does not require it, is a crime against the safety of
the nation.'

. . . . 'We are always saying that "Liberty,
equality, and fraternity" is the watchword of this
century ; this perhaps refers more to the future than
to the present. Was there ever in Europe a more
flagrant infringement of individual liberty than in
this case ? Is it consistent with liberty to try to
compel a Church to forego the exercise of its rights ?
And what sort of equality is that which is not consistent with liberty, or shall we make men brothers
by binding them together with chains ? The legislator ought not to wound even prejudices, unless
forced to do so in the interest of the State ; for what
we call "prejudice" is often with the people a sentiment with which their happiness is bound up. Do

not let us fling the apple of discord into the midst of an excited community, at the moment when we are calling the people to arms for the defence of Freedom and Fatherland.   Are we afraid of the reaction ?   The reaction is dangerous only when it finds some support, some basis.   It is easy to awaken alarm ; to allay it, not force is needed, but winning persuasion.'

CHAPTER XI.

Removal of the seat of government from Presburg to Pesth—Sanguine hopes of the Hungarian Ministry—Deák's forebodings—Causes of his satisfaction in the recent Liberal triumph in Hungary—Deák himself free from anti-Slav prejudices—The bitterness of the debates on the question of the Magyar language to be traced in part to his absence from the Diet of 1843-46—In the Laws of 1848 full consideration shown for the rights and liberties of Croatia—But all hope of restoring harmony between Hungary and Croatia now gone by—Increased difficulties of the Hungarian Ministry—Their authority defied by the imperial troops—Meeting at Agram—The Hungarian Government disavowed by the Croats, headed by the Ban Jellachich—Demand for an independent Croatian Ministry—Movement in Croatia encouraged at Vienna—Rising of the Serbs, or Raitzen, in the south of Hungary—Application of Hungarian Government for military assistance from Vienna—Reluctance of the Batthyány Ministry to take matters into their own hands, notwithstanding the renewed incursions of Serbs on the southern districts, and threatening attitude of the Ban of Croatia—Government strengthened in their position by favourable reception of Hungarian deputation at Innspruck, consequent upon popular triumphs in Germany and Italy—Jellachich disavowed publicly by the Imperial Government.

THE famous Laws of March having received the royal sanction, and the Diet at Presburg having been closed by the King in person, the Ministry had repaired to Pesth full of hope, to enter upon their new functions. The dream of a reformed Hungary, free, united, and independent, for indulging in which at the end of the last century the Abbé Martinovics and his companions had been branded as conspirators and had died upon the scaffold, seemed now realised.

But notwithstanding the general rejoicing and the apparent victory of the National party, Francis Deák foresaw clearly that Absolutism had by no means laid down its arms, and that the Ministry of which he was a member would not long be allowed to carry on quietly the constitutional government of the country.

' People here cannot accustom themselves to the new order of things,' Deák wrote from Vienna even so early as March 1848. Beneath the aspect of bold, cheerful self-confidence which made his countrymen look upon him as a pillar of strength and wisdom, Deák cherished a sorrowful foreboding of the troubles that were coming upon Hungary. ' Whether it be the Russians, or once again the power of Austria, or perchance the direst anarchy, that is to enslave us, God only knows.'

These forebodings were but too soon justified.

The reason that more than any other had contributed to Deák's profound though anxious satisfaction in the parliamentary victory of March, was the belief that the laws then passed under the joint sanction of King and people would save his country from the calamity of civil war. The same true Liberalism which had induced him to fight resolutely and against powerful opposition for the accordance of freedom, personal and political, to all classes of his compatriots, made him desire with equal earnestness to minimise as far as possible those distinctions of race, the maintenance of which was considered by some of his fellow-Magyars to be the Alpha and Omega of Hungarian patriotism. From first to last throughout his long public career there is no trace in Francis Deák of that national exclusiveness, that scornful contempt for the non-Magyar inhabitants of Hungary, which has so often been laid to the charge of his countrymen, and to which is sometimes ascribed, perhaps not unjustly, the political isolation of the kingdom at the present time.

Deák had not been in the Diet during the embittered debates of 1844 concerning the compulsory employment of the Magyar instead of the Latin tongue by all the members of the Diet, including those from the Croatian counties. By some cool-headed politicans even at that time, as has been seen, the victory then gained by the Hungarian Opposition in the midst of passionate excitement, and at the cost of increased hostility between Magyars and Slavs, was regarded as a dangerous triumph; better calculated to serve the purposes of the Vienna Government than of the Liberal party in Hungary.

Never had Deák's authority, tact, and judgment been more grievously missed than in those violent debates, when many seeds of ill-feeling were sown, destined, when aided by the fostering care of the Austrian Government, to produce so plentiful a crop of discord and misery. In the Liberal Programme of 1847 and the March Laws of 1848 the influence of the large-minded statesman was again to be recognised. With Deák the plea for a Liberal Constitution for Hungary, on the ground that by the concession of this right 'every part of the empire would be invigorated and knit together by a common tie,' was no empty phrase ; he believed in all sincerity that the extension of the parliamentary form of representative government to Croatia would tend not to the extinction, but to the establishment on a broader footing, of the ancient rights and institutions of the little Slav kingdom ; he never imagined that the substitution of a responsible Hungarian Ministry for the Hungarian Council of Lieutenancy, would be resented by Croatia as an act of tyranny and injustice ; especially as in the administration of justice the jurisdiction of the local tribunals was left unaltered.

But the time had now gone by when goodwill or wisdom on the part of either nation or individual could avail to ward off the coming storm. The winds of passion, ambition, and national jealousy had been let loose, and it was to the interest of the 'Camarilla' at Vienna to see that they were not too soon laid.

As the year drew on, the troubles of the Ministry at Buda Pesth increased on every side.

Their authority was set at defiance by the troops, on pretext of loyalty to the Crown. In Agram the Croats, headed by the Ban Jellachich,—himself according to the Laws of March a member of the Hungarian Ministry,—held an assembly, professed openly their disavowal of the Hungarian Government, and presented a petition to the Emperor demanding an independent Croatian Ministry and the union of the kingdom of Croatia with the three Slavonian counties and Dalmatia.

The political movement in Croatia, sedulously encouraged at headquarters, was supplemented by a rising amongst the wild and ignorant Serbs, or Raitzen, on the southern borders of Hungary, incited by their Patriarch Rajaacs.

The Government at Pesth applied for aid to Vienna; the Hungarian troops being at this time in Italy, engaged, according to the traditional policy of 'Divide et impera,' in fighting the battles of the Hapsburgs at a safe distance from the corrupting influence of local patriotism.

In spite of the suspicious reluctance of the Austrian Government to render the needful assistance in suppressing the horrors now being committed by the savage Raitzen in the south of Hungary, the Batthyány Ministry, hopeful of a speedy pacification, risked their popularity with their countrymen

by declining to take matters into their own hands
and put down the Raitzen themselves independently
of the central authority; it was only with a heavy
heart that Deák at length yielded to the determination of the House to proclaim a state of siege in the
southern districts. Meanwhile a fresh influx of Serbs,
excited by appeals to their religious fanaticism,
poured into the Banat.   Jellachich, as the representative of the pan-Slav or Illyrian party, continued his
preparations for the invasion of Hungary; whilst the
Court at Vienna knew well how to turn to the advantage of absolutism the sincere aspirations of some
of the Nationalist party in Croatia for an independent
Ministry.

Thus the aspect of affairs grew daily more
threatening, and it became constantly more difficult
to hold in check the extreme National'st party in
the Hungarian Legislature.

The Batthyány Ministry wished to refrain from
breaking irrevocably with the Hapsburg dynasty,—
one branch of which was believed to be honestly in
favour of constitutional liberty,—and to avoid being
hurried into any illegal step; yet the danger to the
country was imminent, and with their popularity,
Deák and his colleagues were also, it might be
feared, losing the power to influence and control
events.

The position of the Moderates, however, was
strengthened at this critical juncture by the favour-

able reception accorded to the Hungarian deputation sent to Innspruck in June.

The effect of the recent triumph gained by the popular cause in Germany and Italy was also discernible in the Imperial Manifesto, in which Jellachich was publicly disavowed, deprived of his dignities and official command, and himself summoned to justice. Along with this official condemnation, the Ban, however, received privately from the Imperial Government fresh supplies of arms and money.

CHAPTER XII.

THE persistently lawful and constitutional attitude
of the Hungarian Ministry was at once baffling
and irritating to the Court party. Some ostensible
ground for disregarding these repeated and reasonable demands for active assistance must clearly be
found. It was not long forthcoming : the point

at issue between the two Ministries was declared to be the refusal of Hungary to take upon herself a share of the Austrian National Debt ; the fact being, that she had neither received any benefit from the Austrian public loans, nor been in any way a party to the contraction of the debt.   Claim there was none ; though Deák, speaking in 1869, declared that he regretted the action taken by the Hungarian Ministry on this point.   'We were asked to take our share in supporting the burdens of a debt incurred without our consent ; we were not bound to do this, either by law or equity ; the Vienna Ministry were wrong in demanding from us as a duty what on our side could only be regarded as a concession ; but on the other hand we were wrong in raising a difficulty over a mere question of form, and not at once agreeing to a compromise.'

Our sympathy and admiration have often been aroused on behalf of a people striving gallantly to throw off the yoke of a hated authority, the oppression of an illegal government ; but is there not also something pathetic if not heroic in the spectacle of a small knot of men struggling to uphold the cause of law and authority, unsupported either by the material power of a strong despotism or the moral force of popular enthusiasm ?   The Batthyány Ministry had such difficulties to contend with, from discontent at home and hostility abroad, as might well have made the task of maintaining the rights of Hungary, and yet keeping strictly within the bounds of loyalty and constitutional legality, seem hopeless. The state of things tolerated, and even connived at, by the Vienna Government, was enough to make a patriotic Hungarian forget all the obligations which still bound him legally to the Austrian Empire ; but Deák, for one, declined resolutely to lend himself to any scheme propounded on behalf of the national cause that was based on any secret anti-Austrian understanding even with those to whose objects in themselves he might heartily wish success ; the Liberal party in Italy could never succeed in enlisting the secret support of the Hungarian Liberal against the dynasty to which he openly professed loyalty ; Deák could never make up his mind to become a conspirator even in the cause of freedom.

The reassuring promises of the Palatine in his speech from the throne on the convocation of the Diet in July, (the Long Parliament of Hungary, as it has been called), were hardly consistent with the treacherous weakness shown by the imperial troops in repressing the Raitzen, and the evident collusion of the Austrian general Puchner with the Wallachian insurgents in Transylvania.

One of the first acts of the Ministry on the re-assembling of the Diet was to propose through the Finance Minister, Louis Kossuth, a vote of 200,000 men and 40,000,000 florins, for ' the defence of the country, the restoration of order, and the security of the throne.' The proposal was hailed with enthusiasm, as was also the action of the Hungarian Government in despatching a deputation with an offer of alliance to the representatives of the German Confederation at Frankfort, and of diplomatic envoys to the Governments of England and France.

Measures of national defence were organised, the command and organisation of the new levies being entrusted to four Hungarian officers, amongst them the ill-fated Gorgei.

Still there was no open rupture between the Governments of Vienna and Buda Pesth; on the contrary, the Hungarian Ministry, in order to meet the Austrian Cabinet half way, had even consented to compromise still further their popularity with a large part of their countrymen, by inserting in the address to the throne a passage to the effect that 'Hungary would do its best to bring about an understanding in Lombardo-Venetia, which, while compatible with the dignity of Austria, should at the same time insure liberty to the Italians, on condition that Austria would restore peace in Hungary.'

But with the victories of Radetzsky in Italy and Windischgrätz at Prague, the prospects of the restoration of peace in Hungary grew fainter. The King, emboldened by these recent successes, refused to sanction the measures with regard to the levy of national troops; the Ministry, hoping against hope for the advent of a better state of things, persevered nevertheless in their determination to remain on strictly legal and constitutional ground ; but the intention of the Court party, now relieved from immediate danger in other quarters, to ignore, and eventually to stamp out, that new system of government in Hungary which five months earlier had received the royal sanction, had become by this time only too apparent. It was clear that Hungarian patriots must look not merely to the defence of their country against the invasion of Croats and Raitzen, but to the preservation of their dearly loved and hard-won liberties from the revengeful wrath of the absolutist power.

Still one more attempt was made at reconciliation —an appeal was addressed to the Sovereign himself. In September, Count Batthyány and Francis Deák, accompanied by a deputation of two hundred magnates and deputies, journeyed to Schönbrun, implored the King to admonish the military commanders of their duty, and invited him to come himself to Pesth, thereby to lend to the regulations of his loyal ministers the support and sanction of his own presence.

After keeping the Hungarian deputation waiting for two hours in an ante-room, Ferdinand gave an equivocal, ungracious reply, and the deputation returned to Pesth to find that Jellachich had crossed the Drave, and that, so far from being discountenanced by the Vienna authorities, he was encouraged in an imperial decree ' to pursue his loyal undertaking.'

The decree of the preceding June which had disavowed his conduct was annulled, and Hungary was forbidden to take further defensive measures against the Ban of Croatia.

In the following month the Batthyány Ministry resigned. In order that the country might not be left without any sort of executive government, a Committee of Defence was nominated by the Diet, with Kossuth as president.

Deák's state of distress and perplexity at this juncture is shown in a letter addressed to his brother-in-law: ' How could I be the minister of a power which is carrying on war against my country, and which exacts as a condition of peace the sacrifice of all that is most absolutely essential to our national independence and constitutional freedom? Under a monarchy the minister is always the minister of the king, and as such is responsible to the country; but if war is made upon my country in the name of the King, how can I be that King's minister? You answer perhaps that I might be the minister of the nation; but under a monarchy, a separate national ministry apart from, and in opposition to, the sovereign, is inconceivable.' . . . ' The country may have a provisional government, a dictator, but that implies a revolution.'

Not the blackest treachery on the part of the Sovereign and the Camarilla could shake Deák's determination to do all in his power to keep his

country as long as possible on the firm ground of
constitutionalism—to insure, that whatever the sins
of the Hapsburgs and their advisers, the people and
Government of Hungary should by a faithful adherence on their side to the Laws of 1848, establish
the strongest of all claims to the ultimate fulfilment
of those royal engagements which were being now
so shamefully broken.   Even in the midst of the
bewildering crisis that succeeded the resignation of
the first short-lived Hungarian Ministry, and indeed
to the end of his life, Deák held firmly the belief that
keeping in view not only the disastrous present, but
also the past and future of his country, it was better
for Hungary, better for the historic Magyar nation,
to preserve its connection with the Empire of
Austria.

This was the key-note of Deák's action throughout
the terrible events that seemed at one time as though
they must of necessity be fatal either to the continuance of the Hapsburg rule in Hungary, or to the
preservation of the Hungarian Constitution.   On
looking back to this year of war and revolution in
connection with the years that followed, the position
then taken up by Francis Deák appears perfectly
intelligible ; but it is not surprising if at the time
the man who, on whatever ground, shrank from taking
a foremost part in the desperate struggle of his
betrayed and injured country to free herself from
all connection with the Hapsburg dynasty, should

seem to have forfeited justly all claim to a place amongst the recognised leaders of Hungary.

But in truth, apart from political scruples, Deák had not in him the makings of a revolutionary leader. He felt himself that he had not the power, like his famous contemporary Louis Kossuth, to stir the hearts and feelings of the people, to fire their imaginations and incite them to action by burning denunciations, clothed in a language of poetic imagery that seemed more akin to the fervid exhortations of the Hebrew prophets than to the political oratory of modern days. When requested to compose the revolutionary appeal to the nation, Deák replied: 'I do not understand that kind of thing; give me the making of your laws.'

The nation had good cause to acknowledge in later years that in the exercise of such weapons as could be drawn from the armoury of law and reason, the hand of their great lawyer-statesman had not lost its cunning.

CHAPTER XIII.

THE outburst of popular rejoicing over the
repulse of the Croats, and the deliverance of Buda
Pesth by the victories of Perczel and Gorgei, seemed
the last flickering of the nation's hopes before their
final extinction.

The Diet continued to sit; debates were still
held on questions of domestic interest, on the
amount of compensation to be adjudged to landlords under the new urbarial law. Even when at
length the troubled state of the country made the
further continuance of these peaceful discussions
seem incongruous and impossible, Deák,—who had
felt that in the absence of a Government appointed
by the Sovereign it was needful that there should
be some authority entitled to act in the name of the
nation,—moved by his ineradicable regard for legality
and constitutional forms, opposed the intention of

Parliament to declare itself in permanence, on the
ground that such a declaration was needless, because
in accordance with Article IV. of the Laws of 1848
a Diet could never be dissolved 'until the address
had been passed and resolutions on the Budget
been voted.'

To the last, the Government of Hungary—now
represented by the Diet and the Committee of
Defence—strove earnestly to avoid taking any
action that might give excuse to the Austrian
Government for the declaration of an open rupture.
In face of recent events—the proclamation of
Jellachich as Governor of Hungary, the treachery
of Austrian officers in command of Hungarian
regiments on the plea of loyalty to the Emperor,
the sudden flight of the young Palatine from the
Hungarian camp, and the subsequent discovery
amongst his papers of a plan containing suggestions
for the use of his imperial uncle on the most
effectual means of subjugating Hungary,—it was no
easy matter to brave the passionate reproaches of
the nation ; and to continue to act upon the theory of
Austrian good faith, even to the extent of restraining
the Hungarian army from crossing the Austrian
frontier in pursuit of Jellachich, until it was too late
to be of any avail ; for the Ban, taking advantage of
the three days' truce granted him by the Hungarians
after his repulse before Pesth, had marched on Vienna
with the intention of joining Windischgrätz.

After suppressing the rising in Vienna, the Austrian general was free to devote his whole energies to the 'pacification' of Hungary.

At the end of October a battle was fought at Swechat between the Austro-Croatian troops and the small Hungarian army, now reinforced by some thousand inexperienced recruits brought by Kossuth as Plenipotentiary Commissioner of the Diet. The national troops were defeated, and Windischgrätz was appointed Viceroy of Hungary.

Still the Diet clung to the hope of averting the final crisis; such an awful calamity as civil war was not to be entered upon with a light heart.

A deputation, including the Archbishop of Erlau, Counts George and Anton Mailáth, Count Batthyány and Francis Deák, was sent to Windischgrätz to protest solemnly against his conduct, and entreat him in the name of justice to desist from his treason to Hungary and not bring ruin upon the dynasty.

The celebrated reply of the commander-in-chief, 'I do not treat with rebels,' put an end to these negotiations. A deputation of Hungarian bishops who travelled to Olmütz, there to beg for peace, and to remind the King of his coronation oath, received no better treatment, but were dismissed with the contemptuous injunction 'to go and pray for their country.'

This was the last intercourse between Ferdinand II. and his Hungarian subjects. At the beginning of December he abdicated in favour of his nephew Francis Joseph, the young prince whom the Hungarian nation only three months before would gladly have welcomed as their king, on the sole condition of his breaking with the traditions of absolutism and ill-faith with which the Camarilla had identified the House of Hapsburg.

The Diet, acting on behalf of the country, and mindful, it would seem, of Deák's counsel 'never to suffer their national rights to fall into abeyance through indifference, cowardice, or despair,'—declared that, in conformity with an ancient law which affirms 'that the King of Hungary cannot be discharged from the duties of his sovereignty without the consent of the States, and that in case of resignation the Diet has the appointment of a regency,' the abdication of Ferdinand and the accession of Francis Joseph were, as regards Hungary, illegal; consequently no allegiance was due to the new Emperor, so long as he was not crowned King of Hungary with the consent of the nation.

In the manifesto published by the young Sovereign there was little comfort to be found.

The Emperor announced, amidst profuse promises of future good government, that he assumed the Crown of Hungary by virtue of the Pragmatic Sanction, making, however, no allusion to reciprocal obligations imposed on King as well as people by that famous document.   The only reference to the 'Gravamen' of Hungary was a declaration on the part of his majesty of his intention to quell the disturbances in his troubled provinces by force of arms.

The invasion of Hungary was decreed, and the Austrian army poured into the country.

The Diet resolved to make one last effort to save their country from the horrors of war.   A deputation, headed by Count Batthyány and Francis Deák, was sent to the Austrian headquarters to treat for peace. On Deák's requesting permission from the commander-in-chief to return to Debreczin (whither the Diet had now withdrawn) to confer with his colleagues upon the terms proposed, Windischgrätz replied that the permission should only be granted on condition that Deák would give his word of honour to use all his influence to persuade Kossuth and the Diet into unconditional surrender.   It was not difficult to predict the failure of negotiations conducted in this spirit.   The Hungarian envoys refusing to become the tools of the Austrian Government against their own countrymen, were at once put under arrest, and Hungary found itself compelled either to submit unconditionally to the form of government designed for subject provinces by imperial wisdom and clemency at Vienna, or to embark upon a war of self-preservation, even at the risk of being branded as 'rebels,' and abandoned to the ready vengeance at the disposal of a powerful military despotism.

Of the attitude of the Hungarian Diet during the past year, so full of danger and perplexity, Kossuth himself could say with truth in a letter of instruction addressed to the Hungarian envoy in London, M. Francis Pulzsky, in February 1849 : 'We have rebelled against no Government, we have not broken our allegiance ; we have no desire to separate from the Austrian Empire, we desired no concessions and no innovations ; we were satisfied with what was ours by law.'

But the time had now come when no prudence, no painful adherence to strictly legal and constitutional forms, could avert the impending crisis, and the parliamentary revolution of 1848 was followed by the War of Independence of 1849.

CHAPTER XIV.

THE chief events of the tragical year of 1849 are too fresh in the memories of Englishmen to need more than the briefest recapitulation here : the taking of Buda Pesth by Windischgrätz in January, the brilliant but unfruitful successes gained by the Hungarian levies under Generals Bem and Dembinsky; the occupation of Transylvania by the Russians, influenced solely, as Count Nesselrode explained to the Czar's ambassador in England, 'by motives of humanity,' and with no thought of armed intervention in the internal affairs of the Austrian Government.

The struggle for self-preservation and the maintenance of Hungarian independence became a truly national war; all classes of the population, from magnates and prelates down to herdsmen and common soldiers, threw themselves eagerly into the contest, each ready with their quota of self-sacrifice,

for the sake of the liberties of their country and
the defence of the Kingdom of Hungary. This
spirit of fierce resistance and absolute confidence in
the strength of a good cause, which made the task
of the powerful invader so difficult, is illustrated
in the well-known prayer of the Hungarian
artilleryman on the eve of an engagement with
the imperial forces : 'O Lord, I pray Thee
only not to help the Austrian, and then my work
will be done.'

At Vienna the war in Hungary was officially
represented as a struggle against the entire revolutionary party in Europe, and the demand of the
Imperial Government for the military assistance of
Russia, was justified on the ground that it was
consequently to the interest of all other States to
assist Austria in her efforts to suppress the danger.
An interesting commentary upon this official view
of the character of the Hungarian 'rebellion' is
to be found in the report of one of the English
secretaries at Vienna to Lord Palmerston. 'With
respect to the Hungarian rebellion,' wrote Mr.
Magenis, in May 1849, 'I may here state a
curious fact, which your Lordship will doubtless
have seen mentioned in the newspapers, but which
I have it in my power to confirm on the authority
of persons who are well informed on the subject of
Hungary. The population of Hungary are almost
universally royalist, but Kossuth has succeeded in

persuading them that the late Emperor Ferdinand has been dethroned, and that the present Emperor is an usurper, so that they are convinced they are fighting for the cause of their rightful Sovereign.'

On the 4th of March a new Imperial Charter was promulagated at Olmütz, containing many excellent provisions, but having this fatal defect, that in it Hungary was merged completely in the Austrian Empire, and all its ancient institutions obliterated.

On the 14th of April the Imperial Decree was answered by the Declaration of Independence, in which the Hapsburg dynasty was proclaimed to have forfeited all right to the Hungarian throne, and to be banished for ever from the country.

Kossuth was appointed Governor, and a new Ministry was chosen, under the Premiership of M. Szemere, the late Minister for Home Affairs in the Batthyány Government.

For a while the national army was victorious; Comorn was relieved, and in the south the Raitzen were once more dispersed by the Hungarian troops under Perczel.

But the despotic princes of Europe were now recovering from the panic that had demoralised them and their principles in 1848; the time had come for absolutism to rally its forces and reassert itself after the old fashion. Acting on the maxim that 'La raison du plus fort est toujours la meilleure,' the Emperor of Austria, after previous arrangement with his imperial brother in St. Petersburg, felt at liberty to disavow and ignore the arguments for constitutional government which had seemed so cogent to his predecessor, and the enactments of the Diet in 1848 were treated with as much contempt as though they had been mock laws, passed by a stage parliament for the temporary entertainment of an excited audience.

In July the Czar's troops a second time entered Hungary, this time with no disavowal of political motives, but on the ground that 'His majesty, having always reserved to himself entire freedom of action whenever revolutions in neighbouring States should place his own in danger, was now convinced that the internal security of his empire was menaced by what was passing and preparing in Hungary ; every attack upon the integrity and union of the Austrian Empire being one on the actual state of territorial possession which is in accordance with the spirit of treaties, the balance of power in Europe, and the safety of his own States.'

In August, Gorgei, the commander-in-chief of the national army, who had been nominated Dictator in the place of Kossuth, was invested with full powers to treat for a peace, and instructed to act according to the best of his ability to save the national existence of Hungary.   At Vilagós, on the 13th of August, the Hungarian army, by order of the new Dictator, laid down their arms, and surrendered—not to the Austrians, but to the Russian general Rudiger.

Thanks to the united efforts of 300,000 of the flower of the Austrian and Russian troops, the Hungarian rebellion was at an end. The good news reached the young Emperor of Austria on his birthday, and, by an equally fortunate coincidence of dates in Russia, the standards and colours taken in the Hungarian war arrived at St. Petersburg in time to be paraded through the streets and deposited in the Winter Palace on the festival of St. Alexander Newsky. 'The victorious arms of the Emperor have overcome the thousand-headed Hydra of the Hungarian Revolution,' announced the Austrian commander-in-chief in impressive language. 'La Providence divine a béni nos efforts,' piously ejaculated the Russian Chancellor.

Compliments and decorations were exchanged between the two victorious Governments, and Francis Joseph received the congratulations of his brother sovereigns on the pacification of Hungary,—the English Government not forgetting to express a hope that the ancient constitutional rights of the conquered country would be duly regarded. But as might perhaps have been expected, the representations of Lord Palmerston on this head, as well as his remonstrances against the ferocious measures of the Austrian general in Hungary, made small impression at Vienna. When, in due time, Prince

Schwartzenberg thought fit to take notice of the subject, it was only to retort with that invariable allusion of continental politicians under similar circumstances, to 'la malheureuse Irlande'; the English Government, it was further intimated, had always known how to maintain its own authority, when threatened, at the cost of torrents of blood, and yet the Austrian Government had never presumed to express an opinion on the methods adopted, in the belief that it is easy to fall into grave mistakes in criticising the complicated situation of a foreign country. His Excellency considered that this conduct on the part of the Austrian Government gave it a right to expect that Lord Palmerston would be good enough to observe in this respect a 'complete reciprocity.'

The conquered country was thus left entirely to the tender mercies of the Imperial Government. General Haynau presided over the Bloody Assizes of Pesth and Arad, and the long roll of Hungarian patriots condemned to death at the hands of the Austrian hangman was headed by such names as Count Batthyány and General Damyanics, the wounded leader of the 'Redcaps,' the famous student brigade. Those who escaped death found a refuge in England, America, or Turkey, whither they carried with them bitter memories of wrong and suffering inflicted, and an undying love for the country of their birth. Those bitter memories have happily died away, under the healing influence of time, and still more of that great work of reconciliation which a wise generosity on both sides has effected between the two countries; and of the patriotic men who then fought and suffered for the cause of Hungary and of Freedom, many are still living to render their tribute of loyal service to the Austro-Hungarian Monarchy.

PART III.—REACTION.

CHAPTER XV.

Condition of Hungary at the conclusion of the war—Deák recognised as the guide and counsellor of the nation—Residence in Pesth—The System—Passive resistance in Hungary—Position of Deák in the estimation of his countrymen—Personal characteristics—Methods of keeping alive public spirit in Hungary—Agricultural Union—Academy.

AT the close of the war in August 1849, the pecuniary resources of the country were effectually crippled by means of a general confiscation of property, ruinous taxation levied by armed force, and the promulgation of an imperial decree cancelling the paper money issued under the late Hungarian Government. The land was placed under military rule, seconded by imperial commissioners; the right of domiciliary visitation was entrusted to foreign spies, and all the old institutions of Hungary—now divided into thirteen military districts—were completely abolished.

The storm of war and revolution had swept over the country, leaving a scene of terrible devastation behind it. The flood seemed to have carried away all that was best and noblest in Hungary ; to have left nothing that might even serve as a point of leverage for future action. The leaders of the revolution had staked their own lives, and the independence, nay, the very existence, of their country on the desperate venture of the 14th of April. The Hungarian Republic proclaimed at Debreczin had been extinguished in blood ; and with it, to all appearance, the national existence of Hungary, notwithstanding the heroic efforts which for three months had kept at bay the two great despotic powers of Europe.

But amidst the excitement, the bewilderment, the terror of the crisis that the country had passed through, since the young Emperor had openly set at defiance past engagements, and asserted his claim to the crown of Hungary, not by right of law, but of force, a talisman had been preserved, which force had been unable to destroy, and which in the end proved effectual even against Haynau's troops and Bach's officials.

Owing partly to deliberate choice, partly, as he himself owned, to outward circumstances, Francis Deák had taken no share in the events that followed upon the arrest of the Hungarian deputation sent by the Diet to Windischgrätz on the eve of the Austrian invasion. He remained living on his estate at Kehida, not seeking to hide himself, but not taking any active part in public events ; he was not present when the Diet, amidst tumultuous applause, had declared the independence of Hungary, and the severance of all connection with the House of Hapsburg.

Such a step as this, popular though it might be at the time, and strong as were the arguments that might be urged in its justification, was not one of which Deák could honestly approve. Like many a true patriot before him, he saw the strong tide of passionate feeling carrying his country in a direction that was opposed, as he believed, to its best interests.

The current had become beyond his strength to stem, but at least he could refuse to be carried away by it against his better judgment. For a time it seemed as though he had been left hopelessly stranded, and had lost for ever, by thus holding aloof, the influence he formerly possessed as one of the acknowledged leaders of the people. The name of Francis Deák was not known as one of the gallant band of Hungarian gentlemen whose struggle in defence of the liberties of their country was watched with such sympathy and interest in England.

It was only when the lurid light of war had died away, and Hungary was left sunk in the darkness and silence of despair, that his countrymen recognised in Deák a leader who, by loyal unswerving adherence to law, was destined to win back for them, step by step, every iota of their ancient rights, and restore that mutual confidence between king and people which recent events had seemed to make for ever impossible.

During the years following the 'pacification' of Hungary, Deák lived permanently in Pesth, having sold his estate that he might have no temptation to return to the quiet country life which he loved so well.

His presence in the capital at this time was a constant source of strength and encouragement to his fellow-citizens; they knew that they had still amongst them a Hungarian patriot, who, whilst he won the respect even of Austrian statesmen by his strict regard for law, by his generous recognition of the difficulties of his opponents, and his manly honesty of purpose, might yet be safely trusted to abate nothing of his assertion of the lawful rights of Hungary, nor to despair of gaining his cause in the end. From the outset of that long period of passive resistance which the country entered upon in 1849, Deák had his object—the restoration of the Hungarian Constitution—clearly before him, and no conciliatory overtures on the part of Herr v. Bach and his colleagues could ever induce him to be drawn into a discussion which he foresaw would be based on premises that he could never accept. To the urgent request of the Austrian minister on one occasion, that Deák, as the representative of his country, would consent to negotiate with the Vienna Government, the sturdy champion of Hungary replied, ' I must beg your Excellency to excuse me, but I know nothing of any Constitution but the Hungarian. So long as that is not restored, I can do nothing, for I am nothing—I have no political existence.'

It was now seen that the long contest which the Liberal Opposition of Hungary had been carrying on during the past twenty years, both in and out of the Diet, had not been without its results : the fruits of the victory consummated in 1847 had not been destroyed even by the war, which might have appeared to blot out all previous events. The Hungary that emerged from the disasters of 1849 was at least a united Hungary ; the nation which now looked to Deák as their guide and counsellor in the new campaign of passive resistance, was no longer weakened by class distinctions, nor hampered by the cumbrous relics of an obsolete feudalism.

Deák and his friends never lost heart and hope, and yet cheerfulness in those days was no easy virtue. The 'dismal cold dead uniformity' of the System weighed heavily upon the Empire, and the grip of the central Government at Vienna was firm and relentless.

To the royal and aristocratic despotism—somewhat out of favour in Europe since 1848—there succeeded another form of personal government. The period between 1850 and 1860 was the golden age of the bureaucratic *régime*. Charters and constitutions were no longer unfashionable words, even in the most exalted circles ; the designing of various fanciful and attractive systems of government was a favourite amusement with active-minded and ingenious officials, and it had moreover the happy effect of keeping a certain portion of the Liberal world harmlessly occupied in the discussion and contemplation of political theories which, it was evident to the authorities, could never be realised under the existing conditions of the Empire.

The system of Herr v. Bach had at first sight the appearance of being a distinct improvement upon the old *régime* of Metternich and Schwartzenberg, but the fundamental principle of government, 'administrative unity,' remained the same ; the sole difference, in truth, consisted in the fact that whereas formerly the centre of the State system was to be found in the royal cabinet, it was now transferred to the minister's bureau. In deference to the march of Liberal ideas, a too obtrusive imperialism was replaced by a system of German officialism, but the strings of the whole Empire were still worked from Vienna.

Hungary, like all the other provinces of Austria, was ruled entirely by German officials ; the local organisation of the Counties remained totally ignored ;

justice was dispensed by newly established Austrian tribunals, and the country was overrun with armed spies, charged to detect and suppress the faintest symptoms of national revival.

But no official vigilance could prevent the remembrance of 1849 from burning fiercely in the minds of every shepherd and fisherman toiling on the hot plains or beside the broad rivers of Hungary; and in the humblest peasant homes the recollection of the national Constitution, now so ruthlessly trampled under foot, was never suffered to die out.

On-lookers in Europe saw clearly that though Francis Joseph might have succeeded in turning Hungary for the time being into a dependency of Austria, he had not succeeded by this means in turning the Hungarians into good Austrian subjects; and many were the prophecies that the 'pacified' country would prove the weak point in the armour of the great military despotism.

Nevertheless, the people of Hungary, under the influence of their guiding spirit in Pesth, refrained with striking unanimity during these trying years of alien rule from isolated acts of violence or lawlessness. All classes of the nation entered into the spirit of Deák's policy, relied on the justice of their cause, kept alive the memory of their past freedom, and looked forward to regaining it one day by lawful means under the guidance of their law-abiding champion.

A plate fixed into the wall of one of the long corridors of the 'Queen of England' Hotel at Pesth, marks the apartment occupied at this time by Francis Deák. The modest room became the 'head-centre' of the country, where were concocted, no plots and secret conspiracies, but openly avowed schemes for the spread and encouragement of such germs of national life as not even the Vienna Government had been able to root out. Here assembled men of all shades of opinion, bringing tidings from all corners of the country, and learning to sink political differences in a common patriotism. The only parties in the land whose representatives were never to be seen at these gatherings were those pledged either to the reaction or to revolution. From this rendezvous went forth messengers of hope, carrying to their countrymen in distant parts of Hungary the cheering assurance that 'Deák Ferencz' was alive and active, that he did not despair, 'that he was to be seen going about his business in good spirits.'

The very sight in the streets of Pesth of his stalwart figure and shrewd kindly face, with its bright eyes flashing from beneath their shaggy overhanging brows, was a satisfaction to his countrymen ; and his humorous pithy sayings were passed on from mouth to mouth for the benefit of a wider circle than his own immediate friends and acquaintance.

Never perhaps did a public man occupy quite the same position as that which Deák held in the intimate affection and respect of his countrymen. The English traveller in Pesth was surprised to find that the grave, quiet-looking Hungarian gentleman whom he passed constantly on the staircase of his hotel, and whose name perhaps he had never heard until introduced to Francis Deák through the good offices of some chance acquaintance, was the idol of his fellow-countrymen ; the single-minded patriot, the able statesman and jurist whose wide knowledge, sound sense, and keen intellectual power were at length to carry the day against the arguments of German lawyers, and the still more formidable logic of 'accomplished facts.'[1]

But Deák's influence with his countrymen was due to other causes besides respect for his ability and absolute confidence in his political honesty ; they loved the man as much as they honoured the statesman, and it was perhaps owing to this mixture of personal affection with political hero-worship, that in later years the portrait of Deák Ferencz was commonly to be found enshrined amongst the household gods of the Magyar peasant.   To the

---

[1] 'But Deák cannot surely demand,' an Austrian statesman had once exclaimed, 'that after such a series of "accomplished facts" we should begin affairs with Hungary all over again !'   'Why not?' returned Deák: 'if a man has buttoned one button of his coat wrong, it must be undone from the top.'   'The button might be cut off,' said the minister.   'Then,' replied Deák, 'the coat could never be buttoned right at all.'—Csengery.

warm-hearted, impressionable Hungarians there was something singularly attractive in the character of the statesman who, with the self-confidence and unsparing candour that never shrank from denouncing political errors and facing popular misunderstanding or royal disfavour, was yet uniformly fair and courteous towards his opponents, genial and friendly in his personal bearing towards all classes of his countrymen, and lastly—no contemptible distinction—a universal favourite with children. It did not lessen their regard for their national champion to know that the same man who refused, with a persistence which his enemies called 'obstinacy,' to yield an inch, in matters where he thought the interests of his country were involved, was yet so weakly indulgent when the appeal was one demanding merely a personal sacrifice of time or money, that his friends were occasionally forced to intervene to prevent him from becoming the victim of his own kindliness and the importunities of place-hunting mediocrities or begging letter-writers.[1]

Like Cavour under similar circumstances of political extinction, Deák did all in his power to keep alive the national spirit, by promoting those literary and agricultural enterprises which presented

---

[1] Deák's method of almsgiving would have scandalised the members of a modern Charity Organisation Society. Every night was to be seen arranged on a table in his room a little pile of money destined for the purpose of indiscriminate distribution the next day amongst his poorer fellow-citizens.

no handle of offence to the Government officials,—
ever on the watch to suppress the least semblance of
an attempt at political association,—and which at the
same time offered a basis for united action such as
the quick-witted Hungarians were not slow to take
advantage of.

In this way the 'Köztelek,' or National Agricultural Union, came to serve in some respects the
purpose of a club, offering a place of meeting for the
Hungarian gentry, now debarred from the exercise
of all public functions, and deprived of those opportunities of political and social discussion which had
been afforded by their favourite national institution
of the County Assemblies.

The Academy at Pesth, founded originally by the
magnificent generosity of Count Széchényi, owed
much also to Deák and his friends, who felt that
everything which contributed to mark and to preserve the individuality of the nation, whether social,
literary, or political, deserved the gratitude and
support of all patriotic Hungarians.

Deák himself was a man of considerable literary
culture; his earnest desire, so far back as 1838, for
the promotion of the scientific study of the Magyar
tongue, and its introduction as the official language
in the place of Latin, was to him a matter not only
of political but of literary interest; and in his younger
days he had spared no pains to make himself master
of the intricacies of his mother tongue, and to extend

a thorough knowledge of it amongst all classes of his countrymen.

On one occasion during the era of official despotism, Deák, who in 1837 had been elected a member of the Academy, came gallantly to the assistance of his learned colleagues. The Government, uneasy at the distinctively national character of the institution, made an attempt to obviate this by requiring the directors so to change their statutes as to place the Academy under the direct control of the Government. From the noble founder of the Academy, Count Széchényi himself, came a message of protest and remonstrance, and Deák at once drew up a memorial protesting in such vigorous and uncourtly terms against the proposed alteration that the council shrank from presenting the address to the authorities, some members suggesting that the remonstrance might prudently be couched in milder terms. In the end, however, Count Desewffy took the memorial in its original form under his protection, and undertook to present it ; with the result, as it proved, of inducing the Government to abandon their projected interference.

CHAPTER XVI.

New aspect of parties — Conservatives — Liberals — Distinguishing principles of the present Conservative party—Memorial of 1850 refused by the Emperor—Second visit of the Emperor to Pesth, 1857—Petition drawn up by Count Desewffy to be presented by Cardinal Szitowsky also refused.

In a country like Hungary, it was not to be expected that misfortunes however crushing, national effacement however complete, should destroy those ingrained political tendencies which lead to the formation of opposing parties even amongst men united in the fellowship of a common suffering and a common patriotism.

But in considering the party conformation existing during the decade that followed the war of 1849, we are struck with the fact that the nomenclature of the period before 1848 is no longer applicable.

The terms Conservative and Liberal are still in use, but the men to whom they apply are not the same that we recognised under those denominations in the Diet of 1847.

Prior to 1848, the chief strength of the nation, both moral and intellectual, had been represented by the large and powerful Liberal party, the political descendants of the old Hungarian Opposition of 1825 ; in the ranks of this historic party had been included such men as Francis Deák and the framers of the Liberal Programme of 1847. But the name of the popular leader was no longer for the time to be found amongst the politicians who now claimed the honourable title of the Liberal party of Hungary. These looked rather to the exiled Louis Kossuth as their chief, and they it was who in later days played the game of the German Centralists at Vienna by the demand of unconditional autonomy for Hungary —a demand that could only have been met either by a complete concession, which would have meant separation from the Austrian Empire, or by a blank refusal, to be followed by a more stringent centralisation. It was these Liberals who subsequently headed the vehement, and in one instance successful opposition to the proposals tending towards compromise and reconciliation which Francis Deák had the courage to advocate, at a time when popular opinion was running strongly against the Austrian Government and everything connected with it.

Another great change in the aspect of parties might be observed in the complete disappearance of the genus 'Conservative,' in the pre-revolution acceptance of that term.

Where was the party that had once so vigorously maintained that the abolition of class privileges would infallibly entail the ruin of society and the downfall of the Constitution ?   It had vanished as completely as the old world institutions it had vainly sought to preserve.   The party, as a party, no longer existed ; side by side with those distinguished men who now by hereditary succession, as it were, found their place amongst the ranks of the present Moderate Conservatives, were some whose political companionship would have sent a shudder through many of the stately bearers of that designation under the old *régime.*

So far as Deák at this time belonged to any party more limited than that of all patriotic men throughout the country, it was to the Conservative party, as thus understood ; though no doubt he occasionally disapproved of their method of action, and was annoyed at finding his name identified with measures which he regarded as inopportune, and therefore as harmful to the cause he had at heart.

But on the whole it may be said of the Conservatives at this period that they represented the true force and wisdom of the country, as the Liberal Opposition had done in 1847.

The distinguishing principles of these modern Conservatives may be briefly described, first as a recognition of the fact that the just demand of Hungary for the full restoration of her rights, must be based upon an acknowledgment of the necessity of insuring not only the integrity and administrative independence of Hungary, but also the unity of the

Empire; secondly, as a conviction that even should the complete autonomy demanded by the extreme Liberals be attained, a strong and permanent consolidation of the monarchy could never be accomplished so long as genuine constitutional freedom was not enjoyed by the other provinces of the Empire.

The party that supported these principles—whether under the name of Conservative or Liberal—was in any case faithful to the Programme of 1847; and it was from the members of this party—equally obnoxious to the extreme advocates both of independence and incorporation—that came the first protest against the unlawful authority of the Vienna Government in Hungary.

In 1850, a memorial bearing the signatures of some of the greatest names in Hungary—Esterházy, Széchényi, Josika, Batthyány, Desewffy, Andrássy—was presented to the Emperor. "You are playing with your heads," the imprudent memorialists were warned by a high official; but judging from the outspoken language of the address, the warning produced small effect on the Hungarian magnates. With all due reverence and loyalty to the Emperor, the memorial declared plainly that the course taken by the Government would never lead to the pacification of Hungary, and a demand was boldly made for the restoration of the constitutional institutions of the country, and of the municipal administrative and legislative rights of the Hungarian people. 'In the revolution which has passed over the country,' said the memorial, 'much has been destroyed, and much uprooted, but the ground on which the Throne and Constitution of Hungary has stood firm for so long remains unshaken.' 'On this foundation alone can a new edifice be safely built up.' 'The universal desire of the country to have an influence in the settlement of its future relations, does not spring from a desire to draw back from the path of needful reform, to throw obstacles in the way of the constitutional development of the Empire, or to claim for Hungary rights and constitutional forms, which might be dangerous to the common welfare of the monarchy or injurious to the strong action of the Supreme Power.'[1]

Already the note is struck so constantly recurred to by Francis Deák in his exposition of the claims of Hungary—'It is likewise fully and universally acknowledged that Hungary, by virtue of the Pragmatic Sanction, is indissolubly connected with the monarchy, and that it is indispensable that the relations of the former to the Empire, as well as its internal constitution and administration, should be regulated upon a secure basis, and in such a manner as to offer strong guarantees against the renewal of the events we have lately witnessed.'

The result of this memorial might have been

---

[1] *Drei Jahre Verfassungsstreit.*

K

foreseen. Not only were its protests disregarded, but the imperial officials in Hungary were charged to watch closely the dangerous agitators who were thus defying and bringing into contempt the measures of the supreme Government, were impairing the authority of the administration, and rendering. the task of consolidating those social conditions which had been so seriously shaken by revolutionary anarchy, more difficult, by their intrigues and machinations.

The signatories of the memorial, having been thus held up to the official world as conspirators and revolutionists, were, by a truly masterly stroke of misrepresentation, exhibited to the people, through the medium of a docile press, as bigoted Conservatives and aristocrats, who, irritated at the paternal Liberalism of the Austrian Government, were agitating for the recovery of their class privileges and exclusive national rights.

Seven years later, on the occasion of a visit of the Emperor to Pesth, the Hungarian Conservatives resolved once more to approach the Sovereign as loyal subjects with a prayer for justice to their country. A petition was drawn up by Count Emil Desewffy, setting forth the grievances of Hungary under German official rule, especially with reference to the newly introduced system of taxation.

'We do not doubt,' said Count Desewffy, 'that your Majesty will in the course of your inquiries arrive at the conviction that it will be possible to bring into harmony those historic institutions which are bound up with the life of the nation, and to which the people are devoutly attached, with the requirements of the age, the necessity for the unity of the monarchy, and the conditions of a strong Government. We will readily co-operate with the other subjects of your Majesty in everything that may be needful to maintain the security of the monarchy, to heighten its prestige, and to increase its power. In the greatness of your Majesty and the strength of the Empire lies our own security, and in the general welfare of the monarchy our own prosperity. The unity of the monarchy is the result of centuries; it comes from the co-operation of all the natural forces of the Empire. A people which has had a past is never able to forget its history. This country has learnt the great lessons which history teaches, and the interest of your Majesty demands that it should not forget them. Our Fatherland feels and acknowledges the obligations it is under to your Majesty and to the common monarchy; it is ready to discharge these obligations, to do everything but this—to be untrue to itself, to renounce its individual existence, and abjure the creed which is itself founded upon its dynastic feelings and its devotion to the dynasty.' During the three days that the Emperor remained in Buda Pesth, more than a hundred influential names of burghers and

nobles were privately affixed to the above petition.
But it was never presented to the Emperor.   The
time had not yet come when Francis Joseph was to be
allowed, according to Count Széchényi's expression,
' to see with his own eyes, and hear with his own
ears.'   The Ministers at Vienna got wind of the
affair, and at once urged upon his Majesty the
imprudence of encouraging so grave a breach of
the law as would be involved in the presentation of
such a document ; indeed so great was their alarm
that Count Buol and Herr v. Bach travelled to
Pesth and intimated that, should the Emperor
consent to receive the petition, they should feel it
their duty to resign office.

The Prince Primate of Hungary, Cardinal
Szitowsky, who had undertaken to present the
memorial, was careful always to take it with him
when he appeared at Court, in the hope that an
occasion might some day arise for presenting it
formally to his Majesty ; but the opportunity never
came, and at last the document found itself en-
tombed amongst the archiepiscopal archives at
Gran, where for a time all hope of the restoration
of the liberties of Hungary seemed buried with it.

PART IV.—REVIVAL.

CHAPTER XVII.

Outlook not altogether hopeless—Favourable disposition towards Hungary of the Emperor and some of his German ministers—Deák on the permanence of the System—Effect of Austrian defeat in Italy in 1859—End of the System—Offer of Ministry of the Interior to Baron Josika—Count Rechberg and Baron von Hübner—Difficulties of carrying into execution the Emperor's intention to grant constitutional government to the whole empire—Competence of commissioners for revision of Bach's Municipal Law not acknowledged in Hungary—Difference between Deák and the Hungarian ministers—Enlarged Privy Council—Refusal of Eötvös, Vay, and Somssich to attend—Attitude of the Hungarian magnates in the Council—Majority in the Council for Constitution based not on centralisation but on recognition of national rights.

BUT nevertheless the outlook was not altogether so hopeless as it might appear to some desponding patriots in Hungary. Above all, the Emperor Francis Joseph was not the ' perjured young Nero ' whom Kossuth, burning with the recollection of his country's wrongs, was wont to denounce with bitter indignation, and in Shakespearian English of entrancing eloquence, before sympathising audiences in this country.

Even amongst the German ministers of the Crown there were some who recognised the unsatisfactory character of the existing state of

the Empire—a recognition that was intensified
as the prospect of war with a powerful military
state like France became more imminent.

Deák had never believed in the permanent
establishment of the System ; his opinion as to the
probable influence of a European crisis upon Herr
v. Bach's political structure is expressed in the
significant little anecdote which he once related by
way of answer to the gloomy prognostications of
some of his compatriots. On consulting his gardener,
he said, who was also an authority in architecture,
as to the solidity of a certain vine-dresser's hut
which had just been erected on his estate, the man
expressed the sage opinion that the building might
stand for a long time, if the wind did not blow.
'Yes,' Deák had answered, 'but suppose it does
blow—and that often?'[1]

Before ten years had gone by, the storm had
come that was destined to test the durability of the
political fabric, and prove how different is union by
compression from that union of voluntary cohesion,
which alone gives strength to the State.

As the victories of Radetzsky in Italy in 1848
had once sealed the fate of constitutionalism in
Austria, so in 1859 the news of his defeat came
like the first dull crash of melting snow that heralds
the break-up of the long frost-bound winter and the
advent of spring and freedom.

[1] Csengery.

All through the Empire there passed a thrill of
life and movement ; loyalty to the throne remained
unshaken, but a breach was plainly discernible in
the hard crust of official absolutism that had
overspread the land. The era of the System was
at an end.

A significant symptom of the new spirit at work
in the imperial councils was to be seen in the offer
of the portfolio of Minister of the Interior to Baron
Josika, one of the Conservative magnates who had
signed the petitions of 1850 and 1857. But the
Hungarian magnate, true to his principles, declined
the honourable proposal. The words in which he
explained his reasons for so doing deserve to be
noted as a remarkable instance of the manner in
which some Hungarian statesmen have combined
with their intense and deeply rooted patriotism a sense
of consistency and justice towards other nationalities
than their own. 'We are persuaded,' said Baron
Josika, 'that no man, however great his talents, is
able to enter so completely into the various relations,
opinions, feelings, inclinations, and peculiarities existing in the two halves of the Empire as to be
capable of managing, rightly and successfully, the
internal affairs of the whole monarchy. On the
same principle that I would not credit any man
who had not devoted a lifetime to the study of the
peculiar relations of the lands under the Hungarian
Crown, with the power to rule those provinces well,

so I do not consider that a conscientious Hungarian statesman ought to undertake the control of the internal administration of the German and Slav provinces.'

On the return of the Minister President and Count Rechberg from the seat of war in Italy, and the conclusion of the Peace of Villafranca, Herr v. Bach resigned ; and after a short interval a Polish nobleman, Count Golouchowski, accepted the office of Minister of the Interior which the Hungarian magnate had felt bound to decline.

Meanwhile the evidence of goodwill shown in the recent offer made to Baron Josika was not disregarded, and a constant though unofficial intercourse was kept up between certain Austrian and Hungarian statesmen.

Deák himself had little faith in the practical success of the projects of reconciliation sketched out by Count Emil Desewffy and amicably discussed over Count Rechberg's tea-table—a scepticism in which, as it proved, he was only too well justified.

At the same time it was a fact, not without importance, that at this early stage of affairs there should have been two Austrian statesmen, namely, Count Rechberg and Baron v. Hübner, who approved in the main of a programme that was based upon a frank recognition of the impossibility of maintaining the present system of internal administration, and the need for a thorough reconstruction of the State. However, as Deák had foreseen, the vast complication of imperial politics was not to be thus easily unravelled in the course of a few private conferences.

Outside the minister's sanctum matters went far less smoothly. In consequence of too pronounced views on the subject of the rights of Hungary, Baron v. Hübner found himself compelled to resign ; and the difficulties of carrying into execution the Emperor's generous intention to establish constitutional government in Austria, in such a manner as to satisfy the various sections of the Empire, became daily more formidable.

Whilst in the German and Slav provinces the Commissioners who were entrusted with the revision of Bach's Municipal Law, and were invited to give expression to their free opinion on its working and results, acknowledged gratefully the confidence thus reposed in them, and set to work obediently upon their prescribed task,—the Hungarian Commissioners, on the contrary, declared themselves touched by the honour done them, but unable to undertake the flattering office, 'since the revision of the Municipal Law was undoubtedly the function of the Diet, and of the Diet only.' Here was the rock on which all attempts at a private settlement of the Hungarian question split. It was from his firm resolution to accept no compromise that could be effected only by dint of ignoring that primary factor in the Constitution of Hungary—the lawful authority of the Diet—that Deák became pre-eminently distinguished as the national champion of Hungary. 'First arrive at a reconciliation with the Imperial Government, and you will then be in a position to summon the Diet, and do full justice to the special claims of Hungary'—so argued the Hungarian magnates, whose valuable services to the nation at this juncture few of their countrymen would deny.

'First recognise the lawful status and authority of the Diet,' insisted Deák, 'and then by all means let the Diet acknowledge the paramount necessity for harmonising the distinctive rights of Hungary with the requirements of the common monarchy.'

There was much to be urged on either side, both from a purely national and from an imperial point of view. The former policy promised best for immediate fulfilment; but the latter has been crowned, as it deserved, with the success due to the patient, far-seeing statesmanship of its great exponent.

Checked in the attempt to prepare the way for the establishment of the promised Constitution by means of the proposed Royal Commissioners, owing to the refusal of the Hungarian people to acknowledge the legal competence of such functionaries, the Emperor determined to carry on negotiations through the aristocratic rather than the popular element in the monarchy—to begin the work of reconstruction in the upper instead of the lower strata. The permanent Reichsrath, or Privy Council, was enlarged, leading men chosen from every province of the Empire being summoned to Vienna to deliberate with the Sovereign on the fitting measures to be taken for the proposed re-organisation of the State.

Of the six Hungarian magnates nominated by the Crown to represent their country in this enlarged Imperial Council (Verstärkte Reichsrath), only three, Counts Apponyi, Barkóczy, and Mailáth, answered the summons ; Baron Eötvös, Baron Vay, and M. de Somssich declined, considering the present Reichsrath, however well-intentioned, to be only a fresh means of avoiding direct consultation with the nation through the Diet.

The Hungarian representatives at Vienna—though the very fact of their presence in the Imperial Council, under present circumstances, was in itself contrary to the general wish of their countrymen— could in no other respect be charged with betraying the national independence of Hungary. Through-out the whole course and conduct of the discussions they maintained a firm dignified and attitude, and never shrank from using all the influence conferred by their independent position and natural aptitude for debate in asserting the just claims of their own country, and of the cause of national liberties in general. It was greatly owing to the ability and eloquence of the Hungarian magnates that the majority of the Imperial Council, including representatives of various sections in the Empire, declared themselves strongly in favour of a Constitution founded, not upon centralisation, but upon a recognition of the national and historic rights of the several lands and provinces of the Empire.

In the celebrated October Diploma of 1860, in which the Emperor of Austria announced the abolition of the absolute system, and his intention henceforth to admit the peoples of Austria to a share in the government of their country, this principle received the royal sanction; and Baron Sennyei and Count Mailáth were summoned to Vienna by their compatriots, with the assurance that this time 'things were really in earnest.'

CHAPTER XVIII.

Anxiety as to Deák's view of the October Diploma—Respect for his
opinion amongst his countrymen—Deák acknowledges the benefits
of the diploma in restoring the municipal institutions of Hungary,
but declines to pledge himself to his future course before the
convocation of the Diet—Provisional Statutes of Count Golouchowski—Discontent both of Hungarians and German Liberals—
Resolution of the Hungarian ministers at Vienna to remain in office,
in hopes of re-establishing a better system through help of the Diet
—Fundamental harmony between them and Deák—Refusal of the
latter to accept any scheme based upon theory of Forfeiture of
Right—Consequent demand for preliminary recognition of Laws
of '48—Judex Curiae.

WHAT would Deák say to the October Diploma?
For ten years the great representative of Hungary
had kept silence, leading the ordinary life of a citizen
of Pesth, going quietly about amongst the people,
ever ready with a word of encouragement or hope
when it was needed, but never volunteering an
opinion or suggestion on the course of public events
either by speech or writing. And yet when the
crisis of 1860 came, ministers on both sides of the
Leitha, friends and foes alike, felt instinctively that
to this silent, unobtrusive man they must look for
an answer to the momentous question : 'Will the
people of Hungary accept the provisions of the

royal Diploma in so far as these affected their own country ?'

The strange influence exercised by Francis Deák over his countrymen seemed only to have increased during those years of inaction in which his name had been unknown in Europe.

'In the eyes of the people,' writes one of his compatriots at this time, 'Deák is the type of justice, the organ of truth, the touchstone of true law. It is not enthusiasm that he inspires, for he has never sought to captivate by his speeches or writings ; but the entire nation believes that from him alone it can take the "mot d'ordre." No party could suceeed in carrying the nation with it without the assent of Deák, for all think that he alone can say when it would be prudent and right to proceed to action. The exiles, however popular they may be, would find no response in the country if Deák were to hold aloof; but once let him come forward, once let him give the word, and all Hungary will obey his voice like one man.'[1]

On the promulgation of the October Diploma, Deák abandoned his attitude of silent observation, and entered heartily, though still in the same un-assuming, unofficial manner, into active political life.

He frankly acknowledged the great step gained by the restoration in the October Diploma of the

---

[1] Quoted by Laveleye. *L'Autriche et La Prusse.*

municipal institutions of Hungary, and fully hoped that an opening had now been found for future discussion and for ultimate reconciliation through the Diet; at the same time he would not, prior to the convocation of the Diet, consent to pledge himself or the country as to the course he should take with regard to its further application.

Unfortunately the tendency of events was such as gradually to widen instead of to diminish the breach which had seemed at last on the point of being closed between the two halves of the Empire.

To the profound disappointment of the Hungarian magnates at Vienna, the imperious provisions by which the October Diploma was carried out departed widely from the spirit of the original document and the intention of the majority in the Imperial Council.

The 'Statutes' issued by Count Golouchowski to all the various provinces gave equal dissatisfaction in the Hereditary States and in Hungary; to the advocates of centralisation, as well as to those of nationality. With the publication of the arbitrary statutes—affecting the constitution of the Provincial Diets—a system was introduced that was neither to the taste of the Hungarian Conservatives nor of the German Liberals.

The principle of national self-government was, to a certain extent, recognised in the convocation of the Provincial Diets, but at the same time the intimation that local institutions would be carefully regulated by the Crown, in such a manner as not to interfere with existing relations, considerably lessened the value of this concession.

On the other hand, whilst the creation of a single Legislative Assembly at Vienna was in theory consistent with the views of the German Centralists, the powers of the new Legislature were ill-defined ; and the fact of its members being for the most part nominees, chosen by the Crown from amongst the delegates of the Provincial Diets, deprived the proposed Reichsrath of a genuinely popular or representative character.

It appeared as though events would justify the warnings and the silent abstention of those Hungarians who considered that when, in the praiseworthy desire for a reconciliation with Austria, Count Apponyi and his colleagues had consented to waive the due recognition of the Hungarian Diet, they had been tempted into sacrificing the just pretensions of their country, without gaining for the common monarchy that genuine constitutional freedom which they had looked for in return.

But in spite of the unfavourable turn of the reform movement, the Hungarian ministers determined to remain at their posts, in the well-founded belief that by dint of tact and perseverance they might still bring about the meeting of the Diet, where the country might decide its own fate, and perhaps succeed in removing those flaws in the new arrangement which individual efforts were powerless to eradicate. They still maintained, in spite of recent discouragement, that whatever the form of the Constitution designed for the whole Empire, nothing would meet the interests both of the monarchy and of the various provinces composing it which was not founded on the principle of the October Diploma—namely, common constitutional treatment of the common affairs of the monarchy, combined with as much regard as possible for the historical autonomy of the separate provinces, and their political and national individuality.

Thus there was no essential difference of opinion, as to the ultimate object to be gained, between the Hungarian ministers and Francis Deák. Both held that the 'rights' of Hungary, those peculiar constitutional privileges, which required that laws should not be imposed upon the land without the consent of the Legislature, could not be ignored without destroying the political existence of the country; that no change, however desirable, should be 'octroyé' upon Hungary, but should be carried out with the free consent and co-operation of the Diet. Both held that no devotion to their national rights would justify the Hungarians in weakening the authority and influence of the common monarchy. But the Hungarian magnates aimed first at the attainment of common constitutional government for the whole Empire, in the hope that the recognition of the rights

L

of individual states would follow in due course; whilst Deák believed that a genuine constitutional *régime* for the common monarchy would never be established until the constitutional rights of these individual states had first been fully and legally acknowledged. He had no faith in the power of the Vienna Government to construct a Constitution that should be based upon the theory, in favour with some German Liberals, of 'forfeiture of right.' It was because he believed, on the contrary, in the vital and universal importance of the opposing theory of the 'continuity of right,' not only for Hungary, but for all the provinces of the Empire, that in November 1860 he gave as the *mot d'ordre* in the impending negotiations 'recognition of the laws of 1848,' and thereby brought upon himself the charge of endangering the successful attainment of a little by demanding too much.

'How can I be your Judex Curiae?' said Deák to the Hungarian ministers when they would have persuaded him to take office under the existing *régime*. 'You forget that I am your Minister of Justice, and that my resignation, which I sent in in September 1848, has never yet been accepted.'[1]

---

[1] Rogge, *Unsere Zeit*, 1876.

CHAPTER XIX.

Resignation of Golouchowski—February Patent issued by Baron von
Schmerling, Minister of the Interior—Triumph of Centralist party—
The Hungarian ministers still anxious to bring about a reconciliation—Office of Court Chancellor accepted by Baron Vay—Hostility
of the County Assemblies of Hungary to the Austrian Government
not encouraged by Deák—His efforts to moderate the violence of
the ultra-National party — Remonstrance against the disavowal
of existing judicial authority by the County Assemblies dangerous
to the liberty and the rights of individuals—Excitement in
Hungary before the opening of the Diet—Deák's forebodings—
March 1861, Deák elected deputy for Pesth—His influence over
the Pesth County Assembly ; over the extreme Nationalist deputies
—Solution of difficulty as to place of meeting of the Diet.

BETWEEN October 1860, and February 1861, the
constitutional problem in Austria assumed a new
phase. Count Golouchowski was succeeded by
Baron v. Schmerling, and the Patent of February
issued under the auspices of the new minister
marked the triumph of the Centralist policy of the
German Liberals, and the inauguration of an attempt
to establish the Constitution upon an entirely
different principle from that laid down in the
October Diploma.

For the changed aspect of affairs in Austria, the
Hungarian ministers were no more responsible than
was Francis Deák for the uncompromising and

violent attitude of the Hungarian County Assemblies, which had undoubtedly contributed to bring about the present estrangement between the two countries.

Though seeing with regret the direction in which matters were tending—thanks to the arbitrary application of the October Diploma—the Hungarian counsellors of the Crown had resolved not to give up too soon the hope of arriving at some arrangement to which their country might with justice to itself agree.

Baron Nicholas Vay, a Protestant magnate, and one of the most popular men in Hungary, who in 1849 had been three times summoned before General Haynau's military tribunal, twice acquitted, and the third time condemned to two years' imprisonment in the Fortress of Theresienstadt, was proposed by the Hungarians at Vienna for the office of Court Chancellor.

The Emperor consenting to the appointment, Baron Vay was summoned to the capital, where he arrived still in ignorance as to the purport of his journey. Whilst he was being enlightened by his compatriots, Count Mailáth and Baron Sennyei, on the present state of the negotiations, the Chancellor elect was called away to an audience of his Majesty.

The interview was short, and no definite scheme of future policy was agreed upon, but the wished-for result was obtained : the Hungarian magnate consented to forget past wrongs, and to come loyally to the help of his Sovereign in the new attempt to restore harmony and confidence between Hungary and the Imperial Government.

Never did a sovereign more abundantly deserve the loyal support and self-sacrifice of his subjects, be they of what nationality they might. For more than five hundred years the Hapsburgs have exercised a stronger and more personal influence upon the destiny of States and nationalities than any other reigning house in Europe. But the power and prestige of the ancient dynasty, which for centuries bore exclusively the Imperial title, were too often employed with baleful effect by princes who chose to make the name of Austria synonymous with bigotry, despotism, and oppression, a byword for blind resistance to liberty and progress amongst all the freedom-loving nations of Europe. The Emperor Francis Joseph has shown that the magic power of the Hapsburg dynasty has not become extinct even in this democratic age; that it is a power which can be used for good with as great effect as it was once used for evil. The truly royal patience and magnanimity displayed by the Sovereign throughout the long and difficult endeavour to reconcile the claims of his various subjects upon the basis of constitutional and national freedom, was an element in the ultimate success of the attempt which none but a strong personal influence could have supplied.

In enumerating the causes that in the opinion of some foreign critics must speedily lead to the dissolution of the heterogeneous Empire of Austria, the great Catholic State of Europe, sufficient account is not always taken of the strength of the uniting bond of dynastic loyalty. In looking back at the principal changes which have passed over Europe during the last twenty years, and comparing the present position of Austria with her position at the time of the Italian war of 1859, it seems at least open to question whether the personal influence of the last Hapsburg emperor has not tended more to strengthen the foundations of the monarchy than Solferino and Königgrätz, the Treaty of Versailles, or the Peace of San Stefano, have done to endanger them.

The line of uncompromising hostility to the Austrian Government taken up by the provincial assemblies on the re-establishment of the County organisation of Hungary formed no part of Deák's policy of legal resistance. He had, as we have seen, been prepared to welcome the disposition towards reconciliation evinced in the original scheme of the October Diploma, and the long interview which he had with the Emperor at Vienna in the following December confirmed him in the earnest desire to find a 'modus vivendi' acceptable to all parties in the State.

On his return to Hungary, Deák, not for the first

time in his life, risked his popularity in the attempt
to moderate the unreasoning violence of the ultra-
National party in the County Assemblies, who
would have exercised their newly restored power in
sweeping away every trace of Austrian rule, and
refusing all recognition of officials appointed under
the central Government.

The lawyer in Deák, as well as the statesman,
was alarmed at the prospect of anarchy involved in
the ill-considered conduct of the 'ultras' in thus
suddenly disavowing all existing judicial authority.
He acknowledged, he said, the importance that
should be attached to public opinion, even when
excited, but he should consider it an injury to
the State if private relations were to be decided
under the stress of a political agitation; 'the voice
of the private person who has been unjustly dealt
with is far too weak to make itself heard above the
tumult of excitement, and individuals suffer without the State being in any way benefited thereby.'
'After ten years of absolute rule under Joseph II.,
it was easy to restore the old order of things, for
then nothing but the organisation of the courts of
justice had been altered; the law itself had not been
changed, no foreign code had been introduced into
our country, no new regulations founded upon a
basis distinct from the law of Hungary. But now
the case is entirely different; old legal principles

have disappeared ; with new laws, new principles
of law have been established ; the legal relations
between private persons, both in our own country
and abroad, have been modified, and that to some
extent in the direction which in principle we ourselves acted upon in 1848. And can any one with
the smallest idea of truth and justice doubt for an
instant that the legal relations which have arisen
out of the new laws must be judged by the same
laws under whose sanction, and in accordance with
whose ordinances, they came into existence ?'[1]

Deák's ideal of liberty was rather that of the
English than of the French reformers. No one
realised more keenly the advantages of a strong
central authority, whether for his own country or
for the common monarchy ; but in his conception
of a well-ordered political community, the State
played a less prominent part than in the schemes
of most constitutional reformers in France ; he was
ever a most jealous guardian of the freedom of
individual citizens.

'The struggle between Liberty and Depotism,'
he once said, 'is as old as history ; and it is always
a striking feature of the contest that that party has
invariably succumbed which did not fulfil its promise
to the nation. The absolute system held out the
prospect of order, peace, and material prosperity ;

[1] Csengery, *Franz Deák*, p. 148.

liberty, on the other hand, promises the enjoyment of individual and civic freedom.'

For his part, Deák might fairly claim to have spared no pains in the attempt to prevent the advocates of constitutional liberty in his own country from belying this promise of perfect individual freedom without prejudice to race, religion, or nationality.

Altered circumstances, both at Vienna and in Hungary, had made the approaching assembly of the Diet seem far less promising of a successful issue than when Deák had first hailed the proclamation of the October Diploma.

He felt oppressed with the difficulties attending the harmonious settlement of the great question affecting the future of his country, at a time when at home and abroad the most extravagant hopes and fears were rife, and the political atmosphere was so charged with electricity that the slightest friction might produce an explosion such as would shatter the whole framework of the empire.

' I have lived through many hard times,' said Deák—' hard for the Fatherland, and hard for the political position of individuals, but I have never before known a time when I have not been able to look forward, frankly, boldly, and with inward contentment, to coming events, with at least the satisfaction of knowing, understanding, and feeling what was my duty as a citizen. But now, my brain reels, my heart fails me, when I look into the chaos of possibilities that lies before us, in emerging from which a single false step may plunge the country into ruin.' 'You write that the eyes of the country are turned expectantly towards me,' he wrote to a friend at this time. 'So much the worse for me and for the country; for the evil has come to such a point that neither I nor any one else can save the Fatherland from it.'[1]

In spite of his gloomy forebodings, Deák worked manfully at the attempt at least to minimise the perils he realised so forcibly. In March 1861 he was elected deputy for the town of Pesth, and very shortly had an opportunity of using his great influence in the interests of moderation and prudence; he even succeeded in inducing that ardently patriotic body, the Pesth County Assembly, to vote the measures necessary for the levying of recruits and the collecting of taxes—a concession to an unconstitutional Government which most of the officials of the newly restored County Assemblies had refused to sanction, not without serious detriment to the public service. In warning his countrymen of the futility of trying to establish a more satisfactory state of things in Hungary by a resort to violent or aggressive measures, Deák would remark, 'You may blow up whole fortresses with gunpowder, but you cannot build the smallest hut with it.'[1]

[1] Csengery, *Franz Deák*, p. 152.

The Diet had been convened to meet at the royal palace at Buda, in disregard of a law of 1848 which provided that for the future the Legislative Assembly should be held in Pesth.

For a time it appeared as though all chance of reconciliation were to be wrecked on this comparatively trifling question, the Left being anxious to refuse all compliance with the royal summons until a concession should have been made to them on this point.

But Deák, having once entered on the campaign, was determined to exercise the rightful prerogative of a leader in choosing his own ground, and he resolved to occupy a more tenable position of defence for the coming contest. He quietly announced that for his part he should go to Buda for the opening sitting of the Diet, whether the other deputies should follow him thither or not. The extreme party, who in this instance were numerically in the majority, agreed to a compromise; the opening ceremonial was attended by all the deputies at Buda, and the subsequent debates were carried on at Pesth.

CHAPTER XX.

On the 6th of April 1861, the Diet was opened by the Royal Commissioner, Count George Apponyi.

Nothing could have been more gracious than the tone of the speech from the Throne. His Majesty, it was said, felt deeply the mistrust to which the remembrance of the past eventful years had given rise in Hungary, and was persuaded that harmony, confidence, and sincere reconciliation could only be brought about by reciprocal respect for rights, and mutual consideration of interests. After announcing

that the principal object of the Emperor in con-
vening the Diet was 'to deliberate with the
legislative bodies on the restoration, maintenance,
and remodelling of the Constitution, to receive the
consecration of the Holy Crown, and issue the
Inaugural Diploma preliminary to his coronation,'
the speech proceeded to explain the reasons that
rendered it imperatively necessary to carry out the
first provisions of the October Diploma, without
previous consultation with the Hungarian Diet,
and that 'compelled his Majesty to hold certain
ordinances of the laws of the land in abeyance
until the constitutional system should, after a renewed revision, come into full force.'

In short the October Diploma and the February
Patent, with all that they entailed, were regarded
in the royal speech as the irrevocable Constitution
of the Empire; and the Hungarian Legislature
was simply invited to discuss subsidiary details,
and to express its opinion on the mode in which
the definite organisation, rendered necessary by the
change in the internal affairs of Austria, might be
brought into accordance with such of the constitutional rights of Hungary as might be not
incompatible with the new Constitution of the
Empire.

'In Hungary,' said Lord Brougham, speaking at
Dublin in 1861,[1] 'the ancient Constitution as it

---

[1] *Addresses of the Hungarian Diet in* 1861, translated from the
Hungarian by J. Horne Payne, Esq.

existed before 1848 is restored, and the establishment of that which was formed in a season of civil
war is alone refused.'

Not so thought the Hungarians.

The extreme Nationalists, who now constituted
the Opposition party in the Diet, had been growing
constantly more powerful since the first assembly
of the Legislature; and the ardour of hostility to
the Vienna Government was not checked by the
tragic death of their leader, Count Teleki, on the
eve of the opening debate. His place was at once
filled by M. Ghyczy and M. Tisza, their party
numbering a slight majority in the Lower House.

On the 13th of May Francis Deák, who for the
past few weeks had been hard at work in collabora-
tion with his friend M. Csengery (known in Pesth
as 'Deák's pen'), read to the House the proposed
reply of the Diet to the speech from the Throne—a
reply couched in the loyal and respectful language
which the tone of the Emperor's gracious message
amply demanded.

It was the first of those famous Addresses in
which Deák, with the wide knowledge of a historian,
the logical reasoning and clear argument of a
jurist, and the dignified moderation of a statesman,
set forth in the name of his country the reasons
why Hungary, with all grateful acknowledgment
of the Emperor's good intentions in conferring
constitutional government upon the Empire, yet
could not consent to the provisions of the October

Diploma, and the system of government there laid down for Hungary as well as for the other provinces of the Empire.

Great indignation was expressed by Liberals in England as well as in Germany against the Hungarian leader, for thus continuing his policy of resistance in face of the new Constitution proffered by Francis Joseph and his advisers.

'Here,' it was said, 'is a nation declining to accept liberties of infinitely wider extent and more liberal character than those it had enjoyed under the provisions of its ancient charter. Not only does it injure itself by this obstinate refusal to accept an improvement upon its antiquated Constitution, but by this selfish abstention it prevents the successful working of the new Imperial Constitution, which would have established parliamentary government, and secured to all the different provinces of the Austrian Empire the ample enjoyment of their rights and local privileges.'

This is a serious indictment, but on closer examination it will be acknowledged that there was more justification for the conduct of the Hungarian people than would be apparent from the foregoing view of the situation.

To appreciate Deák's line of argument as presented in the two Addresses of 1861, and to understand the force of his objection to the assertion that the new Constitution offered Hungary a boon more

valuable to his country than the rights which she
was asked to sacrifice, it may be well to recall what
had been the position of things before the political
earthquake of 1848 had shaken the mutual relations
of states to their foundation.

According to the Pragmatic Sanction of 1723, it
had been definitively agreed, in the interest both of
Hungary and of the Hapsburg dynasty, that, as
regarded the rest of Europe, Austria and Hungary
should constitute one State, but that, as regarded
the internal relations of the two countries, each
should maintain its separate national existence and
distinctive form of government—the bond of union
between them, the pledge of their identity in all
dealings of the State with foreign Powers, consisting
in the person of the hereditary sovereign, who in
matters of internal legislation and administration
formed the sole point of contact between Hungary
and the other provinces of the Empire. Such was
the theory of the relations between Austria and
Hungary.

No doubt, in the course of a hundred and fifty
years, *force majeure* and the natural tendencies of
absolutism on the one hand, political subserviency
and the blinding influence of class prejudices on
the other, had frequently caused an infraction of the
original stipulations, and had warped or obscured the
ideal theory of the unity of the State and the independence of the nation, recognised in the Pragmatic

Sanction, and embodied in the Constitutional Laws of Hungary. Too often, it is true, the Hungarian nobles, in their dread of losing any fraction of their caste privileges, had played into the hands of the Vienna Government, and by their connivance at, or actual participation in, illegal and unjust proceedings, had seemed to sanction a theory of government in which all question of Hungarian independence was disregarded.

But with all the servility and treachery which had sometimes brought discredit upon the Hungarian aristocracy, and had imperilled the national independence, there had never been wanting patriotic men to assert the rights and interests of their country ; men who refused to use the letter of the Constitution as a weapon for destroying the spirit of it ; who, whilst clinging to the loyal observance of the law themselves, demanded that others should do the same.

Francis Deák and those who thought with him, might in this respect claim their descent from the Magyar patriots who formed the small but far-sighted band of reformers in the Diet of 1791 ; from those magnates who, like Zichy, Urményi, and Batthyány in 1792, succeeded in wringing from the Government, even amidst the excitement of an approaching European war, the acknowledgment of the constitutional independence of their country ; from Paul Nágy and the "Old Guard" of the Opposition in 1825.

M

It is not difficult to show that the rights and
privileges claimed by the Hungarians were frequently
overridden by their powerful neighbours ; but on
the other hand there is abundant evidence to prove
that though the Austrian Emperor may often have
used his giant's strength like a giant, he was always
ready to acknowledge that by right he was bound
to consult with Hungary and not to command her ;
that the refractory country with its Diets and County
Assemblies could not be treated in the same arbitrary
fashion as the Hereditary States ; and there had
always been separate Hungarian ministers to per-
petuate, in name at least, what was too often merely
the fiction of national administrative independence.
The responsible Hungarian Ministry established by
the Laws of 1848 was but the modern development
of the old system of Hungarian Courts and Chan-
celries ; not, as Lord Brougham had said, the creation
of a season of civil war.

Even during the crisis of the Napoleonic Wars,
the Emperor dared not disregard the Constitution
he would so gladly have abolished.

The popular Archduke Charles, a great favourite
with the warlike Magyars, had even then felt that
his only hope of carrying out the important changes
in the military system of Hungary, which he
earnestly desired, was through the Diet, which was
accordingly summoned for the first time after an
interval of ten years. The subject had to be ap-

proached cautiously, being introduced in a speech from the President of the Lower House ; but in the end the Diet, indignant at the inadequacy of the Royal Propositions with reference to the redress of long-standing grievances, and at the fresh burdens which it was sought to lay upon the nation, refused absolutely to gratify imperial wishes by transferring to the Austrian War Minister the unconditional control of the Hungarian army, and the Archduke was forced to be content with receiving the military aid of the Magyars on their own terms.[1]

As regards the financial relations theoretically existing between Hungary and the Empire, it is a significant fact that in the Diet of 1811 the Emperor Francis failed entirely to induce the representatives of the nation to vote an extraordinary levy for the purpose of guaranteeing the 100,000,000 florins of paper money then to be found in the Imperial Treasury. The demand was met with the reply from the deputies that in no case would they consent to give the required guarantee, inasmuch as the Government had committed the mistake of confounding the finances of Hungary with those of the Hereditary States ; moreover, it was impossible that under present circumstances they could give their approval to the proposed financial operation, because it was forbidden them to impose upon their country

---

[1] See Sayous, *La Hongrie depuis* 1790.

prospective taxation. The Diet maintained its point, and the royal proposition was withdrawn.[1]

During the critical year of 1807, when Napoleon, relieved from anxiety on the score of Russia by the interview at Tilsit, was making Austria feel the precarious nature of the peace lately signed at Presburg, the military preparations of the indomitable Empire in view of a possible renewal of hostilities had to be carried on with the utmost secrecy. Under these circumstances the attitude of Hungary was of vital importance. The eloquent harangues of Paul Nágy, the patriotic leader of the Opposition in the Diet, now assembled at Presburg, must be silenced at all costs. But what were the means resorted to? Any interference on the part of the Austrian Government would infallibly have roused the Hungarians to a more dangerous pitch of excitement. The King of Hungary alone could hope to influence the conduct of his Magyar subjects.

Paul Nágy was summoned to Vienna, and in a private audience with the Emperor was admonished to be more circumspect in his language. Loyalty to the Sovereign prevailed for the time over all other considerations; Paul Nágy promised to observe a discreet silence, and henceforward no perilous allusions to the French Empire in the Diet at Presburg complicated the foreign policy of Austria.[2]

[1] See De Gérando.   [2] Sayous.

That the Constitution of Hungary stood in great need of reform to fit it for the requirements of modern times and altered circumstances no one recognised more fully than Francis Deák himself, when in 1833 he first entered upon public life.   For twenty years he had laboured heart and soul to free it from the defects which had furnished adversaries of contrary opinions with a pretext for aiming at its destruction ; but once convinced that the reformed Constitution of Hungary was the best form of government for his country, he might well feel justified in straining every nerve to uphold and hand down unimpaired to his successors that noble heritage which for centuries had distinguished Hungary amongst the despot-ridden States of Europe.

Hence in answer to the charge that in refusing the ' octroyé ' Constitution of 1861 the Hungarians were refusing what was in fact an immeasurable improvement upon their own, it might fairly be urged that the ancient national system which they were required to supersede by Baron Schmerling's German Parliament had been changed by the Hungarians themselves, with the sanction of royal authority, into a Constitution that was now valued not only by the nobles but by all classes of the people, and which was as much superior in the eyes of the Hungarians to the new Constitution introduced into the Empire as the latter undoubtedly was to the absolute system which had preceded it.

CHAPTER XXI.

THE pith of the objections raised by the Hungarians to the new parliamentary system in which they were required to take part is to be found in the following clause of the First Address:[1] ‘This Diploma would rob Hungary for ever of the ancient provisions of her Constitution which subject all questions concerning public taxation and the levying of troops throughout their whole extent solely to her own Diet. It would deprive the nation of the right of passing in concurrence with the King

[1] From the translation by J. Horne Payne, Esq.

its own laws on subjects affecting the most important material interests of the land. All matters relating to money, credit, the military establishment, customs and commerce of Hungary, these essential questions of a political national existence, are placed under the control of a general Council of the Empire (the Reichsrath),—a body the majority of whom would be foreigners. There, these subjects would be discussed from other than Hungarian points of view, with regard to other than Hungarian interests. Nor is this all ; in the field of administration this Diploma makes the Hungarian Government dependent upon the Austrian, on a Government which is not even responsible, and which, in the event of its becoming so, would render an account not to Hungary, but to the Council of the Empire, which would give no guarantee for our interests where these should come into collision with those of Austria.'

By elaborate reference to historical acts and treaties, and to the former political relations between Hungary and the Hereditary States, Deák essays to prove that from the time when Austria and Hungary were united under the same ruler, none but a 'personal union,' consisting in the identity of the reigning sovereign, had legally existed between the two countries.

Once again the principle is asserted which throughout his life forms the cardinal point in Deák's political creed : 'Sanctioned laws can only be abrogated by the power which brought them into existence. In a constitutional country only the entire Legislature can create a law. For one member of the Legislature to set aside the same, or whilst professing Constitutionalism to hold in abeyance statutes which were suspended by the absolute power because incompatible with that system, is a proceeding which militates against every constitutional conception. . . . A parliamentary government, a responsible ministry, freedom of the press, with its concomitant trial by jury and the right of self-taxation, are the strongest guarantees of constitutional liberty.

'Our sanctioned laws have given us those guarantees, and never shall we consent to their abrogation or curtailment, however modified; we shall always regard a temporary suspension of these laws as a suspension of the Constitution, as a denial of the constitutional principle itself.'

But the spokesman of the Hungarian people was a practical statesman as well as a jurist and a patriot. Even whilst asserting in these uncompromising terms the theoretical position of Hungary, Deák was careful not to close the door upon the hope of eventual reconciliation by claiming the actual concession of all that might be demanded on the strength of 'légalité formelle.' 'We do not wish,' said the Address, ' to endanger the existence

of the monarchy; but are prepared on a basis of
equity and from considerations of expediency to go
beyond what strict legal obligations would require
of us, to do all that a due regard for our independence and constitutional rights will allow, in
order that the crushing burden resulting from the
reckless policy of the hitherto existing absolute
system may not annihilate at once the prosperity of
the Hereditary States and our own, and that the
ruinous consequences of the past hard times may
be averted from us both.' . . . 'The King of
Hungary,' concludes the Address, 'becomes only
by virtue of the act of coronation, legal King of
Hungary, but the coronation is coupled with certain
conditions prescribed by law, the fulfilment of which
is indispensably necessary. The maintenance of
our constitutional independence, and of the territorial and political integrity of the country, in-
violate, the completion of the Diet, the complete
restoration of our fundamental laws, the restoration of
our parliamentary government and our responsible
ministry, and the setting aside of all the still sur-
viving consequences of the absolute system, are
the preliminary conditions which must be carried
into effect before deliberation and reconciliation are
possible.'

The calm and dignified language of the State
documents in which the controversy between the
Government and the Hungarian Diet was carried

on, would give but a faint idea of the turmoil of excitement raging at this time in Vienna and Buda Pesth.

The extravagant spirit of anti-Austrian hostility to which many of the County Assemblies in Hungary had recently given vent, aroused a corresponding feeling of irritation in the Cis Leithanian provinces, where perhaps not enough allowance was made for the fierce reaction which twelve years of silent enthralment was likely to produce amongst such a people as the Hungarians.

The random declamations of patriotic orators, luxuriating once more in the free display of their native eloquence before an enthusiastic and sympathising audience, made more impression in Austria than the moderate language and reasonable propositions of the national leaders. An angry expression such as that attributed to the Hungarian orator who was said to have exclaimed, ' What do we care about Austria ? ' when caught up and spread abroad through the newspapers, was more widely read and produced more effect on the public mind than all the careful arguments and historical references by which statesmen on either side sought to 'ménager' the national sentiments of both parties.

Amongst politicians in Vienna, and indeed amongst all the advocates of Herr v. Schmerling's idea of a centralised parliament, the indignation against the Hungarian ' obstructives ' was naturally very great; for it was the German Liberal party, now in the ascendant, who had procured the addition of the February Patent to the original Diploma, for which latter the Hungarian ministers and the majority of the non-German members of the Imperial Council had been chiefly responsible.

The belief held at one time by the German Liberals, that the extreme Nationalist party in Hungary might be enlisted as an ally in the attempt to establish a central parliament at Vienna, on 'progressist' and separatist principles, was now entirely dispelled by the union of all parties in Hungary in support of Deák's First Address, which made it abundantly clear that the form of government devised by Herr v. Schmerling had not the remotest chance of being accepted at Pesth by those whose demand was seen to be not for *a* Constitution, but for *the* Constitution of Hungary.

It was inevitable that the German Liberals, being now in power, and having acquired a position in which they might at last hope to put in execution their favourite scheme of a central parliamentary government in which the German element would be predominant, feeling keenly moreover the necessity on financial grounds for bringing the present state of uncertainty to an end,—should resent bitterly the conduct of Hungary in thus preventing the immediate introduction of an uniform settlement for

the whole Empire. Nor was the disapproval of
Deák's policy confined to politicians at Vienna.

By many English Liberals the position of
Hungary was declared to be false and illogical.
She was warned that the reputation of her people
for statesmanship and patriotism had been seriously
damaged, and was advised to accept without selfish
resistance the state of things which Providence had
imposed upon her in the birth of new institutions in
Austria. As for the arguments and suggestions
based upon Francis Deák's 'legal lore,' they were
declared to be of a ludicrous impracticability ; one
writer demonstrating conclusively by reference to
a passage from Lord Macaulay that the idea of
two parliaments was a manifest impossibility, and
a scheme that could not last half a dozen years.

In Pesth, on the other hand, the fever of agitation
ran no less high than in Austria. The scenes in the
Diet were such as to remind the spectator of the
debates in the County Assemblies during the great
reform battle of 1840. All the fire of Hungarian
eloquence was aroused ; youthful orators, clad in
the picturesque national costume, addressed stirring
appeals to the galleries ; the House rang with the
cries of ' Eljén ' that greeted the vigorous outburst
of some patriotic assailant of the Vienna Government ; the old uncompromising opposition fervour
of pre-revolutionary days seemed to have got sole
possession of the Assembly ; recollections of 1849

were evoked, and a new era of civil war was freely
prophesied.

Any one who was present at the first meeting of
the Hungarian Diet in the spring of 1861 would
acknowledge that it must have required something
more than the 'legal lore' and ingenuity of a jurist,
to frame an address which should have satisfied the
imperious demands of the Hungarian Legislature
and nation for an unyielding assertion of their
rights, and yet at the same time have left an
opening for further negotiation with the Imperial
Government.

Indeed it appeared at first as though even Deák's
influence and authority were powerless to keep the
nation to the course in which, as his instinct told
him, lay the sole hope of a future reconciliation.

The party in the Diet in favour of presenting the
Address as it stood, led by Deák himself, was opposed
by the extreme Nationalists, headed by M. Tisza
and Baron Podmanicky, who proposed to reply to
the Royal Speech (or Rescript) simply in the form
of a Resolution, stating, that until he should have
been crowned in accordance with the Laws of 1848,
Francis Joseph could not be regarded as the legal
sovereign of Hungary. On this point, after long
debate, the Ultras, or 'Resolution party,' were
defeated by a majority of three ; but they succeeded
in carrying an amendment to the effect that in the
address the Emperor should be styled simply by the

title of Majesty, leaving out the words ' Imperial Royal.' This victory of the ' Resolution party' in the Diet was a severe blow to the hopes of the Hungarian ministers at Vienna. All chance of reconciliation was at an end if the Emperor should resent—as was not unnatural—this discourteous rejoinder to the well-disposed and even gracious tone of the Royal Rescript, and yielding to the advice of his German ministers, should renounce all idea of coming to a reasonable understanding with his Hungarian subjects, and at once dissolve the Diet. To accept the Address as at present worded would be derogatory to the dignity of the Crown ; to refuse it absolutely, would be to give a most undesirable triumph to the extreme parties both in Pesth and Vienna.

Thanks however to the goodwill and the ingenuity of some of his advisers, a most characteristic method of escape from the dilemma was discovered.

It was suggested that by reference to an act of 1790 a precedent could be found in Hungarian history for addressing the Monarch as ' Imperial Royal' before he had been formally crowned King of Hungary. On the strength of this discovery, the Address was returned to the Diet with a Rescript countersigned by Baron Vay and M. Szédenyi, intimating that it could only be received by His Majesty when addressed in a manner becoming his royal dignity.

Backed by all the weight of a well-authenticated precedent, the 'Address party,' or Moderates, after repeated conferences, succeeded in carrying their point ; the amendment was withdrawn, and the Address sent back to Vienna in the original form.

CHAPTER XXII.

MEANTIME the preparations of Herr v. Schmerling and his coadjutors for a Constitution upon the ground of purely parliamentary institutions, went on apace. The representations of the Hungarian ministers, to the effect, that at least the number of delegates to be sent by Hungary to the new Parliament House at Vienna should be left to the decision of the Diet, were unavailing. A complete 'octroyé' Constitution was now the order of the day, and the amendments and remonstrances of the Hungarians were disregarded, or overruled by an appeal to the majority which the German ministers could now command in the Imperial Council. The

bureaucracy was entirely on the side of Schmerling,
as was the German element throughout the country,
reasonably confident of a preponderating influence
in the future administration. The claims of provincial Diets—including the Hungarian Legislature
—might well, it was considered, be required to
subordinate themselves to the dispositions of a
Ministry which was prepared to give them in exchange
for local autonomy the advantages of a central
Parliament, organised on the most approved Liberal
principles. That the Reichsrath at Vienna appeared
likely to be an Imperial Parliament only in name, in
consequence of the refusal of Bohemia, Hungary, and
Galicia to send to it the prescribed quota of representatives, was perhaps no fault of Baron Schmerling
and the advocates of the new Constitution ; it was
the fault of historical facts, and of human nature.

The paramount ascendency of the parliamentary
Centralists was plainly evident in the tenour of the
Royal Rescript of July in reply to the First Address
of the Hungarian Diet, which no longer bore the signatures of Baron Nicholas Vay and Count Szédenyi,
but of Count Forgách and M. Koloman Beke.

The Hungarian ministers at Vienna, with little
sympathy for the ultra-Nationalists in the Diet in
their demand for the unqualified restoration of the
Laws of 1848, and with a sincere desire to bring
about an understanding between their country and
the Imperial Government, were yet forced reluctantly

to acknowledge that the measures taken by the Austrian ministers, and the new aspect now given to the controversy in the reply to the First Address, made it impossible even for Deák himself, supported as he was by the whole strength of the Diet, to advance a step further towards a compromise.

It was in vain that the late Hungarian chancellor and his colleagues had urged upon the German ministers, that the necessity for some closer bond than a mere personal union having been practically conceded by Francis Deák in the recent Address, the settlement of the future relations between Austria and Hungary might safely be left for discussion in the Diet, with full reliance upon the statesmanship and good sense of its leaders. It was in vain they pointed out, that, by taking as the basis for further negotiations the principles established in the Pragmatic Sanction, a means might still be found for reconciling a due respect for the undisputed rights of Hungary with the equally undisputed necessity for united action in the common affairs of the monarchy; and in vain they proposed that to meet the pressing exigencies of those questions of common concern which required immediate settlement, a deputation should be appointed by the Diet to confer upon such matters with the Government and the Reichsrath.

The plans of the German ministers and their supporters were too far advanced to be disorganised by a return to what would have been in effect an application of the October Diploma, now eclipsed by the Patent of February.

The draft of the second Rescript was drawn up with such complete disregard of the representations of the Hungarian ministers that the latter had no choice but to resign ; with the melancholy consciousness that the step about to be taken by the Imperial Government would only widen the breach which they and the Deák party in Hungary had been labouring so earnestly to heal.

The sting of the Royal Rescript of July lay in the insistance upon the unqualified acceptance by the Hungarian Legislature of the Austrian Constitution, as formulated in the Patent of February. There was no question here of the Diet consenting to 'suspend' the Laws of 1848 ; they were simply abrogated ; there was no recognition, even in form, of the undoubted validity of the claims of Hungary, of that 'légalité formelle' which Hungarian statesmen had acknowledged might with reason be subordinated to a regard for the common good of the monarchy. The favours conferred by the Sovereign were impressively dwelt upon, whilst the maintenance of the existing and old-established laws of the nation was treated as a question not of right but of expediency. 'We indeed acknowledge,' said the Rescript, 'that agreeably to the contents of our former Diploma the Hungarian Diet will, in deviation from former law, deliberate on all questions concerning taxation, the liability to military service and its regulations, henceforth only in common with the other constitutional representatives of the Empire.' But this summary abrogation of ancient rights was not to be without its compensations. 'We at the same time call the attention of the Estates and representatives, in Diet assembled, to the circumstance that until now their influence extended over but a small area of the field of taxation, and not, as will be the case agreeably to our said Diploma, over all matters of taxation and finance.'

To some this might appear a tempting prospect; but Hungary being Hungary, it was as improbable that a new scheme of government, however perfect, thus 'octroyé' upon the nation should be gratefully accepted, as that Englishmen should consent to discard the ancient British Constitution in favour of a system recommended to them by the President of the United States as better suited to the political requirements of the Anglo-Saxon race in its modern development.

The Second Address of the Hungarian Diet, in answer to the July Rescript, is a masterly and exhaustive statement of the position of Hungary in relation to the Sovereign and to the rest of the Austrian Empire, and a spirited vindication of the conduct of the country in refusing obedience to the royal commands.

With a force of argument and an animation of style that carry the reader with unflagging interest through a State paper over a hundred paragraphs in length, Deák in this remarkable document replied point by point to the arguments and assertions of the Rescript, and showed the inconsistency of grounding the royal demands on an appeal to the Pragmatic Sanction, when the stipulations of the Pragmatic Sanction were actually being violated in the suspension of the Constitution and laws of the country by the sole force of absolute authority.[1] The demand that representatives should be sent to the Imperial Parliament (created without the consent of Hungary), there to deliberate on matters —such as taxation—which concerned the internal affairs of the kingdom, was in itself, Deák pointed out, contrary to a clause in the Third Act of 1715, which declares 'that his Majesty will not rule and govern the Estates in any other way than according to the own laws of Hungary heretofore made, or hereafter to be made, through its Diet,' and that ' Hungary shall not be governed according to the manner of the other provinces.'

[1] It may be objected that, considering the proportions of this Memoir, too large a space is devoted to the purely legal and historical questions involved in this and the foregoing Address of the Hungarian Diet. But on the other hand, to attempt an account, however brief and superficial, of Deák's work, without entering at some length on the great state controversy of 1861, in which he played the chief part, would be to write the Life of Wellington with but a cursory allusion to the Peninsular Campaign. The quotations throughout are from the translation by Mr. Horne Payne.

In answer to the assurances contained in the Rescript that the guarantees of the constitutional independence of the country would not be endangered, but on the contrary further secured, if Hungary were to discuss the questions of taxation and military service in common with the representatives of the Hereditary States,—the Address boldly declares : ‘ We find in these words no ground whatever for the least reassurance.   The constitutional independence of the country is seriously infringed by the very fact that your Majesty, without the previous consent of the Diet, of your own might takes from the land this cardinal right ; that your Majesty of your own authority ordains laws, and without once asking the Diet whether it accepts these essential alterations of its ancestral Constitution, treats the same as an accomplished fact, and commands us straitway to send representatives to the Council of the Empire (Reichsrath), which will take the place of our Diet in exercising those rights with regard to Hungary.’ . . . ‘ Where would be the guarantee of the constitutional independence of Hungary, if at a future period a successor of your Majesty, appealing to this precedent, should act in the same manner with our other laws and rights, and should by a command of his own power and authority suppress or modify these without the previous consent of the nation, and then instruct the Diet to complete these mandates in the field of legislation ?’

After showing by reference to former Acts, notably those of 1715, 1790, and 1827, that Hungary through her Diet had always in reality possessed and exercised the right of herself disposing of the lives and money of her citizens, and had never shrunk from heavy sacrifices, when threatened danger to the monarchy had made them necessary[1]—the Address grapples once more with the question of the relations established by the Pragmatic Sanction between Hungary and the Hereditary States, in consequence of the identity of the common sovereign.

The particular Acts quoted in the Royal Rescript are declared not to demonstrate a more intimate real union, but on the contrary, to confirm the political and administrative independence of Hungary. ‘The methods, the conditions, and the forms prescribed by law, by which the prince becomes King of Hungary, are one thing, the steps by which he ascends the throne of the Hereditary States are another.’

The present arrangement existing in the Dual Empire of Austria-Hungary is foreshadowed in the passage referring to the necessary unity in the

[1] A right which the Sovereign had no reason to grudge the nation. It could certainly not be maintained that a rigid respect for constitutional laws had the effect of making the Hungarians niggardly with their contributions in times of danger to the monarchy. The campaigns of 1799 and of 1800, in which Hungary took a foremost share, cost the Kingdom 100,000 men and 30,000,000 florins. (See Sayous.)

administration of foreign affairs. ' The sovereign
rights in Hungary being vested by the Constitution
in the person of the King of Hungary, who is at the
same time ruler of the Hereditary States, it follows
as a matter of course that rights of this nature should
be exercised, both in relation to Hungary and to the
Hereditary States, by the same sovereign. Such a
royal prerogative is the right of the King of Hungary,
by virtue of which he decides of his own sovereign
will the external relations with foreign Powers, and
foreign affairs generally.'

That questions of peace or war should be subject to the influence of Hungary, that Hungarians
should not be excluded from the administration of
foreign affairs, and should be admitted to the foreign
embassies, had indeed been stipulated by various
laws for the past two centuries ; but the supreme
control of foreign affairs had always been placed
in the hands of the King ; and the country, satisfied
with its highest and amplest guarantee in its right
to grant taxes and levy recruits, only desired that
Hungarians should have their due influence in their
administration.

' This principle too in reference to foreign affairs
was carried out by the Diet of 1847–48, which
respecting the said royal right, and maintaining it in
its full integrity, established no special Hungarian
Ministry for Foreign Affairs, but considered it
sufficient that the minister attached to the person

of his Majesty should exercise the influence secured
to the kingdom by the laws above enumerated.'

The military and financial aspect of the relations
between Hungary and the Hereditary States is next
dealt with; the legislative and administrative independence of the kingdom in these matters being
demonstrated not only by reference to the sanctioned
laws of the Diet, but to the evidence of historical
facts, which show that the Emperor had in times
past recognised, not only theoretically but practically,
the necessity for separate dealings with Hungary.

As to the former (the military relations), an
enumeration of the various important matters which
had always been subject to the decision either of
the Hungarian Council of Lieutenancy or to commissioners appointed by the Diet, 'places it beyond
a doubt that the law of 1848 which entrusted to
a responsible minister the administration of the
military department, without prejudice to the royal
prerogative of the Hungarian king, was passed in
accordance with the spirit of the former laws.'
With regard to the latter (the financial relations),
also, it is carefully shown that by law the administration of the income of the country was independent
of, and separate from, the administration of the
other 'provinces.' The determination of the taxes
belonged to, and was settled by, the Diet, without
any influence being exerted on it by the Hereditary
States.

Having refuted in detail the various statements quoted by the Royal Rescript from former Acts to prove the existence of a central Government having a right to direct matters relating in common to Hungary and the other provinces,—Deák explains that he had entered thus fully into the former rights and position of the country in order to lay before his Majesty the true and firm basis of the legitimate wishes submitted in the First Address, and to prove that 'the rights of the country did not owe their origin to the legislation of 1848, but have existed according to older laws.' 'The Laws of 1848 have only given the rights of the nation a newer, clearer, and more determined form, a form more adapted to the requirements of the times. With regard to the relations between the nation and the Sovereign, no new rights were created or established.'

After making the daring assertion that, 'if the Laws of 1847–48 did create new rights, if they had altered the Public Law of Hungary not merely in form but in substance, we should still have the right to demand—as we do demand—all that they contain; for these laws were enacted by the constitutional Legislature, by the common consent of the King and the nation, and are therefore binding, until repealed by the same common consent of the Sovereign and the nation,' Deák proceeds to vindicate the aforesaid Laws of 1848 from the charge of having caused the convulsions which in that eventful year had agitated Hungary in common with the other provinces of the Empire. The Constitution bestowed upon the Hereditary States in 1848 contained none of the separatist tendencies with which the Hungarian laws are reproached, 'yet this bureau-born Constitution, whose principles had been established by royal power, was speedily revoked, convulsions followed there also, and there too the absolute system was introduced. Croatia, which had taken up arms against the Laws of 1848, and is certainly not open to the same reproaches made against them, suffered the same fate as Hungary and the other provinces, and lost too all its constitutional rights.' 'The convulsions, the dangers, and the introduction of the absolute system were then not the consequences of the Laws of 1848, for the absolute system was imposed beyond the jurisdiction of the Hungarian Laws, nay, even where they met with resistance.'

The promise of the Monarch in the Royal Rescript to restore the Constitution, and that conditionally, by the exercise of royal absolute authority, is declared to give no confidence whatever in the stability of even that partial restoration which it boasts of having already effected ; there is no guarantee that rights acknowledged to be dependent on royal authority may not on the strength of the same authority be again revoked or suspended.

'Did our holiest duty and our conscience not

mask of constitutionalism the attempt at incorporation which the absolute power had so often, though unsuccessfully, attempted, was to be renewed. This anxiety and its invariable companion, mistrust, would at every step impede the progress of deliberations, and often make them impossible; would finally either dissolve the Council of the Empire, or lead the majority to conduct productive of bitterness and hatred, not between individuals, but between people and people, land and land. This without doubt would be the greatest blow that could reach the Empire.'

Whatever may be the opinion of politicians as to the probable stability of the present Dual system, few will deny that Deák has been justified in his belief that the concession to Hungary of her long-sought rights would not loosen but strengthen the bonds uniting her with the Empire.

The following protest against enforcing the 'centralised unity' of the Empire is based not only on the opinion of a Hungarian patriot as to the form of administration best suited to his own country, but on a broad principle of government applicable to all states, and in all times: 'A forced unity will never make the Empire strong; the outraged feeling of the individual states, and the bitterness arising from the pressure of force, awaken the desire for separation, and therefore the Empire would be the weakest just at the moment when it would be in

want of its united strength and the full enthusiasm
of its peoples.   The position of an empire as a
great Power whose unity can only be maintained by
force of arms, is precarious, and least safe in the
moment of danger. . . . Feelings and ideas will
extend themselves; and because a "centralised unity"
is in opposition to the past of the individual lands
to which they look back with pious recollection,
because it is opposed to the hopes they nourish for
the future, the practical carrying out of " centralised
unity" will have to contend not only with hostile
feelings, but in the course of open deliberations with
opposition and considerable difficulties.   If therefore
your Majesty wishes your Empire to be free and
really strong, your Majesty cannot attain that object
by a compulsory unity, but by a mutual understanding
arrived at through the free consent of the nation.'

Something of the same idea as to the true nature
of a strong empire had been expressed in very
vigorous English eighty years before :   ' Perhaps,
sir, I am mistaken in my idea of an empire as
distinguished from a single state or kingdom.   But
my idea of it is this, that an empire is the aggregate
of many states under one common head, whether
this head be a monarch or a presiding republic.   It
does in such Constitutions frequently happen (and
nothing but the dismal cold dead uniformity of
servitude can prevent its happening) that the
subordinate parts have many local privileges and

command us to protest against this "octroi," we should still cling to our own ancestral Constitution, because that Constitution, which has sprung from the existence of the nation, and concurrently with the nation, has grown to maturity, developed, and extended itself, according to all precedent, answers its purpose better, and is more durable than an " octroi." We could appeal in this respect to history, and quote examples from other countries ; but we will only call to mind how many constitutions or systems taking their place have been introduced into the Austrian Empire since 1848, of which some have never come into operation, others have survived but a short time.'

Had the Address ended here, the Austrian and Hungarian statesmen who so earnestly desired in the interests of the monarchy to bring about a speedy reconciliation between the two countries, might justly have complained that, whilst establishing beyond dispute the 'légalité formelle' of Hungary's position, and giving eloquent expression to the strong constitutional and patriotic feelings of his countrymen, Deák had yet shown himself incapable of appreciating the true nature of the situation as it affected not only the Hungarian Constitution, but the safety and well-being of the whole Austrian Empire.

But Deák had not ignored this side of the question, and was prepared to show that in fighting thus stubbornly for the rights of Hungary he was not endangering the true interests of the Hereditary States.   Although taking his stand on the theory of a 'personal union,' he was willing to modify it in the direction of a 'real union,' so far as this might be done lawfully and with the free consent of the nation. 'We have no desire,' so ran the Address, 'to endanger the existence of the Empire; we do not wish to dissolve the union lawfully existing through the Pragmatic Sanction. The "personal union" is a bond from which common relations spring, and these relations we wish to bear in mind.' After pointing out that the Third Act of 1848 had made special provision for the settlement of those relations which affect 'the common interests of the country and the Hereditary States,' the Address declares the willingness of the Hungarian Legislature from time to time freely and openly to confer with the constitutional peoples of the Hereditary States. . . .

'By such means it will be much more easy to settle in special cases matters affecting our joint interests than by a common Council of the Empire, to which we could not send deputies without sacrificing our most essential rights and our constitutional independence, and which Hungary would moreover enter with the anxious fear that in spite of all verbal assurances she would be considered as an Austrian province; that under the immunities.   Between these privileges and the supreme common authority the line may be extremely nice.   Of course disputes, often too very bitter disputes, will arise.   But though every privilege is an exemption (in the case) from the ordinary exercise of the supreme authority, it is no denial of it.   The claim of a privilege seems rather "ex vi termini" —to imply a superior power.   For to talk of the privileges of a State or of a person who has no superior is hardly any better than speaking nonsense.

'Now, in such unfortunate quarrels among the component parts of a great political union of communities, I can scarcely conceive anything more imprudent than for the head of the empire to insist that if any privilege is pleaded against his will or his acts, that his whole authority is denied ; instantly to proclaim rebellion, to beat to arms, and to put the offending provinces under the ban.   Will not this very soon teach the provinces to make no distinctions on their part ?   Will it not teach them that the Government against which a claim of liberty is tantamount to high treason is a Government to which submission is equivalent to slavery ? '[1]

But Burke's words of remonstrance and warning fell unheeded, and the American Colonies ceased to form part of the British empire.

---

[1] Burke's *Speech on Conciliation with America*, 1775.

To return to the Address.   With reference to his Majesty's declaration, that he has given validity to one part of the Laws of '48, but 'never has and never will' acknowledge the other part, asking the Diet at the same time to modify a part of those laws and submit to the Royal Sanction Acts for their repeal, the Address, whilst announcing the readiness of the Diet, when completed, to transform and more clearly define certain points in the Laws of 1848, protests absolutely against the assumption that his Majesty is entitled to repeal of his own authority any part whatever of the existing laws. Above all, the Diet demurs to the unconstitutional principle that his Majesty does not consider himself personally bound to recognise the Laws of '48.

After vindicating elaborately the claims of the Hungarian Diet with respect to the administrative reunion of Transylvania, Croatia, and Fiume, and explaining the position which the legislation of 1848 had established with regard to the non-Magyar peoples of Hungary, Deák adds : 'But we know that the constantly developing feeling of nationality deserves respect, and must not be weighed by a measure derived from former times or older laws. We shall not forget that the non-Hungarian inhabitants of Hungary are in every respect citizens of the country, and we are prepared sincerely and readily to secure to them by law whatever their own interests or that of the country demand.'

Francis Deák was not one of those whose theories of patriotism are framed exclusively to suit their own race or country. In condemning the pride of race, the perhaps over-zealous patriotism, which is sometimes laid to the charge of the Hungarian people, it is well to remember that Count Széchényi, Baron Josika, and Francis Deák are Magyars who have at least as much right to be cited as typical representatives of their nation, as the vehement ultra-Magyar orators who are sometimes regarded abroad as the only true exponents of Hungarian opinion.

After summing up shortly the foregoing arguments and defining the present attitude of the country, the Address ended with the declaration that 'in consequence of the Royal Rescript we are compelled with the greatest sorrow to regard the thread of negotiations through the Diet as broken of.'

Those who knew Francis Deák, not only as the dauntless champion of the national rights, and the accepted leader of a united party, but as the far-sighted careworn man who realised with a painful intensity of personal feeling the dangers and difficulties that beset his country, were well aware that the closing passage of the Address was no mere rhetorical peroration, but the genuine expression of sad though not hopeless foreboding: ' It is possible that our country will again pass through hard times ; we cannot avert them at the sacrifice of our duties as citizens. Constitutional freedom is not our possession in such a sense that we can freely deal with it; the nation has with faith entrusted it to our keeping, and we are answerable to our country and to our conscience.

'If it be necessary to suffer, the nation will submit to suffering, in order to preserve and hand down to future generations that constitutional liberty it has inherited from its forefathers. It will suffer without losing courage, as its ancestors have endured and suffered, to be able to defend the rights of the country; for what might and power take away, time and favourable circumstances may restore; but the recovery of what a nation renounces of its own accord from fear of suffering, is matter of difficulty and uncertainty. The nation will suffer, hoping for a better future, and trusting to the justice of its cause.'

In the debates on the First Address, Deák had been forced to defend himself against the charge of excessive caution and even cowardice, and had been driven to declare in words which made a deep impression upon his auditors: 'He who is careful about his own personal safety when the interest of his country is at stake, is indeed timid and cowardly; but the man who with no fear for himself is anxious solely for his Fatherland, who is prudent not for his own sake, but to avert danger from his country, he is neither timid nor a coward. When we are acting only for ourselves, we may run what risks we please ; but when it is a question of acting on behalf of those who have entrusted their destiny to our hands, of the fate of the country itself, then we must run no risks ; prudence is a duty. We are bound to hazard our all for the country, but not the country itself.'

On the present occasion, however, the Diet acknowledged, that the man who had preached caution, when the prevailing excitement amongst his countrymen was all in favour of a spirited policy, who had braved misunderstanding and even suspicion rather than endanger the interests of his country and disobey the voice of conscience, could speak out boldly enough when he believed that the right time had come.

The Second Address was carried unanimously, and sent to Vienna accompanied by a protest from both Houses of the Legislature against a breach of the Fourth Act of 1848, which decrees that ' the Diet cannot be dissolved until the Ministry has submitted to it the accounts of the past year, and the estimates for the ensuing one, and until the Diet has passed resolutions.'

The result of this Address, the last will and testament of the doomed Assembly, was a foregone conclusion.

In spite of the efforts of Counts Mailáth and Apponyi at Vienna, the Diet was dissolved, and the provisional laws and ordinances in force before the

commencemant of the recent negotiations re-established. Protests against the dissolution of the Diet
were sent in from many of the County Assemblies,
amongst others from that of Pesth, where a general
congregation was summoned for the 30th of September. But the short interlude of municipal liberty
had gone by, at least for the present.

On the members of the Assembly appearing on
the appointed day, to the number of seven hundred
and fifty, the hall was found in possession of
Austrian troops, and the Hungarians were forced
to disperse without having held their meeting.

At the beginning of November a Royal Rescript
was published suspending the Hungarian Constitution, the existing authorities in the counties
were removed, and military tribunals re-established
throughout the country.

Once more Deák warned the nation not to be
betrayed by these arbitrary measures into acts of
violence, nor on any pretext whatsoever to abandon
the ground of legality.

'This is the safe ground,' he said, 'on which, un-
armed ourselves, we can hold our own against armed
force. Law endues men with such serenity that in
holding closely to it they can await in confidence
the most critical events; it is this which supplies
the oppressed with their chief need, the power to
suffer with dignity; for dignity is conferred by law,
and by law only.'

On the sudden rupture of all negotiations through the Diet, the leader himself, the representative of the nation, relapsed again into private life.

The summer at this time he spent mainly on the estate of his brother-in-law at Szént-Lászlo, the winter in the 'Queen of England' hotel at Pesth.

At the height of his fame, Deák could never be brought to assume the habits and surroundings of a political personage. The 'wisest Hungarian,' the distinguished statesman, whose able defence of his country's rights had drawn upon him the attention of Europe, continued always to lead the same life of homely simplicity as the young deputy who came up to the Diet at Presburg thirty years ago.

On the very day on which Parliament was dissolved and all hope of further negotiation was therefore at an end, Francis Deák, it was said, might be seen, playing bowls and chatting with a knot of intimate friends, at one of his favourite haunts in the environs of Pesth, as though no 'bon bourgeois' in the capital were more entirely innocent of all share in the political events of the time. If he disliked and avoided all ostentation and unnecessary publicity, it certainly could not be said of the 'sage of Kehida' that he affected to enhance his reputation by any mystery of seclusion. Day after day he was to be seen, either pacing the streets of Pesth, his hands folded behind his back, the inevitable cigar between

his lips, deep in conversation with one of his
numerous devoted friends; or strolling over the
beautiful grassy slopes of the hills that overhang
the western banks of the Danube; or listening to
the lively political gossip in the dining-room of the
' Queen of England ' hotel, occasionally breaking
into some heated discussion with a humorous
commentary or warning, that had more effect in
forming the public opinion of Pesth than half a
dozen leading articles.

Notwithstanding his apparent disappearance from
the prominent place which he had occupied during
the past few months in the face of Europe, Deák
had by no means let go the reins which none but he
could handle with such masterly power, and was
quite prepared to undertake again the guidance of
his country's course when the times should seem
ripe for a fresh advance.

' We can wait,' the German minister had proudly
said, when thwarted in his schemes by the opposition
of Hungary.

' We can wait,' was Deák's motto, as he quietly
resigned himself and his country to a second period
of political inaction.

CHAPTER XXIII.

FOR four years the Austrian Constitution as organised by Baron Schmerling maintained a difficult and precarious existence.

It was a strong proof of the ability and dexterous management of the Minister of the Interior, that so exceedingly artificial and one-sided a piece of mechanism, should have worked even this length of time without breaking down.

The theory of a 'Full Reichsrath,' to which the various provincial Diets should all send their representatives in obedience to the regulations of the February Patent, remained a theory and nothing more, in consequence of the refusal of Hungary and Croatia to comply with the commands of the Imperial Government.[1]   During the first two sessions of the new Parliament, the Legislative Assembly was supposed therefore to be only the Lesser (or Diminished) Reichsrath ; though to satisfy his Liberal supporters, the Constitutionalists, Baron Schmerling, braving the remonstrances of Czechs and Conservatives, allowed the Lower House to discuss the 'estimates of the State expenditure' as though it were the Full Reichsrath, which alone was entitled to decide upon affairs common to the whole empire.

In the session of 1863 an expedient was found for gradually transferring to the actually existing 'Lesser Reichsrath' the functions that should, according to the Constitution of February, have been exercised by the unfortunately non-existent 'Full Reichsrath.'

The Diet of Transylvania, based on the newly introduced electoral laws, and composed entirely of the Saxon and Rouman nationalities, dutifully

---

[1] 'The sphere of action of the Full Reichsrath embraces (according to Art. II. of the Diploma of October) all subjects of legislation which have reference to rights, duties, and interests common to all the kingdoms and lands, including military service, regulation of money, customs and commerce, imperial finance, and general estimates of the State expenditure. To the Diminished Reichsrath belong, with the exception by the matters mentioned above, all subjects which are not expressly reserved of the Provincial Ordinances for the several Provincial Assemblies represented in the Diminished Reichsrath.'— *Patent of February* 1861.

accepted the provisions of the February Patent, and sent delegates to the Reichsrath at Vienna.

The presence of the Transylvanian deputies was declared to constitute a Full Reichsrath; on their withdrawal from the Chamber, the scene changed, and the Assembly became at once the Lesser Reichsrath; thus with a respect for the 'Unities' worthy of the classical drama, subjects pertaining to one or the other body could be dealt with on the same day, in the same place, and by the same persons. No more ingenious method could have been devised for reconciling the exigencies of theory with the realities of fact.

In the end, however, the task of satisfying the demands of the Centralist Liberals in the Lower House, and at the same time preserving a good understanding with the non-German representatives and Conservatives, became too hard even for Baron Schmerling. His position was a peculiar one, the chief supporters of the minister and of the Constitution, as identified with the February Patent, were the advanced German Centralists, who, owing to the provisions of the Patent, had acquired such control over the finances as to give them an influence which they were not backward to take advantage of, when the Budget came to be submitted for discussion in the Lower House.

But the minister was aware that if the Constitutionalists made too free a use of their privileges in this respect, and pressed too strongly for important changes—such as recognition of ministerial responsibility—which were beyond their legitimate scope to effect, and were moreover highly distasteful to the Cabinet, the whole scheme of parliamentary government 'octroyé' by one minister might be withdrawn by a more favoured successor.

Thus, both to refuse and to concede the demands of his Liberal supporters, was equally dangerous to the position of the chief author of the Constitution.

With the financial embarrassments occasioned, or at least heightened, by the perpetual disputes over the Budget in the Lower House, discontent with the existing state of things increased amongst the non-German populations; a desire for some change, the conviction of the necessity for coming to some agreement with Hungary, grew daily more pressing.

In those attempts to establish a satisfactory compromise which had taxed the best endeavours of the Hungarian ministers before the publication of the October Diploma, Deák had taken no part, because he believed that events were not then ripe for a solution, which, however desirable in itself, would never be arrived at without the aid of necessity and the sheer force of circumstances.

'He knew,' says M. Csengery,'that peace between the Monarch and the Nation could be firmly established only if the agreement came about of itself, so to speak, as a matter of political necessity.'

But the aspect of affairs in Hungary at this time, even under the Provisorium, was very different from what it had been during the twelve years of Herr v. Bach's *régime*. Instead of a mute, hopeless resistance, there was a feeling in certain circles, not indeed of amity, but of an openness to reconciliation,—a disposition to accept the hand of friendship when it should be cordially held out. The bitter self-contained resentment of former years had subsided, and the relations of the non-German inhabitants of the Empire towards their Magyar fellow-subjects had been rather improved than otherwise by the staunch resistance of the Hungarian Diet to the centralising tendency of the February Patent.

That much discontent and hostility still prevailed throughout the country, was sufficiently attested by the plots and secret negotiations discovered from time to time by the Austrian Government, by the suspicious attitude of Hungary three years later during the Austro-Prussian war, and by the strength and numbers of the party which subsequently carried on in the Diet a strenuous opposition against the Hungarian Government and the Compromise of 1867.

But signs were not wanting in the course of the four years during which Hungary underwent a second period of arbitrary rule to show that though the thread of negotiations through the Diet might have been broken off, yet all channels of communication between the leading statesmen in the two countries had not been closed.

There were at least two men in the monarchy who were determined that, so far as their influence and goodwill could avail, Austria and Hungary should find a means of blotting out past differences, and forming one State, based no longer upon force, but on community of feeling and interest. The Emperor and Francis Deák were steadily pursuing the same object, though from the nature of their respective positions they approached it from a different standpoint.

So long, however, as the chief personage of the present Ministry remained in power in Austria, it was morally impossible that the demands of the united Hungarian nation, as set forth in the Second Address of the Diet, should be satisfied. Baron Schmerling was no less completely identified with the policy of a stringent centralisation than was Francis Deák with the cause of national autonomy and the preservation of historical rights. The very 'raison d'être' of the minister being involved in the successful maintenance of the Constitution as developed in the February Patent, it would have been as impossible for him to yield to the remonstrances of the Hungarian Diet, as it would have been for the popular champion in Pesth to accept a portfolio as minister, and take part in the debates of the Reichsrath at Vienna. It is therefore not surprising that the various endeavours made during the first years of the Provisorium to come to a formal understanding between the two parties in Austria and Hungary should have been unsuccessful; that the programme brought forward by Count Apponyi at the conference of Hungarian statesmen in 1862, even though supported by the *Pesti Naplo*, the organ of the Deák party, should have proved unacceptable at Vienna; that the proposal for a compromise founded on the Liberal Programme of 1847, suggested by Count Forgách in 1863, should have met with no better fate.

So long as Baron Schmerling could rely upon the support of the German Liberals in the Lesser Reichsrath, and insure the toleration if not the cordial acceptance of the existing Constitution on the part of the Court party and the Upper House, so long he could maintain his position without the necessity for such concession to the Hungarians as would in fact have destroyed the symmetry of the present Centralist Government, and diminished the prospect, at best a doubtful one, of its ever striking firm root throughout the Empire.

All suggestions of compromise therefore, however reasonable they might appear to their Hungarian promoters, could from the nature of things be met only with the stipulation that the October Diploma and the Patent of February should be regarded as Fundamental State Laws, from which no appeal was possible.

The reluctance of the Cabinet, moreover, to enter upon an embarrassing discussion of the unsleeping 'Hungarian question,' found convenient justification in the various foreign complications which enabled them to silence the remonstrances of discontented politicians at home with the unanswerable plea, that, in dealing with matters of foreign policy the Government of the day must have all the weight and authority conferred by, at least, the ostensible support and sanction of the various fractions of the State.

But whatever the exigencies of the Government, the Sovereign himself had never wavered in his gracious intentions towards his Hungarian subjects. In 1862, at the request of Count Forgách, and without the intervention of the Cabinet, an amnesty was declared by the Emperor for all political prisoners in Hungary, and about the same time a Royal Rescript announced the grant of a subvention from the Hungarian Exchequer towards the support of the National Museum and Theatre at Pesth.

The few words addressed by the Emperor to a deputation of gentlemen from the Landowners' Association of Hungary made a profound impression in that country, and created a feeling of hopefulness not to be discouraged by the repeated failure of the official negotiations. 'It is my wish,' said Francis Joseph, 'to satisfy Hungary not only in material respects but in other matters also.'[1]

In the autumn of 1864 the question of Hungary's State rights was brought prominently before the public mind by a controversy between the Viennese jurist Dr. Lustkandl', an ardent supporter of Baron Schmerling's policy, and the great Hungarian lawyer.   On this occasion Deák broke the silence of three years with a vigorous reply to the arguments of Dr. Lustkandl', in which he showed the danger of insisting too strongly upon the convenient theory of 'Forfeiture of Right'—a theory that might be turned against the legitimate authority of the Crown as effectively as against the historical rights of the people.   In the following year it became apparent that the Hungarian problem was reaching a stage when it was beyond the scope of professors and jurists, however learned, to solve ; and that political, not legal, arguments were to come into play.

[1] *Drei Jahre Verfassungsstreit.*

CHAPTER XXIV.

A FRENCH writer[1] has ascribed the perilous and unstable condition of Austria to the unfortunate necessity which has compelled her in the course of the past hundred years to take up four successive lines of policy. First the Danubian policy, when the energies of the monarchy were directed against the Ottoman power. This line being abandoned under the present Emperor, and the rôle of patron of the Christian races of Turkey passing exclusively

---

[1] M. de Forçade.

to Russia, an Italian policy was initiated, in which Austrian interests were identified with the maintenance of papal and imperial supremacy over an unwilling people, Austrian troops occupied Florence and Milan, and the black and yellow flag waved over the Castle of St. Angelo.   After the collapse of the Italian policy in 1859, a distinctively German policy was adopted ; and the 'gross Deutsch Idee,' rendered more attractive to German Liberals from its connection with the first establishment of Constitutionalism in Austria, found an able and zealous champion in Herr v. Schmerling.

But the growing influence of the Hohenzollerns in Germany, the failure of Austria to obtain from Europe the recognition of the brilliant position claimed by her at the conference at Frankfort in 1863 as undisputed chief of the German Confederation, the cold indifference of Hungary and the non-German provinces of the Empire,—all combined to convince the Hapsburg Emperor that circumstances did not favour his ambition to become an Austrian Charlemagne.

If it needed Sadowa to bring fully home to the minds of Francis Joseph's advisers the important truth that the safety and greatness of the Austrian Empire were to be found in consolidating, not in extending, the range of its dominion, it would seem as though the Sovereign himself was earlier convinced that the 'Great Germany' policy, pure and simple, could no longer be relied on, if his Empire were to remain a compact and powerful state.

Towards the close of 1864, the question of negotiation with Hungary again coming to the foreground, all eyes were once more turned towards Francis Deák. This time the Conservative magnates, mindful of the difficulties and misunderstandings that had hindered their well-intentioned efforts to render the October Diploma acceptable to the Hungarian people, resolved not again to enter the lists against the German ministers in the capacity of 'generals without an army;' and accordingly Count Mailáth and Baron Sennyei repaired to Pesth, there to take counsel with the true representative of Hungary before embarking on further negotiations at Vienna.

In the famous Easter article which appeared in the *Pesti Naplo* in the spring of 1865, Deák showed in what spirit he was prepared to meet these renewed overtures at reconciliation. From the ministers of the Crown at Vienna he turned to the Sovereign himself. The cause of the disputes, said the Easter article, which had so often arisen between Austria and Hungary, and had threatened at times to break up for ever the unity of the monarchy, might in every instance be traced, not to Hungary, but to those Austrian statesmen who had attacked her Constitution and her laws. The Hungarian Constitution, it was pointed out, had never been opposed to the safe existence of the monarchy ; by its means, the nation in times of danger had always fulfilled its obligations with regard to the preservation of the Empire with energy, and sometimes with brilliant success. After recognising the futility of looking for a reconciliation between Austria and Hungary in a change of opinion on the part of the present ministers, Deák appealed to the wisdom and love of justice of the Sovereign ; declaring at the same time that, 'whilst the Hungarian nation would never give up its constitutional independence, it was prepared, when once this should be restored, to take such legal measures as might be proved necessary for bringing its laws into harmony with the stability of the monarchy.'

When in the First Address of the Hungarian Diet, Deák, speaking in the name of his countrymen, had declared that Hungary was prepared to enter, 'from case to case' and on special occasions, into deliberation with the constitutional peoples of the Hereditary States,—the expression had provoked vehement protests from the Extreme party ; Paul Uzány exclaiming, 'That phrase "from case to case" will take us straight into the Reichsrath.' But Deák had carried his point then, and he did not hesitate now to adopt the same line of good sense and sound statesmanship.

The Easter article acknowledged fully the existence of affairs common to both halves of the

Empire, and even gave to the term 'common affairs' a wider signification than had been expected from the popular champion ; always however with the understanding that their settlement should not be left to the decision of a parliamentary majority in the Reichsrath, but should be arrived at after due consultation between delegations appointed for the purpose.

It was the Deák party that had spoken in the Easter article. After a short interval came an answering voice from the Conservative magnates and their allies at Vienna. As if to show the complete harmony that now prevailed between the Hungarian magnates and the main body of their compatriots, the complement to the article in the *Pesti Naplo* appeared in a series of letters emanating from Deák himself, and published in the columns of the *Debatte*, the organ of the Conservative party.

In the recognition of the existence of 'common affairs' and the proposition to discuss these through delegations appointed for the purpose, a basis of action had been found on which all parties in Hungary, with the exception of the Extreme Left, could agree.

The letters in the *Debatte*, claiming to be the authentic expression of Hungarian opinion, were widely read on both sides of the Leitha, and produced a distinctly favourable effect at the critical juncture, when the relations between Baron Schmerling and his Liberal supporters in the Reichsrath, were becoming constantly aggravated by the inability of the former to satisfy the demands of the German majority in the Lower House, and by the refusal of the latter to replenish the Imperial Exchequer, until their claims had been granted.

The views and wishes of Hungary, as set forth in the *Debatte*, were based on a complete acceptance of the Pragmatic Sanction. From an examination of this fundamental compact were deduced two important and undeniable facts. First, that there are affairs common to all the lands of the Austrian Empire ; second, that all affairs common to the Empire are so only in so far as their being treated as common is necessary to the safety of the monarchy.

After showing that the Pragmatic Sanction regards all the Austrian lands as belonging to one common ruler, and considers the maintenance of the power and dignity of the ruler as a 'common affair,' and that it also binds the several lands to mutual support,— the writer in the *Debatte* argues from hence, that the management of foreign affairs and of the army are 'common affairs.' The providing of money for all such purposes is also declared to come under the same category ; the Hungarian Finance Minister being therefore bound to furnish the proper quota of Hungary to the Imperial Exchequer, whilst leaving to the Diet the settlement of those matters of internal finance which were not common to the monarchy.

From these premises as to the position of Hungary with regard to the Sovereign and to the other lands of the Austrian Empire, the writer draws the conclusion, that a central Parliament at Vienna, legislating not only for common affairs, but for the internal administration of Hungary, is impossible; that a separate Ministry for Hungary is indispensable; and that the two halves of the Empire 'must be considered as two aggregations of lands having a parity of rights.'[1]

No statement of the Hungarian position could have so well succeeded in enlisting the approval and adherence of the best men on all sides in Hungary. The Conservative magnates saw full justice done to their view as to the necessity of common action in matters concerning the dignity and unity of the monarchy. The Deák party and the Moderate Liberals acknowledged that the principles here laid down, committed them to no surrender of that ancient constitutional independence which they had guarded so jealously against the insidious attacks of Baron Schmerling's German Constitutionalism.

There was still a labyrinth of difficulties to be passed through between 1865 and 1867; but Deák had never lost hold of the clue which had enabled him to

---

[1] See *Studies in European Politics*, M. E. Grant Duff, M.P.

guide his country safely through the troubles and complications of twenty years, and which was destined to lead him to the wished-for goal at last. In 1865, Hungary, speaking through the mouth of Deák, was asserting the same principles, claiming the same rights, rendering and demanding the same scrupulous respect for law and justice, as in 1847.

A long interval had passed since the bright hopes which had then seemed so near their fulfilment had been destroyed.

Were the hopes of 1865 to be as speedily extinguished?

The appeal of Hungary to the Sovereign did not remain unheeded. In June of the same year the Emperor of his own initiative (and contrary, it was rumoured, to the wishes of his ministers), undertook a journey to Buda Pesth, this time to stand face to face with his Hungarian subjects in the royal palace at Buda.

The last occasion on which the magnates had assembled in the Hall of Audience was to hear the Royal Rescript which had called upon Hungary to forego the ancient Constitution of the nation, and merge herself in the Austrian Empire.

Instead of the chilling silence that had greeted the message read from the Throne four years before, the hall now rang with the cheers of the assembled nobles, as Francis Joseph, with that perfect mastery of the Magyar language which is in itself a charm in the eyes of his Hungarian subjects, delivered a speech expressing warm sympathy with Hungary, though refraining from rash promises that might have raised undue expectations and made the work of final agreement more difficult.

Cardinal Szitowsky, the venerable Primate of the Kingdom, found at length that favourable opportunity for an interview with his Sovereign which he had sought in vain on the occasion of the last royal visit to Pesth in 1857; at the conclusion of the Emperor's address, it fell to him to declare in the name of his country what Hungary desired of its King, and to assure his Majesty that the hearts of all his subjects would be faithful to the prince who should guarantee to them their rights.

The royal visit to Hungary was of short duration, but it was long enough to prove, if proof were needed, that the chivalrous loyalty of the Magyars was not a thing of the past, and that the experiment of bearding the lion in his den had not been tried too late for success. The King's reception by the mass of the people was no less cordial than that accorded him by the nobles. In the evening of the same day on which he had received the magnates, the Emperor presided at a banquet in the old palace at Buda. As he looked down from the terrace that crowns the Danube, upon the enthusiastic multitude thronging the steep streets and broad quays of the twin cities, now brilliantly illuminated in honour of their unwonted and welcome guest ; as he heard the wild defiant music of Rakoczy's March, played by the imperial band, answered with the stately strains of the Kaiser Lied from the strange half-barbaric instruments of the famous Zigäners, the national musicians of Hungary, Francis Joseph may well have felt that it could only be by a perverse fatality of mismanagement and misunderstanding, if his Kingdom of Hungary did not become the strength, instead of the weakness, of the Austrian Empire.

Shortly after the return of the Emperor from Pesth, the German ministers at Vienna were surprised by the announcement that Court Mailáth had accepted the office of Court Chancellor ; his Hungarian coadjutor, the Tavernicus,[1] being Baron Sennyei, one of the Conservative magnates who had acknowledged most readily the necessity of acting for the future in concert with Deák and his party in Hungary.

The evidence given by these appointments of an intention to treat with Hungary through the medium of the Conservative instead of the ultra-Liberal party in that country, was an additional blow to the already waning power of the Schmerling Ministry ; for it was in great measure by holding out to his supporters the prospect of a speedy settlement with Hungary, on terms acceptable to the ultra-Liberals in both countries, that Baron Schmerling had

[1] Tréasurer.

maintained himself amidst the increasing difficulties of his position.

The finishing stroke to his embarrassment came with the debates on the Budget in the Upper House. A few weeks later the Archduke Rainald, Baron Schmerling, and his whole party in the Cabinet resigned; and Count Belcredi, a Moravian nobleman, became Minister of the Interior in the Cabinet of Count Mensdorff Pouilly.

On the 27th of July the Reichsrath was closed with a speech from the Archduke Rainald, in which, after commending both Houses for the patriotic zeal and unwearied activity which they had displayed in the deliberations, it was announced that important reasons connected with the general interests of the Empire, made it advisable to summon speedily the lawful representatives of the peoples in the eastern parts of the monarchy; and rendered it necessary to refrain in this session from considering the Budget for 1866. An indication of the impending change in the political horizon was visible in the concluding passage of the speech, where a hope was expressed that 'a treatment in common of the rights belonging in common to all the kingdoms and territories, should in the immediate future firmly unite all the peoples of the Empire—a desire based upon a recognition of the conditions of the existence of the monarchy.'

CHAPTER XXV.

In the following September 1865 Europe witnessed
with keen interest the development of a fresh crisis
in the internal history of Austria.

In the desire to establish that form of government
which should be most truly adapted to the welfare
of his complex empire, the Emperor of Austria
had the courage to suspend the Constitution in the
interests of Constitutionalism, and to acknowledge
openly before it was too late, that the provisions

of the February Patent, however excellent in theory, were in practice so ill suited to the requirements of the common monarchy, as to make it dangerous to maintain them in force, even when glorified by the name of the Austrian Constitution.

By the Manifesto of September, the historical rights of the various provinces of the Empire were again fully acknowledged, and the authority of the Diets restored, by the suspension of those obnoxious statutes and electoral laws which had been framed with the avowed object of gradually extinguishing all local self-government, and transferring every vestige of administrative power from the hands of provincial authorities to the officials of the central Government.

The hopes of the Federalists or State Rights party in the Empire ran high. In the suspension of the Constitution of 1861 they, as well as the Hungarians, saw the first obstacle removed that hindered the realisation of their several objects. Czechs, Poles, and Magyars all agreed in their satisfaction at the retirement of the Schmerling Ministry. Indeed in an important article published at this time in a Viennese journal, and attributed to the pen of Count Belcredi himself, one of the chief arguments adduced in favour of the recent Manifesto was grounded ·upon the attitude of Hungary with reference to the suspended Constitution of 1861. The Hungarian Diet, said the article, declined to send its representa-

tives to the Reichsrath, on the ground that the
fundamental State affairs of the country had not first
been definitively settled by the Diet in the sense of
its laws. Now, both in the October Diploma and
the February Patent, such a settlement was distinctly
stated to be the preliminary condition of the validity
of the Constitution of the Empire. Therefore, it
was argued, so long as this condition remains unfulfilled, and Hungary in consequence abstains from
sending representatives to the Reichsrath, there can
be no question that the law respecting the representation of the Empire is 'de jure' inoperative.[1]

Unfortunately, as appeared later, the agreement
between Hungary and the great non-German provinces of Austria was of the negative kind, founded
upon a common dislike of the existing system,
rather than upon any positive harmony of opinion
as to the State policy which should be adopted in
its stead.

But in the first agitation which resulted in the
defeat of the German Centralists, the important
question of Dualism versus Federalism had not
yet come into prominence. In the political campaign that attracted the attention of Europe in
1865, the victorious opponent of Baron Schmerling
was Count Belcredi, the hope of the Federalist party,
not Count Beust, the Saxon statesman who, a year
and a half later, contrived so skilfully to meet the

____
[1] See *Westminster Review*, April 1866.

exigencies of a critical period for the Austrian Empire, by welding together the elements of strength to be found in the German Centralist party and the Hungarian advocates of Dualism.

The babel of political controversy that resounded from one end of the monarchy to the other, formed a strange contrast to the silence that had reigned for centuries past in the great polyglot empire. Assuredly, if complete freedom of speech be one of the chief distinctions of a constitutional State, if unceasing activity of political disputation both with tongue and pen be a symptom of healthy vitality in the body politic, then never was Austria further from her decadence, never was she more truly a constitutional country, than in the autumn of 1865, when the Constitution was suspended, and dismal prophecies were abroad of a new era of despotism and ‘reaction.’

Two months after the publication of the September Manifesto the Diets reassembled. Out of the seventeen Provincial Diets of Austria ten gave a majority of votes in favour of the principles of the Manifesto ; seven, either by resolutions or addresses to the Throne, expressed their disapproval of it.

The one party supported the present Government in the belief that the September Manifesto aimed at a confederation of peoples (*Volkesbund*), whereas the February Patent had tended to create a separate league (*Sonderbund*) amongst the German-speaking

inhabitants of the Empire. The other party pro-
tested vehemently against the recent change of
policy, on the ground that the suspension of the
Constitution was not only impolitic but illegal ; since
' the wilful abstention of some of the representatives
of the Empire, could not be taken as depriving those
who had taken possession of the constitutional
ground, of the further exercise of their legislative
functions.' [1]

This being the position of affairs in Austria, what
was to be the line taken by Hungary ?—a most important factor in the tangled web of Austrian politics.

On the 14th of December the Diet at Pesth was
reopened by the Emperor in person.

With this revival of constitutional life in Hungary
Francis Deák again came to the front, seeming,
from his constant and ever-present activity, to unite
in one the functions of minister, jurist, diplomatist,
and party leader. Now in the royal cabinet at
Vienna, now in the national assembly or in the
clubs and party conferences at Pesth, he devoted
all his energies to making a good use of the fresh
opening for reconciliation presented by the late
ministerial changes, and the publication of the
September Manifesto.

Deák was resolved to consent to nothing that

---

[1] For further information, see a series of highly interesting and
valuable articles on the various constitutional experiments in Austria,
contained in the pages of the *Westminster Review* in 1861, 1863,
1866, and 1867.

would involve dropping a single link in the chain of 'Continuity of Right;' and it had therefore been determined at a conference of the party held in November, before the opening of the Diet, to exact in the establishment of a separate Hungarian Ministry an acknowledgment of the Laws of '48. At the same time he was anxious not to ruin the new hopes dawning for his country, by a persistent refusal to regard the question from any but a purely Hungarian point of view.

Nothing could have proved more decisively the unfaltering consistency of Deák's principles with respect to the sacredness of law, than the tenour of the address drawn up by him on this occasion, and finally accepted by the Diet.

The language of the Emperor in his opening speech from the Throne had been well calculated to overcome the scruples of any loyal subjects less firmly devoted to their constitutional rights, and less deeply versed in the principles of constitutional law, than the Hungarians. 'We are now come,' his Majesty had announced, 'to finish the work which our feeling of the duties of government compelled us to begin. Our object in coming among you in person, is more effectually to remove those scruples which till now have stood in the way of the solution of the political question we have to deal with.'

After pointing out that one of the chief obstacles

to a successful agreement lay in the sharply defined opposition between the different starting-points assumed with a view to the desired understanding— 'forfeiture of right' on the one hand, 'continuity of right' on the other—the Emperor declared that he should himself set aside these obstacles by choosing for a starting-point 'a basis recognised on all sides, viz. the Pragmatic Sanction.'

This famous compact, whilst it guaranteed autonomy for the internal administration and legislation of Hungary, confirmed at the same time the tie which binds the lands and provinces under the same sovereign into one great empire.

The Diet was therefore exhorted, in harmony with the acknowledged principles of the Pragmatic Sanction, to consider the manner in which affairs of common interest should be treated, to deliberate and give their opinion upon the Manifesto of September last, as well as upon the Diploma of October 1860 and the Patent of February '61, and to 'revise or reform that part of the Laws of 1848 which refers to the exercise of our rights of sovereignty and the limitation of the attributes of government.'

'Only when this shall have been done will it be possible for the King, with a quiet conscience, to take the royal Coronation Oath to the Hungarian Constitution duly reformed and confirmed so that it may endure to a late posterity, and be solemnly invested with the diadem of St. Stephen, our apostolic forefather—with that sacred crown in which we would fain insert as its most precious jewel the prosperity of our Kingdom of Hungary, and the unbroken love of its people.'

But the sun had no better success than the wind in inducing the law-abiding champion of Hungary to give up what he considered to be the chief protection, the main guarantee, for the future independence and freedom of his country,—namely, strict respect in every detail for the Continuity of Right. Not even the wish to meet half-way the evident desire of the Sovereign and his present advisers to come to a satisfactory understanding with Hungary, could make Deák consent to include in the accepted bases of negotiation, the provisions laid down in the October Diploma and the February Patent. To regard the Constitution there 'octroyé' upon Hungary and the other lands of the Empire, as an end desirable of attainment in the future by mutual agreement, was one thing ; to lay it down arbitrarily as the starting-point for further action, irrespective of the legal and historical rights of the countries affected by its provisions, was another.

In the Address of February the 24th, Deák therefore felt bound to dwell forcibly on the danger of yielding too far on the plausible ground of 'expediency.' After alluding to the miseries of misgovernment which the country had been doomed to undergo during the past seventeen years under the name of a policy of expediency, he observes : 'The advocates of an "expediency policy" must not be surprised, if, after having been the victims of so many illusions, we are somewhat cautious, and do not enter without consideration on the path which they invite us to follow. It was by holding fast to the law, and not by pursuing a policy of expediency, that our ancestors saved the Fatherland. Leopold I. was forced to restore the Hungarian Constitution in its integrity, without condition or reservation, before the Diet would agree to annul that clause of the Golden Bull respecting the lawfulness of armed resistance, which no well-ordered State could put up with.

'Esau, it is true, when he was in want sold his birthright for a mess of pottage ; he got the pottage he wished for, but there was strife between the brothers all the same.

'This is what those expediency politicians will bring us to, who, under pretext of an amiable concession, are in reality only making matters more difficult to settle.'[1]

The Address acknowledged that there were indeed affairs which Hungary shared in common with the Hereditary States, and promised that the Diet should proceed without delay to the preparation of a bill respecting the definition and treatment of these affairs, as well as take into consideration all

____

[1] See *Unsere Zeit*, Rogge.

the propositions of the Government with regard to the revision of the Laws of '48; but it was stipulated that the recognition of the Continuity of Right must so far take precedence of all else, that the aforesaid propositions should be introduced by a responsible Hungarian Ministry.

'The land still remains under absolute rule,' concluded the Address. 'Sanctioned laws, of which your Majesty yourself allows that no objection can be raised against them on the score of "strict legality," are practically treated as if non-existent. In all branches of the administration the absolute system still prevails; we therefore plead for "Continuity of Right," above all, in respect of our laws; for parliamentary government, for a responsible Ministry, and for the constitutional re-establishment of the municipalities. All we demand is the restoration of the law; for a law not enforced is a dead letter.'

The Emperor could not justly complain that his Hungarian subjects rendered the difficulties of the situation greater by the ambiguity of their language. To a plain request his Majesty returned a plain refusal.

On receiving the Address brought by a deputation from the Diet to the royal palace at Buda, on the 27th of February, the Emperor, after stating shortly that in the interests of the peoples of Austria the principles laid down in the speech from the Throne must be strictly adhered to, quitted the Audience Room amidst profound silence.

Under Deák's influence, however, the Diet, notwithstanding the discouraging reception of the Address, and the somewhat harsh language of the Royal Rescript published a week later, proceeded with the promised revision of the Laws of 1848 ; and a scheme drawn up by the leader, for the regulation of common affairs, was submitted for discussion to a committee of sixty-seven deputies.

But there was no symptom of yielding to the temptations of an ' expediency policy' in the uncompromising, almost threatening, tone of the Second Address of the Hungarian Diet a fortnight later. The draft of the First Address had met with some opposition from the Conservative section of the party, who were in favour of remaining satisfied with a theoretical acknowledgment of the ' Continuity of Right,' and withdrawing the demand for the actual recognition of the Laws of 1848.

Now, however, the discontent awakened by the Rescript of March 3rd was clearly to be seen in the unanimous support accorded to the strong expression of the national views in the Second Address. ' The legislative power,' it was declared, ' is the dearest right of the nation. But if it is to be a reality, it is indispensably necessary that the laws created be maintained in force until they have been legally repealed or altered by the constitutional Legislature.

'If the executive power has the right to leave in abeyance, or to suspend, the force of laws constitutionally enacted ; to replace them by diplomas, and to keep the whole Constitution in suspense until these shall have been revised by the Diet,—then the executive would in point of fact be also the legislative power.

'This is not the Continuity of Right that has been established by laws, royal inaugural diplomas, and princely oaths. True Continuity of Right consists not only in the continued non-abrogation of laws, but in their execution and enforcement.'

On the presentation of this Second Address, the Emperor contented himself with exhorting the Diet to proceed without delay in the discussion on the regulation of common affairs. External difficulties were becoming more threatening, and it was felt that it would be imprudent to follow the advice of some impatient counsellors and undo the work of months by dissolving the Diet in the hope of obtaining a majority that might prove more compliant.

Before three months had elapsed the Austrian army was in the field, Prussia and Italy having declared war simultaneously on the 18th of June.

Meanwhile the Committee of Fifteen in the Hungarian Diet continued its labours on the definition and treatment of common affairs, and the draft measure framed upon Deák's principles was referred for further discussion to the enlarged Committee of Sixty-seven.

On the 24th of June the imperial army gained in the victory of Custozza its only success during a short and disastrous war.

Two days later the Hungarian Diet was adjourned, and in a few weeks Magyar regiments found themselves encamped side by side with Slavs and Germans in the Prater at Vienna.

As might have been supposed, Deák refrained absolutely from all participation in the attempts of General Klapka, and others of the ultra-National party, to force the hand of the Sovereign by raising Hungary in rebellion, at a time when all the energies of the Government were required to meet their formidable northern enemy. Nevertheless the cause at issue between Austria and Prussia was not one that could excite the least sympathy in Hungary.

The wisest heads in the nation recognised clearly the embarrassments that would accrue to Austria, and the dangers to Hungary and the cause of free constitutional nationalities throughout Europe, if the Vienna Cabinet should succeed in establishing even for a time an Austrian hegemony in Germany.

It was not in the nature of loyal subjects and prudent statesmen like Francis Deák and Baron

Joseph Eötvös to pursue the good of their country
at the cost of the general welfare of the monarchy,
or to oppose what they considered an essentially
false policy by means of secret intrigue and con-
spiracy; but none the less, they, in common with the
majority of their countrymen, could not but watch
with cold indifference, it may be with satisfaction,
the military reverses which involved the abandon-
ment of an idea dangerous both to the interests
of Hungary and of the Austrian Empire.

On July 3, 1866, the battle of Sadowa was
fought and lost; on the 18th of August was signed
the treaty of Prague, in which the Emperor of
Austria acknowledged the dissolution of the Ger-
manic Confederation as hitherto constituted; gave
his consent to a new organisation of Germany
without the participation of the Imperial Austrian
State; recognised the Main as the barrier between
the southern States of the German Confederation
that were to preserve an independent national
existence, and those northern States henceforth to
be connected by more restricted federal relations
with Prussia; and lastly transferred to the King
of Prussia all the rights acquired by the Vienna
Treaty of 1864 over the Duchies of Holstein and
Schleswig.

CHAPTER XXVI.

In nothing has the good fortune of 'Austria Felix' shown itself more conspicuously than in her defeats. It will hardly be denied that the military disasters of 1859, and the consequent loss of Lombardy, left Austria a stronger State than she was at the time when every whisper of revolt south of the Alps, found a mysterious echo from half a score of distant provinces, and in as many different tongues east and west of the Leitha. Nor probably will it be denied that the *prestige*, no less than the practical influence, of the monarchy, in the decision of European questions, has been enhanced rather than weakened since the defeat at Sadowa, when the vague pretensions to an impossible sovereignty were definitively abandoned, and Austria concen-

trated all her energies upon the successful execution
of another though not less important rôle.

The new phase of European history presented
by the unification of Germany under the stringent
and somewhat intolerant rule of the 'iron Chancellor'; the crumbling away of the Ottoman power
in European Turkey; the recent successes of
Russian arms and Russian diplomacy, facilitated by
the popular Pan-Slav agitation which an autocratic
Government knows well how to make use of; the
crude efforts at self-assertion, the vague aspirations
towards a recognised national individuality, amongst
the Slav peoples of Eastern Europe—all this renders
more needful than ever, in the interests of civilisation, the existence of a powerful State on the
Danube; a constitutional empire that shall be at
once self-contained and yet capable of expansion,
non-aggressive, and yet with sufficient military
strength to enable it to consider calmly even those
convincing diplomatic arguments that are backed by
standing armies; open to new ideas of freedom and
progress, but yet never departing from that old idea
which holds that in the maintenance of a strong and
respected central authority, based upon true constitutional principles, is to be found the surest guarantee
for the preservation of individual liberty and the
dignity and well-being of the whole community.

The new policy entered upon after 1866 may
have been in the first instance, to use Deák's own

expression on a former occasion, an 'expediency policy,' forced upon Austria literally at the point of the bayonet ; but it is none the less true that when frankly accepted and ably carried out by the statesmen who since that time have had the direction of the foreign affairs of Austro-Hungary, it has seemed destined to prove the commencement of a new and vigorous lease of life for the imperilled Empire of the Hapsburgs.

It was not only in the political history of Austria that the war of 1866 opened a fresh era. As the humiliating Treaty of Olmütz in 1850 had been the signal for the complete reorganisation and improvement of the Prussian army, so the Treaty of Prague was followed by a thorough reform and reconstruction of that brave army which had of late paid so dearly for its inferiority to the enemy in respect of military science and organisation.

Not only the unbiassed opinions of foreign critics, but the still more valuable evidence of facts, tends to show that in the Austrian army, as at present constituted, the Imperial Chancellor has an effective and powerful instrument wherewith to insure due respect for the arguments of a well-considered diplomacy. The variety of races, languages, and creeds, to be found represented in its ranks, has not as yet destroyed the 'esprit de corps' in which consists the main strength and attraction of a standing army. Of the Hungarian at least, whatever his personal opinions, it may be said with truth, that once serving under the imperial standard, he is content for the time being to sink the politician in the loyal soldier of the Austro-Hungarian army.

Two or three days after the news of the defeat at Königgrätz had reached the capital, Deák was summoned to Vienna. Arriving at the palace at midnight, he was ushered at once into the presence of the Emperor, who was standing pale and troubled at the window. Presently turning round, he said abruptly, 'Well, Deák, what shall I do now?' 'Your Majesty,' was the prompt reply, 'must first make peace, and then give Hungary her rights.' 'Will the Hungarian Parliament give me men to carry on the war if I give the Constitution at once?' demanded the Emperor. 'No,' was Deák's answer, thus faithfully representing Hungarian opinion in its repugnance to the war and the whole scheme of policy that it implied. 'Well,' said the Emperor after a pause, 'I suppose it must be so.'

The interview was at an end, and without seeing any one else Deák left the capital.

Peace was made, and now the day seemed not far distant when the second, and—as it appeared to some—desperate remedy, for the ills of the Austrian Empire, was to be tried in good earnest—the restoration of the Hungarian Constitution.

But for the moment the bold importunity of the

Hungarian citizen remained apparently without result. An independent responsible Ministry was not conceded; Hungary declined to abate one jot from her original demands; and the Emperor Francis Joseph was still only the King elect, not yet the duly crowned and anointed King of Hungary.

What he had said in private conversation with the Emperor, Deák did not hesitate to assert openly. A few days after the interview at Vienna, he wrote in the *Pesti Naplo* :—

'The claims of Hungary call for speedy satisfaction; the condition of the monarchy admits of no delay. A large portion of the Empire is overrun by the enemy's troops; Hungary alone is free from them, but Hungary is dead. Everything, or at least a great deal, can be done with Hungary, but she herself can do nothing, for her hands are tied. The one thing, and the only thing, that can set free her hands, and breathe new life into her, is the concession of parliamentary government. If Hungary is to do anything for the monarchy, it can only be under a Government which is the expression of the national will, and is regarded by the nation as a guarantee of its rights.'[1]

On the conclusion of peace, an important change took place in the Austrian Cabinet. Count Mensdorff Pouilly resigned, and was succeeded as Foreign Minister by the late Minister of King

[1] *Unsere Zeit*, Walter Rogge.

John of Saxony, Count Beust, whose bold and successful intervention with the French Emperor on behalf of his country at the close of the war, had rendered him so obnoxious to the victorious Prussian Government as to induce them to insist with the King of Saxony on his dismissal.

At the time when Count Beust transferred his services from King John of Saxony to the Emperor Francis Joseph, it seemed as though the blunders of his predecessors at the Ball Platz, the consummate ability and good luck of the great Prussian minister, had left Count Bismarck with every trump card in his hand.   But amidst the many mistakes committed, there had been one feature in the ' Great Germany' programme—for which the credit was mainly due to Baron Schmerling,—that contained the secret of Austria's speedy regeneration, and of the success with which she was able to reconsolidate the loosened fragments of the Empire.   The proposals of reform brought forward on behalf of Austria at the conference of Frankfort in 1863 had been based upon truly Liberal principles ; and although the conference was a failure so far as it was held with the object of furthering the Emperor's pretensions to Austrian supremacy in Germany, although the broadly liberal character of Baron Schmerling's proposals on this occasion was said to have weakened his position as regards the Conservative members of his Cabinet—yet the constitutional idea

then identified with the House of Hapsburg in its
dealings with the German States beyond the
confines of its own immediate dominions, was the
lever by which Herr v. Schmerling's successor was
enabled to raise Austria out of the perilous condition into which an unwisely ambitious policy had
brought her.

The line to be taken by the new Foreign Minister
was indicated by the fact that Count Beust, on
assuming office, putting all other considerations for
the time into the background, at once advised the
Emperor to come to terms with Hungary.

But in a State like the Austrian Monarchy,
for the Emperor to come to terms with one portion
of his subjects was to arouse deep dissatisfaction
amongst the remainder; and he might not unna-
turally hesitate before acting unconditionally upon
the advice thus offered.

There are times when the highest qualities of
statesmanship can be shown only in a wise choice of
the least amongst many evils; evils so many and so
pressing that to the ordinary mind they seem to
baffle all perception of their true relative proportions.

It is no discredit to the sagacity of Count Beust
that the course which he urged upon the Emperor,
when at the termination of an unsuccessful war he
undertook to guide the foreign affairs of a distracted
empire, should have been received with a chorus of
disapprobation from a hundred hostile critics, each

provided with a distinct and unanswerable argument against the proposed policy.

The great fact however remained, that if there were a hundred good arguments against the policy of Count Beust, there were at least a hundred and one against every alternative scheme suggested by his opponents.

Looking not only to the past and present difficulties of Austria in Western Europe, but to the new dangers that might at no remote period arise in the East, the minister felt persuaded that in the interest of the permanent stability of the monarchy, the Emperor's next move should be in the direction of complete reconciliation with his Hungarian subjects.

It was on this ground that Count Beust resolved to accept the propositions of Hungary, as embodied in the scheme drawn up by Francis Deák for discussion by the Committee of Sixty-seven in the Hungarian Diet, and to use his influence with the Austrian Government to secure its ultimate realisation.

But not even cordial agreement between Count Beust, the Imperial Minister, and Francis Deák, the popular representative of his country and the staunch upholder of the Laws of '48, was enough to insure the wished-for result of a reconciliation between Hungary and the Cis-Leithanian provinces. The fresh attempt to find a basis of common agreement, and an acceptable solution of difficulties, appeared only to have entangled the skein more inextricably than before, and to have made confusion worse confounded.

Austria, the great despotic Empire, the prison house of freedom, where during centuries, thanks to the vigilant exercise of a paternal authority, no unseemly protests had been suffered to disturb the orderly silence in which the work of government was carried on,—seemed now on the point of falling into ruin, amidst a turmoil of confusion, a clamour of tongues loud enough, one might imagine, to reach the ears of the stately worthies of the old *régime*, and cause them to shudder with pious horror in their graves. It seemed as though the Nemesis of History had decreed that the Hapsburgs, who in a greater degree than any dynasty in Europe had represented the theory of absolute power, and been accustomed to rule the fate of their manifold dominions according to the arbitrary dictates of a single will and voice, should now be condemned to see the very existence of the Empire endangered by a multiplicity of counsellors, and by the innumerable conflicting elements that claimed loudly to have a voice in the settlement of great State questions. On all sides the peril of the internal situation was acknowledged, whilst impartial observers abroad shook their heads gravely, and declared it highly doubtful whether the Austrian Empire could survive Sadowa.

The days had gone by when the union between two men, each so influential in his own sphere as Count Beust and Francis Deák, even when strengthened by the tacit sanction of the Sovereign himself, could suffice to insure the triumph of a given policy.

If statesmen propose, it is now the people that dispose. The objections of the Austrian provinces on various grounds to the Dualism involved in the satisfaction of the Hungarian demands, were not to yield at once either to the diplomatic finesse of Esterházy, the persuasive eloquence of Andrássy, the straightforward representations of Francis Deák, or the unwearying exertions of the Foreign Minister,—to any, in short, of all those combined influences which opponents wrathfully described as 'Hungarian intrigue.'

CHAPTER XXVII.

MEANWHILE in Hungary, the Diet, that faithful
barometer of public opinion, pointed to ' stormy ;'
and as the autumn months of 1866 wore away
in fruitless negotiations between the Hungarian
magnates at Vienna and the Imperial Government,
in which Count Belcredi still held office as Minister
of the Interior, the dark cloud of discontent and
sullen resistance seemed once more to be settling
down over the eastern half of the monarchy.

Never was Deák's influence over his countrymen more severely tested than now, when he might
have fairly hoped that he was at last about to see
the fruition of his long and patient labours for the
restoration of harmony and confidence.

The guiding, enlightening, and moderating influence of the popular leader was never more imperatively needed than in the course of the debates which occupied the Diet during the autumn of 1866. With all the political instinct and governing faculty of the Hungarians, it could scarcely be said of their Legislative Assembly, as has been said of the English House of Commons, that it was wiser than any man in it; and the debates were apt sometimes to partake of that extremely animated character which is commonly thought to distinguish the parliamentary discussions of our neighbours across the Channel. Indifference to the political affairs of his country, is a crime of which the Hungarian can rarely be accused; and at this critical period it was only natural that intense excitement should prevail, and that opposing views on the future position and relations of Hungary should come into strong relief.   Every honourable deputy was prepared with a distinct opinion upon the merits of the important State question at issue; every honourable deputy, moreover, possessed a fatal facility in giving expression to his opinion; a circumstance which did not tend to accelerate a final settlement.

Deák was no orator, and yet whenever he rose to speak he exercised over the assembly an influence so marked and so powerful that he himself could only account for it by the modest

explanation, 'that he was so fortunate as to hold
the same opinions as were shared by the great
number of his compatriots.' In addressing the
House, he did not carry his hearers with him
in a burst of splendid eloquence, nor enchain their
attention by the beauty of studied or poetic language, nor rouse their enthusiasm by stirring the
easily kindled flame of national patriotism ; he
did not attempt by the aid of epigram and satire
to bring special points into brilliant relief, to
force a given conclusion upon his auditors by
means of a series of irrefutable logical syllogisms,
and arguments founded upon strict law ; his aim
was rather to place the whole subject of discussion
in broad and clear light before the House, taking
into careful consideration every argument *pro*
and *con.* that might be brought to bear upon it,
and bringing gradually into view the underlying
principle on which, in his opinion, the final action
of his countrymen with regard to it ought to be
guided.

The quiet unaffected delivery, the full deep-
toned voice, sinking at times, when the speaker
was moved, into a low tone that thrilled his
hearers as no elaborate rhetorical pathos could
have done,—these suited well the character of
the man who with all his dry logical faculty, his
imperturbable common sense, could yet feel as
deeply as the most excitable of his compatriots,

and who never spoke upon any subject without such perfect honesty of purpose and conviction, such a single-minded desire for the good of his country, that opponents as well as friends invariably listened to him with attention and respect.

But after all it was not so much what Deák said, as what he was, that gave to this simple, plain-spoken citizen, who had never—except for one short interval during the troubled year of '48—held any official position, who belonged to no 'governing family,' who possessed no advantages of wealth or station, such extraordinary influence amongst his brilliant and headstrong countrymen.

'Deák's speeches,' says M. Csengery, 'excited in the minds of his auditors a peculiar admiration that can hardly be shared by those who only read them in later days; for the effect of his eloquence was heightened not only by the charm of his dignified presence, but also by the consciousness that the speaker was the leader of a great party, at one time indeed of the whole nation.' His hearers could not disconnect the present from the past, nor forget that the Deák who strove so earnestly to bring about a compromise, to moderate the vehemence of the Opposition in the debates of 1866, was the same Deák who for more than thirty years had been spending his life in the disinterested service of Hungary, labouring in the cause with a zeal and a wisdom that had always been able to mitigate, sometimes to avert, the misfortunes besetting his country.

The nature of the compromise to which the leader sought to win the consent of the Diet, was indicated in the rescript prepared by himself and Count Mailáth in the foregoing August at a private conference at Szént Lászlo, after an unsuccessful interview between Francis Deák and Count Beleredi at Vienna. The basis of agreement here laid down, *i.e.* the Report of the Committee of Fifteen, was such, it might reasonably have been supposed, as would have met with the approval of the most vehemently patriotic party in the Diet ; inasmuch as it provided expressly for the maintenance of a separate national control over all questions of trade, customs, the State debt, and indirect taxation, and, above all, stipulated that the appointment of a responsible Ministry should precede the revision of the Laws of '48.

But the temper of the House had become embittered by the inevitably protracted course of the negotiations with the Imperial Government, and the only hope of seeing any sort of compromise carried successfully through the difficulties and objections now rising on every side, lay in the skill and tact of the far-sighted national leader, who, whilst entering fully into the views and sentiments of his own countrymen, could yet look beyond the frontiers of

Hungary, and take into account the difficulties and the opposition which the Imperial Government also had to encounter on their side of the Leitha.

The fate of Deák's compromise seemed threatened on all sides. One party thought that the scheme proposed went too far in the direction of union with Austria ; another (including the extreme Conservative section of those broadly known as the ‘Deák party’) considered that the species of Dualism involved would threaten the safety of the common monarchy ; whilst a third opposed the compromise on the fundamental ground that the maintenance of any bond whatsoever between Hungary and the Empire was contrary to the interests of their country.

The most formidable resistance came from the compact body which, under the leadership of M. Koloman Tisza, constituted for seven years the recognised Opposition in the Hungarian Parliament. Indeed so strong was this party, that when M. Tisza, giving expression to the widespread feeling of weariness and discontent, proposed to break off all further negotiations, the Deák party only succeeded in averting this fatal proceeding after a sharp debate, and a division in which the leader of the Opposition carried one hundred and seven members with him.

To control and guide the Diet under these circumstances was a task demanding not only a strong will, but a light hand. In drawing up the various

Addresses presented by the Diet during this anxious session, Deák's skill in political composition was exercised in no small degree; it being necessary to frame a document that in the first place should prove acceptable to the majority in the Hungarian Diet, and in the second place should avoid being so defiant in its terms as to provoke a complete rupture of negotiations between Vienna and Pesth. Thus, in spite of the victory of the Moderates in the recent division on M. Tisza's motion, Deák saw himself compelled, under pain of forfeiting entirely his position as leader, and losing his hold over the excited assembly, to draw up an Address, presented on December 15, in which the views of the majority were stated in dangerously harsh language. No allusion was made to a revision of the Laws of '48; and the Diet expressed its fixed determination to postpone all consideration of the Royal Propositions contained in the last Rescript, until the Report of the Committee of Sixty-seven should have been passed by the Diet, and ratified by a legally constituted responsible Ministry. 'Between absolute power on the one side, and a nation deprived of its constitutional liberties on the other,' declared the Diet, 'no compromise is possible.'

The year 1866 closed with little apparent prospect of a final reconciliation between Hungary and the Imperial Government; nor did 1867 open more auspiciously.   From Pesth came still the same persistent unyielding demands, the national discontent with the existing state of things being further increased by the publication of the recent decree upon the subject of compulsory military service for the whole monarchy.

'Let his Majesty cancel these decrees and all other measures sanctioned by absolute power in defiance of our Constitution ; and let him restore our Constitution in its integrity, and as speedily as may be.   The aim pursued, with the object of securing the moral as well as the material welfare of the Empire, can only be attained, if Constitutionalism, both in Hungary and in the other lands of your Majesty, is allowed free and full activity.'

Judging by this, Hungary's 'last word,' the end of the long and tedious negotiations was as far off as ever.

But the tone of the royal reply a fortnight later showed plainly that in some quarter at least, if not in Pesth, a marked change had taken place.   The Hungarian deputation bringing the Address above quoted, received a gracious reception, and a hope was expressed that all grievances would shortly be removed.

The counter effect of this conciliatory spirit was seen in the action of the Committee of '67, which at once set to work to amend their report in the sense desired by the Crown.

On the 7th of February Deák himself brought the report thus amended to Vienna ; and a day or two later he had an audience of the Emperor, with regard to the formation of a Hungarian Ministry,— now no longer to be discussed, as in the interview six months earlier, as a theoretic if legal right, but as a question of practical politics demanding immediate settlement.

It was not in vain that Francis Deák had held with patient tenacity to the thankless office of leader during the protracted and wearisome debates of the past autumn, and had striven successfully to prevent the Diet from committing itself absolutely to a fatal ' non possumus.'

On the 18th of February 1867, in the great hall of the National Museum at Pesth, amidst an outburst of enthusiastic cheers, the House listened to the Royal Rescript, in which the Emperor restored the Constitution of Hungary, suspended the arbitrary military service decree, and entrusted to Count Andrássy, as President of the Council, the formation of a responsible Hungarian Ministry. Francis Deák had waited to some purpose.

CHAPTER XXVIII.

Causes of the change in the imperial policy regarding Hungary to be sought elsewhere than at Pesth—Result in appearance of the resignation of Belcredi in February, in reality culminating point of the policy initiated by Beust on first taking office at Vienna five months before—Difficulties encountered by Austrian Foreign Minister in prosecution of his policy equal to those of Deák in Hungary—Natural disappointment of the Federalists at the introduction of Dualism—Deák not responsible—His advocacy of Dualism based on grounds of general advantage to the monarchy.

IT is obvious that the causes for the sudden change in the attitude of the Imperial Government towards the claims of the Hungarian Diet must be sought elsewhere than in Pesth, where the line originally laid down at the commencement of the negotiations had been rigidly adhered to throughout. Deák had ably played his part as a General of division, and it may well be questioned whether, but for the tactical skill of the Hungarian statesman, the union and consolidation of the Austro-Hungarian Monarchy would ever have been accomplished. But nevertheless, the supreme direction of affairs being in the hands of the Commander-in-Chief at Vienna, it was on the success or failure of Count Beust to carry out his pre-considered policy, that the ultimate fate of the Compromise depended.

The history of the political campaign in Austria during the autumn of 1866, when the cause of Federalism again found eloquent and statesman-like defenders in the Slavonic provinces—notably in Bohemia, Moravia, and Galicia,—though full of interest, is beyond the scope of the present memoir. Suffice it to say that the concession to Hungary, to all appearance the immediate result of the resignation of Count Belcredi at the beginning of February, was in reality but the culminating point of a policy initiated by Count Beust five months before, but which he had only succeeded in carrying out after a long period of suspense and opposition.

The difficulties to be overcome by Francis Deák and the advocates of the Compromise in Hungary, had been fully equalled by the difficulties of the Foreign Minister in the prosecution of his policy in Austria.

The final triumph of the Hungarian Dualists, now by a turn in the political kaleidoscope grouped in the same combination with their quondam opponents, the German Centralists, was signalised by the withdrawal of the Patent of January 2, (signed by Count Belcredi and Count Beust) summoning the Diets to an ' extraordinary Reichsrath' for the discussion of the future relations of Hungary to the Empire ; and the promulgation in its stead of a decree bearing the signature of Beust alone, convoking a ' Constitutional Reichsrath ' to legislate for the 'Western Half' of the Empire, and accept the recent arrangements with Hungary as a 'fait accompli.'

Even those who hold strongly the opinion, that under existing circumstances Dualism was the least hazardous solution for the difficulties of Austria, must find it impossible not to sympathise with the distinguished leaders of the Federal party, whose hopes of seeing the Constitution based upon federative principles,—unduly encouraged by the Imperial Manifesto of September 1865,—were now so cruelly disappointed by the Decree of February 1867. No candid Hungarian, however deeply pledged for the time to the support of Dualism, would deny that the objections urged by the national leaders in the Bohemian Diet to the compromise imposed upon the Empire by Count Beust and his allies, were based on the same ground as was taken up by the Hungarians in their resistance to the October Diploma.

Hungary indeed might boast with truth that for twenty-five years she had held the same position and demanded the same rights, and that no reproach could be cast upon her, if, in the tardy satisfaction of her just claims by the Imperial Government, the claims of others were perforce disregarded or ignored. Yet it is not difficult to understand the bitter indignation of the Federalists at seeing the Hungarians—whose stubborn resistance to the pretensions of German Centralism when applied to the common monarchy a few years back, had contributed in no small measure to the downfall of the Schmerling Ministry and the publication of the September Manifesto—now consenting to obtain the restoration of their own Constitution by an alliance with their former enemies, and at the expense, as it seemed, of their former friends, the advocates for a recognition of 'historic rights.' To the Federalists it appeared, that not only were their claims sacrificed to the exigencies of a scheme which merged all the national and historical divisions of the Empire in the one artificial and arbitrary division of a 'Western Half'; but that the promise made in the September Manifesto, that the various provinces of the Empire should have a voice through their Diets in the settlement of the future relations with Hungary, had been broken by the convocation of the so-called 'Constitutional Reichsrath' of February, based upon the recent electoral laws which left the National and Federalist element in the Diets inadequately represented. The present Constitution, it was urged, possessed neither the advantages of a genuine centralised Government such as the German Liberals still professed to advocate, nor of a federative system for the whole monarchy, such as the politicians of the Slavonic provinces and of the Tyrol maintained to be the best suited to the needs of the Austrian Empire.

Under these circumstances, it is not surprising that the protests of the majority in the provincial Diets against a 'centralised West Half,' a 'Cis-Leithania under German hegemony,' should have been loud and persistent.

But whatever might be the defects of the Dual system which excited such profound dissatisfaction amongst a large section of the Austrian public, the most ardent opponent of Dualism could not justly accuse its principal author, Francis Deák, of having at any time during his career shown the slightest animus against the Slav nationalities, or of having sought to regain the rights of Hungary at the sacrifice of those of a sister kingdom. 'The day will come,' he had once said, 'when it will be recognised that the freedom of one nation can never by any possibility be opposed to the freedom of another.' His conduct with reference to Croatia, a short time later, whilst the storm of reproach and remonstrance was still raging, gave fresh evidence that his patriotic zeal for Hungary had not made him insensible to the claims of justice and generosity, when the rights of other nationalities were in question.

Nevertheless, at the time when the new Dual system was introduced, Deák's insight as a European statesman, no less than as a Hungarian patriot, warned him that the only firm ground on which to base the ingeniously constructed and somewhat fragile structure, was to be found in a firm alliance between two at least out of the three great parties in the monarchy, namely between Hungarians and Germans. 'Sei nur ruhig Alter,' said Deák cheerfully to the landlord of the 'Stadt Frankfurt' hotel at Vienna, where in the same little room that he had always occupied during his flying visits to the capital for the past twenty years, he now received the crowd of eminent personages who came to seek an interview with the famous Hungarian statesman,—'sei nur ruhig; es wird noch alles gut werden, wenn Ihr Wiener es auch nicht glauben wollt.'

The genial hopefulness of the Hungarian leader was not the mere exultation of a successful party politician who triumphs in having 'scored a point' and defeated his opponents at any cost; he was not thinking of his own party, or even of his own country only, when he declared so confidently, notwithstanding the dark and confused outlook, that 'it would all come right.' His confidence arose from the belief that the system now initiated would, if allowed a peaceful and natural development, prove well adapted to the requirements, not only of Germans and Hungarians, not only of one province or nationality to the detriment of another, but of the Austro-Hungarian Monarchy as a whole.

[1] See *Unsere Zeit*, W. Rogge.

CHAPTER XXIX.

Dual parliamentary government an adaptation of old-established system, not the introduction of a new one—Principle to be traced as far back as 1847—Causes preventing an earlier agreement between Hungary and the Austrian Empire—Three rights demanding equal recognition—Merit of the Dual system of '67 that it took these into consideration—Essentially a compromise, the distinguishing feature being the Delegations, a modification of both the opposing theories of 'Personal' and 'Real' union—By the compromise respect insured for the three rights—Constitutional independence of Hungary — Constitutional government for the western half of the monarchy—Central administrative unity in affairs of common interest—Drawbacks of the Dual system—Complicated machinery—Numerous opportunities for constitutional obstruction—Consequent dependence upon personal influence and ability for harmonious working—The means adopted for carrying into effect a principle not of equally permanent importance with the principle itself—Count Beust and Deák not to be held pledged to perpetual support of Dualism—The secret of Deák's advocacy of the Compromise in 1867—Desire to preserve the Hungarian Constitution—The connection between Hungary and Austria—All his past acts consistent with belief in these principles—But Deák not committed to support a system established originally with his warm approval, if it should ultimately appear that the system then established had ceased to work in favour of the principles on which it had been based.

WHAT, in effect, was this complicated Dual system, whose authors may in any case claim the credit of having attempted a novel if hazardous experiment in the art of constitutional government, of having supplied a plausible, if not the right, solution of the problem of Austrian state-craft.

We have spoken of Dualism as a novel experiment, and so indeed it must have appeared
to those who to all intents and purposes had
regarded the Austrian Empire as a united and
homogeneous country, of which Hungary, though
possessing certain specified rights and privileges, yet
formed an integral part. But a reference to the
past history of the Austro-Hungarian Monarchy,
and to the internal relations between the two
countries now united by this apparently new and
bizarre device of a Dual parliamentary government,
will show that Dualism was in reality an attempt on
the part of Austrian and Hungarian statesmen rather
to adapt ancient institutions to modern wants and
ideas, than to invent a new political system to be
added to the numerous list of Constitutions that
have been on their trial in Europe, with more or less
success, since the beginning of the century.[1]

[1] The Common Ministry for the Austro-Hungarian Monarchy
consists of a Minister for Foreign Affairs, for War, and for Finance.

In each half of the monarchy there is a separate Ministry of
Worship, of Finance, Commerce, Justice, Agriculture, and National
Defence, headed respectively by a Minister President of the Council.

The Lower House in the Austrian Reichsrath consists of 353
members ; in the Hungarian Diet, of 444, now chosen in both cases
by direct election.

The Delegations, composed respectively of sixty members from each
half of the monarchy, are elected annually from amongst their parliamentary representatives of the majority in each province, by the
members of the two Houses of the Austrian and Hungarian Legislatures.

The two Delegations, who meet alternately at Vienna and Pesth,
deliberate separately, their discussions being confined strictly to affairs
of common interest, with regard to which the Delegations have the
right to interpellate the Common Minister, and to propose laws or

The principles underlying the present state system of Austria-Hungary are to be traced with varying distinctness in the programme of the Hungarian Liberals in 1847, in the Sanctioned Laws of 1848, in the provisions of the abortive Austrian Constitution promulgated the same year at Olmütz,

amendments. In case of disagreement between the two Delegations, the question of policy at issue is discussed by an interchange of written messages, drawn up in the official language—German or Hungarian—of the Delegation sending the message, and accompanied by an authorised translation in the language of the Delegation to which it is addressed.

If, after the interchange of three successive notes, an agreement between the two bodies is not arrived at, the question is put to the vote by ballot without further debate. The Delegates, of whom in a plenary session there must be an equal number present from each Delegation, vote individually, the Emperor having the casting vote.

By virtue of the present definition of common affairs, the cost of the diplomatic service and the army is defrayed out of the Imperial Revenues, to which Hungary contributes a proportion of 30 per 100.

With reference to the former, it is stipulated that all international treaties be submitted to the two Legislatures by their respective Ministries ; with reference to the latter, that whilst the appointment to the military command of the whole army, as also to that of the national force of Hungary, is in the hands of the Sovereign, the settlement of matters affecting the recruiting, length of service, mobilisation, and pay of the Honvid army remains with the Hungarian Legislature.

Those matters which it is desirable should be subject to the same legislation, such as customs, indirect taxation, currency, etc., are regulated by means of treaties, subject to the approval of the two Legislatures. In cases where the two parties are unable to come to an agreement, each retains the right to decide such questions in accordance with their own special interests.

In common affairs, the decisions arrived at by the Delegations (within the scope of their powers), and sanctioned by the Sovereign, become thenceforth fundamental laws ; each Ministry is bound to announce them to its respective National Legislature, and is responsible for their execution.

in the Memorial of the so-called 'Old Conservatives' of Hungary in 1850, in the October Diploma and the Addresses of the Hungarian Diet in 1861, in Deák's Easter article and the letters to the *Debatte* in 1865, in the Imperial Manifesto of September, and in the Speech from the Throne and answering Address of the Diet in 1866.

With so much harmony of intention and idea as is discernible on a comparison of these various documents, how came it that for fifty years the relations between Hungary and the Austrian Empire had been such as to form a constant source of exasperation and misery to the one, of weakness and danger to the other? Putting aside for the moment all consideration of traditional prejudice and antipathies of race, it may be said that the great obstacle to a satisfactory agreement amongst men who had so much in common as was the case with the best and wisest of the statesmen of every nationality in the State, consisted in the difficulty of finding a system of government in which three hitherto conflicting claims, three equally indisputable rights, could be reconciled. First, the right of Hungary to her Constitution, implying in this, the acceptance by the Sovereign of laws constitutionally created. Second, the right of the peoples of Austria to the enjoyment of the constitutional government promised, and that not for the first time, in the October Diploma, and to the due recognition of their historical privileges. Last, but not least, the right of the Emperor to insist that the exercise of national autonomy should in no case be allowed to infringe upon the lawful prerogative of the Sovereign, nor weaken the central authority of the State.

The merit of the Dual system, elaborated by Francis Deák, and carried into execution by Count Beust, lay in the fact that whilst it was based upon a consideration for these several inalienable rights, which to the end of time no one of the parties concerned would ever have consented to forego,—it yet required from each a certain measure of concession, not for the satisfaction of a victorious faction, but for the good of the State and in the interests of the common unity.

It was essentially a compromise, open to all the just and severe criticism to which such arrangements are always liable, but having at the same time the strong recommendation of being the one thing possible ; and it is precisely that novel feature of the present system on which so much disapproval has been expended, viz. the Delegations which gave it this necessary character of a compromise, and insured for it when first started the best chance of practical success. By this ingenious device a link was supplied between Hungary and the Cis-Leithanian provinces, which established something different either from a bare ' Personal union,' dependent upon no stronger bond than the personal identity of the Sovereign, or from a 'Real union,' which would have been equivalent to the complete absorption of Hungary and its Constitution into the political system of the Austrian Empire.

In granting the demand of the Hungarians to be governed by a separate responsible Ministry having entire control over the legislation and internal administration of their country, the time-honoured constitutional independence of Hungary was fully acknowledged.

In reintroducing parliamentary government for the Cis-Leithanian provinces, the way was at least prepared for the more complete development of their constitutional liberties, and for a just distribution of political power amongst the various nationalities of Austria.

In establishing a common Ministry for Foreign Affairs, War, and Finance, responsible not to the respective Parliaments at Vienna and Pesth, but to the Emperor and to the Delegations,—a twin body having parity of rights, and representing in proportionate degree the final opinion upon affairs of common interest of the different nationalities included within the two halves of the monarchy,—the all-important principle of administrative unity in the great affairs of state was respected, and the spirit of the Pragmatic Sanction adhered to.

It cannot be denied, however, that though the ground lines on which the new Austro-Hungarian

Constitution was planned might be comparatively simple, the details that required to be adjusted before the elaborate machine could be set in working order were so complicated, as to inspire reasonable doubt whether Dualism could survive the shock of a single ministerial crisis ; not to speak of the more dangerous convulsions to which the variety of discordant elements comprised within the Hapsburg Empire render it peculiarly liable.   It cannot be denied that according to the existing arrangement, favourable opportunities for 'obstruction' at various points in the administration of government are perilously numerous.   The effective action of the State may be impeded, and even threatened, either by a want of harmony between the Delegations and the Legislatures they professedly represent, or by a serious disagreement on a broad question of policy between the Delegations themselves ; or again, by a failure on the part of the Imperial Minister to reconcile one or both of the Delegations to the measures proposed —possibly already taken—by the Government.

Under these circumstances, it is clear that much must depend, first upon the maintenance of a close and complete understanding between the imperial and national ministers, and secondly upon the ability of the latter to retain the support of a majority in the National Legislature.

Whilst ostensibly based throughout upon the

modern theory of popular representation and submission to the decisive authority of numbers, the
present Constitution is, in some of the most important affairs of the monarchy, dependent for its
successful working upon the tact and capacity of
individual statesmen, on the beneficent influence of
the Sovereign, and on that political instinct and good
sense of the people, which makes all parties sincerely
desirous to avoid pursuing their special objects to
an extreme that might lead to the actual dislocation
of the Constitution, and involve the whole monarchy
once again in all the difficulties of a political crisis.

Hitherto the predictions of failure have been
unfulfilled ; the two Delegations have not yet come
into fatal collision, and the fantastic creation of parliamentary Dualism has contrived to survive without
breaking down, the wear and tear of a twelve years'
experience.

Nevertheless it would be unwise to argue that
because an ingenious expedient founded upon sound
principles has answered even beyond expectation
the purpose of its original inventors, it is consequently
to be regarded as having the same permanent importance as those principles themselves, and as being
therefore equally beyond the scope of future statesmen to change and modify in consideration of new
times and altered circumstances. It would be doing
injustice to the political sagacity of Count Beust and
Francis Deák, to imagine that they would have

considered themselves bound irrevocably to the maintenance, for all time, of the state of things laid down in the Compromise of 1867 ; to suppose that they regarded as an end what was in effect a means, and to insist on the preservation of the Dual system of 1867 in all its details, even though it should appear that the object originally held in view, namely, the consolidation of a strong, free, and contented monarchy under the Hapsburg rule, could best be attained by a modification of the original Compromise. Gifted as he was with a large share of that foresight which is one of the chief attributes of statesmanship, Deák himself would have been the last to assume that he could prescribe for his country, or for that shifting if indestructible State the Austrian Empire, a system of government which should defy all necessity for future readjustment. ' I know what I shall do to-day,' he once observed, ' and to some extent what I shall do to-morrow ; the day after to-morrow I leave to Providence.'

To find the secret of Deák's staunch support of the Compromise in 1867, it is only necessary to consider what were the principles that had guided his conduct since he first entered public life. Were they not broadly these ? First, a firm belief in the Hungarian Constitution, that is, in the right of Hungary to entire liberty in all matters of internal legislation and administration ; the right of her people to absolute independence in these matters of all control by officials appointed under a non-Hungarian *régime*, whether popular or despotic. Second, the necessity for Hungary to maintain on honourable terms her lawful connection with the Austrian Empire, if she would continue to exert an influence on the politics of Europe, and not incur the risk of losing her historical identity under the increasing pressure of Slav multitudes within and without her own borders.

The various acts of Deák's long public career will all be found consistent with his belief in these two principles ; his reforming zeal before 1848, his abstention from all share in the proceedings of the Republican Parliament at Debreczin ; his passive resistance under the *régime* of Herr v. Bach ; his stubborn opposition to Baron Schmerling's central Parliament ; his eager advocacy of the Compromise of 1867.

It was because he believed that the best method of securing the end he always had before him, namely, the union of a free Hungary with a free Austria in one powerful and compact European State, was at that time to be found in the Dual system inaugurated by Count Beust, that he exerted all his influence, all his great legal and political abilities, in the furtherance of that complicated scheme of government.

In the case of a State like the Austro-Hungarian Monarchy, which has already, within a short space of time, gone through so many and such strange vicissitudes, any attempt to forecast the probable changes of a remote future would be more than usually ill-advised. And yet to those who have watched with sympathising interest the introduction and gradual development of the present Constitution of Austria-Hungary, the thought will inevitably suggest itself,—may not there come a time when Dualism will no longer fulfil the purposes for which it was designed in 1867? 'I am not a Deákist, only Deák,' Francis Deák once observed. It may possibly be that the statesman who at some future day, under the altered conditions of the Austrian Empire, looks towards the establishment of a new order of things upon the basis of old principles, will be following more closely in the footsteps of Francis Deák, than the thorough-going defenders of the Compromise of which the great Hungarian citizen was the author and champion.

PART V.—RESTORATION.

CHAPTER XXX.

Deák's refusal of the office of Palatine—Coronation of the Emperor at
Buda Pesth—Contrast between 1849 and 1867.

WHEN Deák returned to Pesth after his last interview with the Sovereign, when the famous message
had been read in which the Emperor announced
his determination to re-establish the Constitution of
the Kingdom of Hungary, and with this end to constitute a responsible Hungarian Ministry,—the great
citizen felt that his task was practically accomplished ;
and with the same predilection for doing the solid
work of politics and leaving it to others to exhibit
the results, which had been so characteristic of his
conduct in the Reform struggle twenty years ago,
he would now gladly have withdrawn again at once
into the obscurity of private life. But his compatriots were not content to be as silent in their
eager recognition of his services, as Deák in his
devotion to his country. What could be done to
testify the gratitude of the nation towards the loved
and honoured leader, Deák Ferencz, the popular
hero to whom the present reconciliation was chiefly

owing ? Count Andrássy was consulted on the subject by the Emperor himself; but the Minister President knew his countryman too well to venture on suggesting the offer of any tangible reward, and his reply to the royal inquiry was not encouraging : ' You have at your disposal, Sire, riches, rank, and honour; for any other your Majesty could do much; but for Deák, nothing.' To bestow orders or decorations on the famous citizen seemed equally out of the question; it might as well have been proposed to decorate the Blocksberg. Even the diamond-set portrait of the King and Queen was declined by their most loyal subject; the feeling between Deák and his Sovereign was not such as needed to be gauged or testified by the bestowal of costly gifts; and the staunch old patriot might well be forgiven if his pride took the form of a resolve never, from the beginning of his life to the end, to have gained the smallest personal advantage by his public services. The attempt of the Hungarian Parliament to do honour to Francis Deák, by the unanimous proposal that the man who more than any other had made the coronation possible, should, in the character of Palatine, himself place the crown on the head of the newly anointed King of Hungary, was not more successful. The Palatine-elect at once courteously refused the proffered dignity; and when his friends ventured a second time to urge their request, they found that they were treading on dangerous ground, for, his face flushing ominously, and in language more peremptory than before, the leader reiterated his refusal of the flattering offer, and insisted that the office of Palatine should be filled by none other than the Minister President, Count Andrássy. Deák had cheerfully made many sacrifices, and done much for his country; but there was one thing he could not bring himself to do, and that was, to step out of the quiet retirement of his ordinary life into the glare of a public triumph, to figure as the centre of a national ovation, and become, though only for a day, the observed of all observers. Never was popular hero more intractable.

On the day of the coronation Deák was nowhere to be seen. He had done his work so well that for the time at least no influence of his was needed to smooth away difficulties between King and people, no logical argument to prove, by dry reference to historic documents, the union legally subsisting between a Hapsburg Sovereign and his Hungarian subjects. The crowds that on that memorable 8th of June thronged the streets of the royal city of Buda, testified by their sincere enthusiasm towards the rightful sovereign that in Hungary the triumph of law had in no way diminished the ardour of loyalty.

The gulf separating the Hungary of 1867 from the Hungary of 1849 seemed wide indeed; and yet such had been the dramatic rapidity with which despair, hope, and triumph had succeeded one another during those eighteen years, that the chief actors were the same throughout. The generation that had witnessed the deepest misfortunes of their country, that had listened to the passionate wail of the young soldier-poet of Hungary over his slaughtered comrades,—' the holy victims of Liberty, mown down in the battle,' [1]—were still living to take part in the national rejoicing over the full restoration of Hungarian freedom, and the hearty reconciliation between the once suffering people and their Austrian oppressors. The Emperor, now welcomed to the Hungarian capital by his people as their lawful and constitutional King, was the same who had occupied the throne when the English Ambassador at Vienna could confidently assure his Government, ' Austria will not ever consent to establish the ancient Constitution of Hungary.' [2] Amongst the loyal subjects who came to do honour to the Sovereign on his coronation day, there were many whose names had once appeared on the roll of proscribed traitors, and who might have answered with Count Andrássy, when the Emperor graciously inquired of the Minister President, ' Where have you been, that I have seen nothing of you for so long ?' ' Sire, in exile.'

Regarded merely as a pageant, there has seldom

---

[1] Petöfi, quoted by St. René Taillandier, *La Bohême et la Hongrie.*   [2] Lord Ponsonby to Lord Palmerston, 1849.

T

been a more impressive spectacle than was witnessed
on that bright June day of 1867, in the streets of
Buda Pesth—gay with the once forbidden colours
of the national tricolour—as the long procession
of nobles and ecclesiastics, clad in all the varied
splendour of Hungarian costume, escorted the
Emperor-King Francis Joseph—now for the first
time wearing the sacred crown of St. Stephen—from
the Cathedral of Buda to the Coronation Hill in
Pesth ; where, mounted on his white charger, the
lawful successor of Arpad brandished his sword
towards the four points of the compass, in token
that from whatever quarter the enemy of his country
might come, the King of Hungary was prepared to
repel the invader.

But to those who looked back over eighteen
years to the ill-omened day when on the eve of a
civil war, the same Francis Joseph, now receiving
the devoted homage of his people, had replied to the
last manifesto of the loyal Hungarian Diet with the
harsh declaration of his intention to crush all dis-
turbance in his troubled province by force of arms ;
to those who could recall the bitter experiences of
war, oppression, and mute helpless misery, which
their country had been doomed to undergo since
then ; who had followed with keen anxiety the
hopes and disappointments of the last six years, and
the slow but patient advance of Hungary towards
the recovery of her ancient and never-forgotten

rights ; to them, the ceremony of the 8th of June was something more than an imposing pageant. For beneath the quaint symbolism, the gorgeous trappings, that seemed more befitting the glories of the Field of the Cloth of Gold than the sober usages of the nineteenth century, might be felt the beating of a nation's heart, and every detail in the stately and elaborate ceremony was fraught with genuine significance to those in whose minds the traditions of their past history were so closely interwoven with the events of present politics as to be matters not of antiquarian interest but of actual practical importance. It is not often in this prosaic age that the deepest realities of national life and feeling have their true expression in so picturesque a form as on the coronation day of the Hapsburg King of Hungary ; not often that we see so ideal a harmony between the pomp and outward splendour of a state ceremony, and the sincere inmost feelings of the actors who take part in it.

CHAPTER XXXI.

Value of Deák's services to Hungary in assisting the establishment
of national parliamentary government — Instinctive anti-governmental feeling amongst Hungarians—The parliamentary Opposition—Deák's influence in the settlement of internal questions—Law
of Nationalities—Croatia—Compromise of 1868.

UNLIKE Cavour, struck down not too soon for his
own glory, but sadly too soon for the tranquil
establishment of his great work and for the future
prosperity of United Italy, Francis Deák was spared
to guide his country through the dangerous period
of restless disorganisation and reaction, that usually
succeeds to the concentrated excitement of a great
national crisis.

He had never done better service to his country
and his sovereign than now during the last nine years
of his life, when his name was seldom heard beyond
the confines of Hungary, or within a small circle of
well-informed politicians in all countries of Europe.
Deák would never consent to take office in the new
Hungarian Government. The position he held as
a sort of supplementary and irresponsible Prime
Minister, whose support was well understood to be
so indispensable to the Cabinet that none could

possibly be formed on any other foundation, might, under ordinary circumstances, have proved a hindrance to the healthy development of parliamentary government. But in this case it was no small gain to the newly established institution of a responsible parliamentary Ministry,—quite independent of the persons composing it—that it should have the unfailing sanction and support of the trusted patriot. In a country like Hungary, where the old Nationalist feeling of suspicion and instinctive opposition towards a Ministry in any way connected with the Imperial Government at Vienna, is still so strong, that a young deputy, however able and ambitious to make his mark in the widest political arena, will even hesitate at the notion of winning his laurels in the character of a prominent member of the Pesth Government—it would have been dangerous to the existence not only of a particular Ministry, but of the whole system of constitutional government as established by the Compromise of 1867, if Deák had at any time during these early years been found in the ranks of Opposition.

Meantime the useful element of hostile criticism was well supplied by two parties who carried on the functions of an effective parliamentary Opposition according to the Hungarian fashion, by aid of well-concerted action in the various party clubs. The one, surnamed the Tigers (a terrifying cognomen, derived simply from the name of the hotel at which the meetings of the party were held), led by MM. Tisza and Ghyczy, opposed the Compromise in the interests of the more complete administrative independence to be found under a ' Personal union.'

The other and smaller fraction, led by MM. Bözsömenyi and Madárasz, looking to the absent Kossuth as their chief, represented in the Legislature the extreme republican principles of 1848. To uphold the existing Constitution in the face of this vigorous internal hostility, was as difficult a matter as to protect in its first years the infant Republic in France against the unceasing attempts of Imperialists, Reds, and Royalists, to undermine its gradually increasing authority.

But fortunately in Hungary the love of order, and respect for lawful authority, however distasteful, prevented opposition from degenerating into intrigue ; and the free discussion of differences in open parliamentary debate, led, not to further estrangement between the two chief parties, but to the eventual establishment of an agreement with regard to the fundamental principles of the Compromise. Within seven years from this time the broad division separating the ' Deák ' from the ' Tisza ' party had disappeared ; a coalition had been formed between their respective followers, and M. Tisza is now Minister President under the conditions of a system of which he was at one period the most formidable assailant. Opposition to the Government there is, and always will be, so long as there are Governments at all in Hungary; but that less dangerous stage has now been reached when it is the rightness of special men and measures that is the subject of dispute and criticism, not the right of the Government itself to exist.

With regard to certain internal questions of vital importance to the safety and well-being of the Hungarian kingdom, Deák's influence amongst his political contemporaries was exerted to good purpose in repairing the grievous errors of past years, and introducing a sound principle for the future. To the great satisfaction of all true friends of Hungary, one of the first acts of the Legislature on regaining its lawful rights was to annul the clause in the Laws of '48 decreeing the compulsory use of the Magyar language in all the County Assemblies throughout the country irrespective of nationality, until the further decision of the Diet.

For the last twenty years Deák had been forced to devote all his abilities to the defence of old-established laws, not to the making of new ones ; but the reforming legislator of pre-revolutionary days was not one of those who have a natural bias towards a negative policy of defence and resistance, and as soon as circumstances would allow, he gladly reverted to that more congenial work of progressive and constructive legislation in which he had been interrupted during the dark December days of 1848, by the blare of Austrian trumpets, and the advance of an invading army upon the Hungarian capital.

Before the close of the year of 1867, Deák, in concert with a sub-committee of the Diet, had prepared the draft of a law for regulating the equal rights of the nationalities[1] (*Gleichberechtigung*) of Hungary. But the ultra-Magyar feeling in the House was still too strong for the leaders to succeed in carrying out at once their wise measure of conciliation; the Diet was prorogued without any decision being taken; and it was not till 1868 that the Law of Nationalities was passed by both Houses of the Legislature.

If Deák had shown that he knew how to stand firm in the interests of Hungary, he showed in his treatment of the 'burning question' of Croatia that he knew also how to make concessions. Of all the numerous dangers besetting the new Government of Hungary, none was so threatening as that presented by the attitude of the sister-province, whose bond with Hungary had always been of that delicate description which requires constant easing and adjusting, lest the slightest undue strain or friction should break the link irreparably.

Ever since the days of Gai and Draskovics, and the

---

[1] Magyars, Roumans, Germans, Ruthenes, Servians, Slovacks.

Pan-Slav or so-called Illyrian movement of 1840—a movement skilfully fostered by the Vienna Government of the time as a useful counterpoise to the increasing Constitutional fervour of the Hungarian Liberals,—there had been a party in Croatia disposed to break off absolutely all connection with Hungary and the Hungarian Government, and aspiring towards confederation with their Slav brethren in the neighbouring provinces ; under the ægis of a Hapsburg Emperor if possible, if not— an eventuality seldom contemplated, it would seem, by the violent anti-Magyar counsellors of his Austrian Majesty—under the patronage of the Czar, who, in accordance with historical precedent had never ceased to take a benevolent interest in the fate of such Slav subjects of a brother sovereign, as belonged, not only to the same race, but to the same Church, as the inhabitants of Holy Russia. [1]

Diametrically opposed to these Pan-Slav Nation-

---

[1] The light in which a wisely patriotic Slav regarded these Pan-Slav aspirations and their tendency, may be judged from the words of Count Palacký, the veteran champion of Bohemian nationality and State-rights, when replying to the invitation to attend the German Parliament at Frankfort in 1848. ' You know which is the colossal Power that occupies all the eastern part of Europe ; all but invulnerable on its own soil, we see it already threatening the world's liberty and aiming at universal monarchy. This universal monarchy, though it professes to be for the benefit of the Slav peoples, I, a Slav in heart and soul, should regard as an appalling evil, as an incalculable and immeasurable calamity. I shall be told that I am an enemy of the Russians—but what of that ? Above the interests of race I have always placed the interests of humanity and civilisation, and the bare prospect of a universal monarchy exercised by the Russians has no more resolute

alists—if such a designation be not in itself a contradiction—were those, chiefly to be found amongst the magnates and upper ranks of the country party in Croatia, who not only had from their position more natural affinity with the Constitution-loving magnates of Hungary than with the extreme party in their own country, but who also believed honestly that the old constitutional rights and privileges of Croatia were more likely to be preserved by maintaining a close connection with the Liberal Government at Pesth, than by exchanging the light parliamentary yoke of Hungary for the bondage of subjection to the Pan-Slav idea ; an idea which, implied the obliteration of national individuality, and which, beginning with liberation, might possibly end with despotism.

Between these, was the great body of Croatian patriots, who, whilst they were as firmly resolved to preserve their national individuality and constitutional rights as the Magyars themselves, were at

adversary than myself, not because it would be a Russian monarchy, but because it would be a universal monarchy' (quoted by St. René Taillandier).

Nor had warning against the danger of coquetting with Pan-Slavism been wanting from the Emperor's Hungarian subjects in earlier days. ' Let his Majesty beware,' exclaimed Charles Jezernitzky, the deputy for Nyitra, speaking on behalf of the Diet in 1790, at a time when Leopold II. was encouraging unduly the separatist tendencies of the ' Illyrian ' party of that day, by listening to their proposal for a separate chancelry : ' From the heart of Russia will, at some future time, come races kindred to this nation, and together they will shake the imperial throne to its foundations.'— De Gérando, p. 101.

the same time anxious to uphold for the present the traditional union with Hungary under the Crown of St. Stephen, provided it were made possible for them to do this without surrendering too far the lawful rights of Croatia and her dependencies.

In all his past dealings with Croatia, Deák had not only shown a thorough comprehension of the political bearings of the question, but a wise and generous fellow-feeling for a people who stood much in the same relation towards the Hungarians as did the latter towards the Austrian Government at Vienna. It was with the same large-minded political wisdom that in the Second Address of 1861 he had ventured to declare in the name of his countrymen, 'that in view of the palpable fact' that Croatia, whether wisely or not, wished to loosen the bond that had attached her for centuries to Hungary, 'the Diet, respecting her wishes, was ready at any moment to enter into negotiations for this purpose.' And again, a short time later, it was Francis Deák, the acknowledged champion of the rights of Hungary, who held out to the Croats the famous offer of the 'blank sheet' on which to inscribe their own conditions for maintaining the connection with Hungary; promising that whatever the conditions, they were accepted beforehand, so long as they did not involve the dismemberment of the Kingdom of St. Stephen.

On this occasion, however, the proposed agreement between the Diets of Hungary and Croatia had, owing to various reasons, fallen through ; and in spite of the expressed willingness of the Nationalists at Agram to consent to a union on the terms of local autonomy and central administration of common affairs by the Hungarian Government— the provisions of the February Patent remained in force for Croatia, as well as for the other provinces of the Empire.

Seven years later, Deák, now the moving spirit of an independent Hungarian Government, having full command over the settlement of its relations with the ' partes adnexae ' of the Kingdom of St. Stephen, showed that he still remained faithful to the principles he had held in 1861. At a time when all parties in Croatia, united in profound discontent at the introduction of Dualism and the whole result of Count Beust's German-Hungarian policy, were giving vent freely to the bitterest anti-Magyar sentiments, sending deputations to Vienna to protest against ' incorporation with Hungary,' and refusing to send representatives from the Diet of Agram to the coronation of the King at Pesth,— Deák, with his ineradicable belief in the sovereign efficacy of reason and moderation, undertook the seemingly hopeless task of devising a scheme that should be acceptable to the ultra-Nationalists both in Hungary and Croatia, and yet commend itself to the approval of cooler and perhaps more far-sighted politicians.

The draft of an agreement prepared by Deák and his distinguished friend and ally Baron Eötvös, was submitted to the joint discussion of delegations nominated by the Diets of Pesth and Agram ; and after long debate a compromise was arrived at, so satisfactory to the aggrieved patriots at Agram that the town was illuminated in celebration of the auspicious event, and for the time at least there seemed a fair prospect of restored good-will between the neighbouring countries.[1]

By the end of May 1868—exactly a year from the time when the Croatian deputies had presented to the Emperor their remonstrance against re-union with Hungary—the compromise was an accomplished fact ; and a distinct step was thus taken towards the peaceful establishment of the Hungarian Government.

---

[1] According to the provisions of this compromise the Diet of Agram exercises complete home rule in all matters of the interior, those questions only which are of common interest, such as the army, customs, and finance, being settled at Pesth. Croatia sends to the Hungarian Parliament thirty-one deputies, who in the special sessions devoted to the discussion of common affairs are entitled to vote, and to address the House in their own language. According to the financial arrangement, 45 per cent. of the revenues of Croatia is set apart for the special expenses of the country, the remainder being paid into the national exchequer at Pesth.

CHAPTER XXXII.

But it was not only within his own country that
the tact and judgment of the Hungarian leader,
combined with the prudent moderation of the
Ministry at Pesth, produced wholesome effect.

The Dual system was on its trial ; and had it
not been for the reassuring example and the steady-
ing influence afforded by the successful working
of parliamentary government in Hungary, the
difficulties of Count Beust in Austria would have
been considerably increased.

For months after the conclusion of the compromise and its official acceptance by the Reichsrath,
the success or failure of the new experiment seemed
a question of at least equal probability, and the
most sanguine onlooker could hardly have asserted

that the latest political crisis was safely over for the storm-tossed empire. It still remained to be seen whether in the disasters and convulsions of 1866 Austria had sustained the final blow that was to break up beyond all possibility of reconstruction the vast congeries of lands and provinces which for centuries had owned the sway of the Hapsburg sceptre, or the electric shock that was to send a thrill of new and vigorous life into every corner of the monarchy. During the latter half of 1867 the darkest forebodings seemed justified.

Germans, Czechs, Poles, Croats, Servians, Italians, —Autonomists, Centralists, Federalists, Clericals, Feudalists, Radicals,—each party straining in a different direction, absorbed in the pursuit of its own special object, following its own leaders, and endeavouring to influence the central Government in the sense of its own particular views and interests. A discouraging prospect truly, for those who, being pledged to no special interests, were only desirous to see a strong and united Austria once more take its rightful place amongst the great Powers of Europe. Well might Count Beust say, 'We are climbing a steep mountain; the load we have to draw is heavy; the road is bad and bordered with precipices; if we are ever to reach the top, every one will have to put his shoulder to the wheel.'[1]

[1] Laveleye.

The day seemed yet far distant when the noble words of the Emperor on opening the Reichsrath in May 1867 were to be realised. 'Let us lay to heart,' his Majesty had urged, 'the lessons of the immediate past; but yet let us find in our unshaken courage, the power and the will to restore to the Empire peace and prosperity at home, respect and strength abroad; let us not be influenced by thoughts of retaliation; we shall find a nobler satisfaction in uniting together to transform by degrees aversion and hostility into regard and sympathy. Then the peoples of Austria, of whatever kindred, of whatever tongue, will gather round the imperial standard, and will render glad credence to those words of my ancestor: "Austria shall exist and prosper down to remotest ages, under the protection of the Almighty."'

As time went on, however, it became apparent that the new Constitution, inaugurated amidst overwhelming difficulties and in the face of opposition passive or active in every province and every class throughout the Empire, had been framed on principles so well suited to the circumstances for which it was created, that not only did it take root and grow, but soon developed sufficient vitality to stand the test of severe criticism, and even of alteration, without losing its original character.

It was fortunate for the harmonious settlement of internal politics in the Austro-Hungarian Monarchy, that in those important measures of reform which the Cabinet judged it necessary to introduce, in the interest of the peoples of Austria, the imperial ministers could rely confidently upon the goodwill and sympathy of the Liberal majority and the Liberal Government in the Hungarian Parliament.

Of the three inalienable rights before referred to, as demanding equal recognition in any permanent settlement of the constitution of Austria-Hungary, viz. the right of Hungary to her lawful independence, the right of the sovereign to insist on the maintenance of a strong central authority, and the right of the Austrian peoples to constitutional freedom and the acknowledgment of their historical privileges, this last might seem to have received the least share of justice in the establishment of the Dual system, and the provisions of the Compromise of 1867. But if so, it was not from any lack of appreciation of the validity of this right, on the part at least of Francis Deák, who in 1847 had declared in the name of the Opposition, their conviction, ' that if the Hereditary States of Austria were to regain their ancient constitutional rights and liberties, the conflicting interests of Hungary, and the other lands of the monarchy, could be more easily reconciled.'

The claims of the national party in Bohemia and Galicia are not yet satisfied, nor, to the full extent of their demands, is it probable that they ever will be ; but the electoral reform of 1873, and the subsequent concession, to some degree, of the Nationalist claims, have at least gone far to amend the present Constitution, in a direction where some such alteration was not uncalled for. The rumours that the Young Czech party in Bohemia, weary of their self-exclusion from the constitutional privileges enjoyed by the other nationalities of the monarchy, are seeking to come to some understanding that shall enable them to take their seats in the Imperial Parliament, would seem to show that the Constitution of 1867 is gradually finding acceptance, even amongst those who were originally most opposed to it. But there are wheels within wheels in Austrian politics, as there are parties within parties; and it would be the height of rashness for an outsider to set down as signs of the times, what may be only transitory and misleading appearances.[1]

With regard also to the great question which for upwards of two years engaged the attention of Austrian politicians of all parties and nationalities,—the abolition of the Concordat and the reform of the

[1] The above was written in May 1879. Since then (in October) the Czech deputies have for the first time taken their seats in the Reichsrath. The ministerial changes of the preceding August, when Dr. Stremayr was succeeded as Minister President in Austria by Count Taaffe, and Count Andrássy as Foreign Minister by Baron Haymerle, are not apparently to be taken as importing a departure from the main principles which have influenced the action of Austro-Hungarian statesmen since the Compromise of 1867. Count Taaffe appears resolved, like his Liberal predecessor, to maintain the constitution then established; Baron Haymerle has entered upon his arduous duties at the Foreign Office with the sympathy and good will of the late imperial Chancellor.

confessional laws,—the sympathies of the Hungarian leader were entirely with Count Beust and the great majority in the Reichsrath.

Few subjects could have provided such a broad ground of common interests, or offered to the various peoples of Austria so favourable an occasion for exercising in concert their newly acquired constitutional privileges; few could have given the Emperor Francis Joseph so striking an opportunity for proving to all the world, by his refusal to override the decision of Parliament by the lawful exercise of the royal prerogative, that a Hapsburg Sovereign, when he had once accepted the principles of freedom and constitutional government, was prepared to abide by them, with the same conscientious devotion that his ancestors had displayed in the cause of ecclesiastical tyranny and absolutism.

The unanimity with which the laws tending to emancipate the State,—in such matters as education and marriage,—from the legal jurisdiction of Rome, were in due time passed by both Houses of the Legislature, was remarkable; considering the multiplicity of classes, interests, and nationalities, represented by those who took part in the debates. But the chief cause for satisfaction lay in the illustration thus afforded of the words used in the Upper House by Herr v. Hasner, the Minister of Worship, in reply to the charge, that in altering the provisions of the Concordat, Austria would be guilty of breaking her engagements.   'All is now changed ; the absolutism which treated with Rome is at an end ; a constitutional State has come into existence, which is bound to settle its internal affairs according to its own convenience.   Austria, in taking her stand upon the ground of Constitutionalism, has regained full liberty of action.'[1]

With this development of constitutional activity in Austria, and also with the special object to which in this instance it was directed, Deák, as has been said, had entire sympathy.

Himself a Catholic and a faithful son of the Church, he yet shared to the full that deeply rooted aversion to papal interference in national affairs, that sturdy independence of judgment, which have at all times characterised the relations between Hungary and the Holy See ; and which were conspicuously evident in 1870, when Deák's friend and compatriot, the accomplished Archbishop Haynald,[2] returned in disgrace from the Œcumenical Council at Rome ; one of the few Catholic bishops who had refused to accept the new dogma of Papal Infallibility.

His own opinion as to the ideal relation between the ecclesiastical and civil authority may be best described in the words of Cavour—'a free Church in

---

[1] Quoted by Laveleye.

[2] The Archbishop of Kalocsa, raised to the dignity of Cardinal by Pope Leo XIII., May 1879.

a free State.'   The last great speech that Deák delivered in the Hungarian Parliament, was on this subject, and though already the shadow of mortal illness was upon him, those who heard him speak on that occasion will not soon forget the masterly force, lucidity, and logical argument with which he expounded his favourite thesis.   The days of a purely 'Deák Cabinet' were at that time gone by, and Deák spoke with no more official authority than the youngest deputy present ; but, as in past times, the influence of the old leader was still potent amongst his countrymen, and the Commission appointed by the House, to prepare a 'projet de loi' regulating the relation between Church and State, received instructions to base their scheme upon the principles just laid down by Deák Ferencz.

CHAPTER XXXIII.

Agreement between Austrian and Hungarian Ministers on the subject of peace—Policy of Austria since the Treaty of Prague—Refusal of Count Beust to be drawn into hostility to Prussia on the question of the Main—Count Beust supported in his peaceful policy by Hungary—Harmony of opinion between Beust and Andrássy as to future policy of the Monarchy—Preparation against a possible reopening of the Eastern question—Deák and Andrássy—Resignation of Count Beust—Succeeded at the Foreign Office by Count Andrássy.

THE Emperor, in his royal message of the 17th of February 1867, had declared his reliance upon the political wisdom of the Hungarians, and his confidence that they would not refuse to accord to the lately established responsible Government, the full and exceptional powers rendered necessary by the grave difficulties of the situation.

This confidence was not misplaced.   Above all, in the pre-eminently important and delicate question of the foreign relations of the monarchy, the Andrássy Government, of which Deák was virtually, though not officially, a member, received the steady support of a large majority in the Chambers.

Apart from the general welfare of the monarchy, there was no subject with regard to which, for the sake of the Dual System itself, there existed so imperative a necessity for the preservation of a complete understanding between the two Governments and Legislatures.

The agreement between the Hungarian statesmen and Count Beust, that had resulted in the Compromise of 1867, was no hasty bargain, patched up to meet the pressing needs of the moment, but a compact based on a sincere harmony of opinion with regard to the present and future policy of Austria-Hungary.

The keystone of this policy, with respect to foreign affairs in both countries, was peace.

The short and sharp thunder-storm of 1866, had marvellously cleared the air in Germany; and when the sombre clouds of battle rolled away, Austrian statesmen could see their course lying more clearly before them. The peace that followed the Seven Days' War, was not a 'recueillement' after the Russian fashion,—a mere truce, occupied with thoughts of retaliation and the precautions of suspicious watchfulness,—a state of things well-nigh as exhausting to a nation's strength, and as fatal to internal progress and reform, as one of open hostility; but a genuine peace, frankly accepted in all its conditions, with the dignity of a great empire that has full confidence in its ability to achieve a worthy future, and to carry out its destiny amongst European nations by other ways than those closed against it by the fortune of war, or still more by the irresistible force of circumstances.

But to carry into execution this conception of Austria's true policy, was no easy matter; and it was well for her statesmen that they were cordially supported in their intention to maintain a solid and durable peace by the leading men in the Hungarian Government.

The Treaty of Prague had left a state of things which by a little ingenuity, a slight imprudence, might easily have been made to produce a feeling of chronic irritation, if not a renewal of active hostilities. Between the Austrian Empire on the one hand, and Prussia, with the States of the North German Confederation [1] on the other, lay the States of the Southern Confederation, prohibited from forming any political connection with Austria, and yet not amalgamated completely with the North German Confederation, though connected with Prussia by the tie of a military convention and a common customs union.

'Germany has been divided into three by the Treaty of Prague,' boasted M. Rouher to the French Assembly; and no doubt the minister and his imperial master,—to whose intervention was due the insertion in the Preliminaries of Nikolsburg, of the arrangement relative to the barrier formed by the line of the Main between the German States

---

[1] Bavaria, Würtemberg, Baden.

north and south of that river,—would have been not ill-pleased, if the arbitrary division created by this politic device, should have proved a source of ill-feeling and strained relations between Berlin and Vienna; thereby leaving renewed opportunity for France to make her game out of the rivalries of the two great German Powers, and enable her to fill the honourable post of mediator in their differences.

But in Count Beust, Louis Napoleon had found his match. In vain is the net spread in the sight of any bird. Though sedulously preserving a good understanding with the French people and their emperor, Count Beust resolutely declined to be embroiled with his late adversary. When the 'Great Germany' policy of Count Buol and his colleagues, was given up at Vienna for good and all, the Austrian Chancellor was too accomplished a statesman not to take care, that the Empire should at least reap the advantages of this compulsory renunciation. There was room enough in Germany for Hohenzollern and Hapsburg, and if it were decreed that the former should carry off the prize for which both had been contending, it was surely better that Austria-Hungary should henceforth strengthen her position by securing the firm friendship of the victorious State, and cementing the natural alliance between the two great German dynasties of the Continent, rather than indulge in the doubtful and perilous satisfaction of angry remonstrance, or ungracious resistance to the inevitable tendency of events.   What if Prussia, in course of time, should gradually draw into her orbit those German States south of the Main, which it was certain would never become incorporated with the Austrian Empire, still less revive the traditions of the German Confederation, even should the river barrier, which separated them in diplomatic imagination from the States of the Northern Confederacy, be preserved till Domesday?   Was not Austria-Hungary, now animated with fresh life and vigour, justified in looking forward with calm reliance upon her strength to the new career marked out for her by the events of recent years, and therefore in regarding with the equanimity of a dignified self-assurance, the increasing greatness of a neighbouring, and now friendly State?

Before four years had gone by, Austria-Hungary, the crushed and shattered Empire of 1866, was the object of anxious solicitude on the part of both her powerful neighbours.   But neither pressure nor flattery, was allowed to divert the monarchy from the position of reserve, and strictly impartial neutrality, which had been deliberately adopted on the conclusion of the late war.

' It has always been the misfortune of Austria,' Count Beust once observed, ' to have made a great commotion, and incurred dislike, about things for which she was not resolved to go to war.   To avoid this mistake is the leading idea of my policy.' [1]

---

[1] *Verdict der Thatsachen*, Leipzig, 1878.

In following out this ' leading idea ' the Chancellor of the Dual Empire, as has been already pointed out, found hearty support in Hungary, where the necessity for peace, and the desire to preserve a good understanding with Germany, were naturally stronger than in Austria.[1] Indeed so closely was this aim kept in view beyond the Leitha, that when, on the occasion of a grand festivity of the National Schutz-verein at Vienna, the Imperial Chancellor had ventured to indulge in somewhat more bellicose language than was quite consistent with his avowedly peaceful policy, a voice of remonstrance and warning was immediately raised by the chief organ of public opinion in Hungary. ' The nation of hussars ' was also a nation of politicians ; and having made up their minds that the interests of the monarchy required the preservation of an unbroken peace, the Hungarians were now as pugnaciously vehement in the cause of peace as they had sometimes been on behalf of war.

But in other questions than that of the immediate relations of Austria-Hungary to her Continental

[1] " Comme je l'ai toujours fait pressentir dans nos pourparlers de l'année dernière, nous ne pouvons pas oublier que nos dix millions d'Allemands ne voient dans la guerre actuelle, non pas un duel entre la France et la Prusse, mais le commencement d'une lutte nationale. Nous ne pouvons pas nous dissimuler non plus que les Hongrois, tout disposés qu'ils soient à s'imposer les plus grands sacrifices dès qu'il s'agit de défendre l'empire contre la Russie, se montreront plus réservés dès qu'il s'agit de dépenser leur sang et leur argent pour reconquérir à l'Autriche sa position en Allemagne."—Despatch of Count Beust to Prince Metternich, July 20, 1870.

neighbours, the Austrian Premier had able and sympathising allies, in the Minister President of Hungary, and his great countryman.

Whilst still the chief of the Hungarian Cabinet, Count Andrássy had shown in his views for the future as well as for the present, how thoroughly he appreciated the 'motif' of the policy initiated by the Austrian Foreign Minister. In his manner of regarding the great problem of the relations to be maintained towards the Porte and its Christian subjects in Turkey, in view of the palpable inefficiency of the Ottoman Government, and the constant growth of Russian influence in that quarter,—the Hungarian Minister was substantially at one with the colleague whom he afterwards succeeded at the Austrian Foreign Office.

Fully realising the value to Austria-Hungary of maintaining a good understanding with the Western Powers, and resolved not again to commit the mistake of 1854, when Austria contrived to aggrieve all parties, without in any way improving her own position ; keenly alive to the importance, from a European point of view, of not allowing the Christian provinces of Turkey, as they became one by one detached from the Ottoman Empire, to fall under the exclusive control of Russian despotism ; and from an Austrian point of view, of preserving the influence of the monarchy amongst the rising Slav States of Turkey,—Count Andrássy was yet at no time a blind devotee of the 'status quo,'—that favourite watchword with some anti-Russian politicians,—and would always have been rather disposed to take as his device the sage words of his predecessor, 'Il importe de distinguer ce qui est possible de ce qui ne l'est pas.'[1]

Deák did not live to see the breaking of the storm, against which his far-sighted compatriot had so long been making ready; but he had not failed to appreciate the tendency of those ideas in the Hungarian Minister President, which the Imperial Chancellor has since been working out under no small difficulties. The veteran statesman who had weathered so many European storms, was accustomed to read the signs of the times, and could well understand why Count Andrássy should keep his eyes so anxiously turned towards the East, even whilst the horizon, in that direction at least, seemed calm and cloudless.

It has been related by one who was accustomed to be present at those familiar conclaves, in which Deák would talk over the events of current politics with a circle of intimate friends, that on one occasion, so far back as 1868, the conversation turned upon Andrássy's absurd infatuation on the subject of the Eastern Question. 'We might safely leave that to the Western Powers,' said a deputy present; 'they will take good care that their work of 1856 is not so soon destroyed.' 'Excuse me, my friend,' observed Deák quietly, 'but with all due deference

[1] Despatch of Count Beust, Jan. 1867. See *Diplomatic Sketches.*

to you, I think Gyula [Count Julius Andrássy] sees farther than you do."[1]   Had Deák been spared to aid his country with his counsels, during the critical phase through which Austria-Hungary has been passing during the past three years, would not the weight of his powerful influence have been still exerted on behalf of the much-abused policy of the Hungarian Chancellor ?   Judging by the internal evidence to be derived from an examination of the words and deeds of a lifetime, does it not seem probable that the same principles influencing the unpopular and so-called anti-Magyar, policy adopted by Count Andrássy and M. Tisza, in their attempt to steer the Dual Empire with safety and honour through the perilous shoals of the Eastern Question, would, rightly, or wrongly, have guided the actions of Deák himself ?

With the removal of Count Andrássy to Vienna in 1871, the period of Deák's intimate personal connection with the Hungarian Ministry came to an end ; though his name was still used to describe the Government party, as being that which was emphatically pledged to the support of the Deák Compromise of 1867.

The internal differences in Austria between the supporters of the amended Constitution of 1867, on the one side, and the Conservative and Clerical party advocating the further concession of

<hr>

[1] See *Verdict der Thatsachen.*

provincial independence, on the other, had come to a point under the Ministry of Count Hohenwart; who, in his desire to satisfy the claims of the Czech party in Bohemia, had gone the length of pledging the Emperor to such a fundamental law on the subject of State-rights, as would, in the opinion of Count Beust, have infallibly broken up the recently consolidated empire.

On the urgent advice of the Chancellor, the new fundamental law was revoked, and Count Beust, satisfied with having gained his point, made all the amends in his power to the justly exasperated Czechs, by resigning the important office he had held for five years.

This somewhat dangerous episode in the internal history of the convalescent empire, had at least the salutary effect of showing the solidarity now established between the two halves of the monarchy. In his representations to the Emperor on this occasion, Count Beust was not only supported warmly by the Hungarian Minister President,—his successor at the Foreign Office,—but by a large majority in the two Delegations. It was evident that the relations between Vienna and Pesth were at this time of such a nature, that the opinion expressed only two years earlier by the German Ambassador, 'The Hungarians are still hoping and waiting for Prussia,' would have to be reconsidered.

CHAPTER XXXIV.

THE prudent policy of the leading statesmen on
both sides of the Leitha, though it might be successful in preserving peace for Austria-Hungary
abroad, was of no avail in guarding it against the
dangers of financial crisis at home. The frenzy of
speculation, the reckless plunge into vast financial
and commercial enterprises of all kinds, which prevailed throughout the monarchy in the year 1870,
the sudden haste to grow rich, the feverish anxiety
to develop within an abnormally short time the
hitherto neglected resources of the country,—all this
was a phase of national activity by no means to the
taste of Francis Deák. In his opinion, the Ministry
of Count Lonyay, who had succeeded Count
Andrássy as Minister President, lent itself far too
readily to the encouragement of the universal
mania ; and it was no secret that when, a year later,

the fall of the minister seemed imminent, the influence of the great deputy in the party club was not exerted in his favour.

Under the Cabinet of M. Szlávy, endless questions of State-loans, railway concessions, the formation of companies, and various speculative undertakings, patronised by the Government in the interests ostensibly of the public service, still engrossed the attention of the Hungarian Parliament. 'We have now neither a Deák party nor an Opposition,' remarked one deputy; 'we have only a Grenz-wälder, a Kaschau-Odenburg, or an Eastern-railway party.'

Deák himself expressed his views with regard to the prevailing state of things in the style of forcible and homely allegory peculiar to him. 'In his youth,' he said, 'he had been passionately fond of a certain little pond-fish, the *csik*, until one day when he happened to see in what disgusting places it was caught; and from that time he could never touch it again. It had been the same,' he declared, 'in the matter of these railway schemes; no one could have been more ardently in favour of this means of extending our civilisation, until he came to see in Parliament, what nasty mud the railways were built out of.' Henceforward, if he chanced to enter the House whilst some fresh railway concession was under discussion, his friends would laughingly call out 'Czik, czik!' a signal for Deák at once to retreat into the lobby.[1]

The fall of the Szlávy Government in the spring of 1874, may be said to have been the beginning of the end, so far as the unimpaired and homogeneous existence of the original 'Deák party' of 1865, was concerned. The old leader himself had never spoken in the House again since he took part in the discussion on the relations of Church and State in the summer of the previous year. Though still following with unabated interest the party evolutions of the time, Deák was now quite incapacitated by increasing illness from taking an active share in that busy world of politics, where, for forty years, he had been a prominent and influential actor. At the time of the last general election, his health having slightly improved, he had consented to be returned once more to Parliament; but the improvement was only temporary; and though still nominally a member of the House, he was unable for three years before his death to attend the sittings, and with characteristic delicacy refused to accept the small salary to which as a deputy he was entitled.

The first symptom of a coming dissolution and re-formation of parties in Hungary, was to be descried in the Coalition Cabinet of MM. Bitto and Ghyczy in 1874, formed out of a combination

---

[1] See "Oesterreich seit der Wahlreform," 1873, *Unsere Zeit*, 1876.

between the Right wing of the Deák party, and a
small fraction from the Moderates of the Opposition.
The necessity of infusing a fresh element into the
composition of the Government, began to be so
strongly felt, that in a conference of the leading men
of all parties, summoned by the Emperor on his visit
to the capital in the spring of 1874, with a view to
the reorganisation of the Ministry, M. Tisza, the
chief of the Opposition, was invited to enter a
Cabinet, which, even in the opinion of the new
Minister President himself, had but small chance of
stable existence.   'I am not at liberty to disobey
your Majesty's commands,' M. Bitto had observed,
when charged by the Emperor to form a Ministry on
the principles of the pure Right, 'but if your Majesty
were to command me to speak Arabic, I could not
do it.'   'Try, at all events,' was the Emperor's
laughing rejoinder.[1]

The proposal mooted in some quarters, less than
a year later, of a Coalition Cabinet, to include such
various elements as Baron Sennyei, a prominent
member of the Extreme Right, Baron Lonyay, the
late chief of the Deákist Centre, and M. Koloman
Tisza, the leader of the Opposition—showed still
more plainly to what a pass matters had come.
Though now completely an invalid, Deák continued
to watch the course of public events with close

---

[1] "Oesterreich seit der Waldreform von 1873," *Unsere Zeit*, 1876,
p. 916.

attention, and even from his sick-room the old leader still exercised no small influence in the clubs of Pesth.   His well-known opinion as to the merits of the proposed Coalition Cabinet was not calculated to further the success of that remarkable scheme. 'Tokay,' he was reported to have said, 'is the king of wines; Somlauer and Villanyer are both excellent also; but what sort of a brew they would make if they were all mixed up together, no one can possibly tell beforehand.   You must try it yourself if you wish to know.'

But even had such a combination Ministry been desirable, the refusal of the Opposition leader to enter the Government under such conditions, would have made it impossible.

With sound political instinct, M. Tisza perceived, that for the chief himself to abandon the leadership of the recognised parliamentary Opposition, before the now imminent break-up of the old party formation had been completely effected, and the ground thus prepared for a new and definite arrangement, would only have enabled the ultra-Radicals to acquire an undue importance, by figuring before the country as the sole representatives of Opposition to the existing Government and the policy of the pure Right.

Moreover, the wary politician saw clearly, that for him to identify himself personally with the once triumphant and united 'Deák party,' in its present state of division and dissolution, would be to join the crew of a sinking ship.

The very triumph of Deák's principles had destroyed all necessity for the existence of a 'Deák party.' The Compromise of 1867 was now so firmly established, that the strong phalanx which had rallied round the great Hungarian leader to defend his work—including in its ranks men of various shades of opinion, bound together for the nonce in the defence of a common cause, had now lost its 'raison d'être;' and it was evident that a fresh centre of attraction, a fresh basis of parliamentary action, would have to be discovered, before a strong Government could look forward to a term of steady and profitable administration founded on the cordial support of a united party.

But it was not till the spring of 1875, when experience had shown the futility of attempting to construct a stable Ministry out of the now incongruous materials of the old 'Deák party,' that the fusion took place on which the present Liberal party in Hungary is based. A few months before his death, Deák had the satisfaction of seeing the formal resistance to the principles of his great work, brought to an end, by the union between the parliamentary Opposition led by M. Tisza, (the present Minister President) and the main body of the old Deák party, on the basis of acceptance of the Compromise of 1867.

The newly constituted Liberal party started on

its career with the hearty good-will and approval
of the veteran leader, who had had perhaps in his
day, more experience than any living politician of
the good and evil, the strength and the weakness, of
party government.   One of Deák's last public acts
was to send his name to be inscribed in the Club-
book of the new Liberal party.

After his return in 1875 from his usual summer
sojourn at the Stadtwaldchen in the environs of
Pesth, it became evident that the illness (heart
disease, with dropsical symptoms) against which
Deák had been struggling bravely for the past
three years, was rapidly approaching a crisis.   The
attacks of suffocation, now more violent and more
frequent, were succeeded by a state of semi-torpor ;
though, even to the last, the old vivacity and genial
humour would at times seem quite unimpaired by
the grievous suffering and oppression of long
illness.   The ancient quarters at the Queen of England hotel were given up ; and under the roof of
M. Szell—who had married Deák's ward, Mdlle.
Vörösmarty—the old bachelor was surrounded in
his last days with all that loving friendship could
supply.

The house in the little square facing the University, now the home of Deák Ferencz, was
known to every man, woman, and child in Pesth ; for
his withdrawal from the stage of active life had in
no way lessened the feeling of familiar yet revering

affection, with which he was regarded by all classes of his countrymen.

· Judging by the constant and anxious sympathy felt and expressed for the illustrious patient, it would seem as though the whole population of Buda Pesth must be included amongst Deák's personal friends, from the Minister and the great lady of the Court, to the waiter at the Queen of England hotel, to whose child Deák Ferencz had stood godfather.

Nor were the King and Queen of Hungary behind-hand in showing their regard for the dying states-man, who had served both King and country so faithfully for forty years.

Only a few days before his death, Deák received pleasure from a special message of affectionate inquiry from the royal palace at Buda,—a pleasure which he was at no pains to conceal. In the sentiment with which the veteran citizen regarded the lawful sovereign of Hungary, there was some-thing of the very ideal of loyalty; the stout-hearted patriot, who in the course of his life had spoken more plain truths when face to face with his sovereign than many a demonstrative republican would have dared to utter, was yet not ashamed of owning to a belief in that old-fashioned superstition of personal loyalty, which is sometimes thought to have disappeared as completely from the con-siderations of all rational politicians, as a belief in divine right itself. And the peculiar relations which had subsisted for many years between Deák and the Emperor Francis Joseph, had only served to intensify this abstract loyalty to the constitutional Sovereign,—always so strangely characteristic of the proud, law-loving Magyar,—into a feeling of deep personal affection and respect for the reigning King of Hungary and his beautiful consort. On the death of Francis Deák, there was no one who shared more sincerely in the grief of the Hungarian people over the loss of their great countryman, than the royal lady who had visited the dying patriot on his sick-bed, and who with her own hands laid upon his coffin a wreath bearing the inscription, ' To Deák Ferencz ; Queen Elizabeth.'

The last occasion on which Deák appears before us in the familiar character of the honoured leader and political chief, as well as the friend and favourite of the nation, will be best described in the touching words of a compatriot, who, like Deák himself, has had his share in the troubles and triumphs of Hungary.

' As for years past, so on the last New Year's Day (1876), the members of the party that once bore his name, but who have now coalesced with those who once so energetically opposed his policy, and form the ruling great Liberal party, had decided to go in a body to offer him their best wishes. Though only just recovered from one of those attacks of suffocation which had already become so alarmingly frequent, he insisted on seeing them. There he was, the strong man of former days, who had led with clear intellect and firm hand his willing and trusting followers, prostrated in his arm-chair, which he had scarcely left for the last year and a half; pale, with sunken cheeks and half-closed eyes, while the representatives of the nation stood round him with mourning countenances ; and when the chairman of the party went up close to his chair, and in subdued voice expressed the feelings of the hundreds who crowded the room, Deák raised for a moment his head towards the speaker, his eye revived and passed over those present, and the lips muttered faintly some words of thanks.

'With subdued steps, as if in a place of worship, oppressed with unspeakable sorrow, and the eyes moist with tears, every one withdrew. One long and sad look of farewell was sent to the parting chief, and a mute pressure of the hand, which was exchanged, expressed the general sad conviction that we should see him no more.'

The long struggle was indeed nearly over ; Deák's work for Hungary was at length to end, but to end only with his life.

During the last week of January 1876, it was known that he had become worse, and all through the day crowds of anxious inquirers thronged the square, waiting for the latest tidings of the sick man. On the 28th, his strength failed rapidly, and in the evening of that day, the hurried summons of the Finance Minister, M. Szell, from the House, announced that the end was come.

Deák Ferencz was dead, and Hungary had to mourn the loss of one of the noblest, purest-minded citizens who had ever stood forth to defend the rights of his country, since the kingdom of St. Stephen was first founded on the banks of the Danube.

The veteran patriot was 'the dead of the nation.' In the great hall of the Academy, which nine years ago had resounded with the cheers that had greeted the announcement of the victory which Deák had won for his country, his body lay in state, that his fellow-citizens might come—now in deep and sorrowful silence—to gaze for the last time on the once familiar form,—the broad brow and rugged features ennobled with the mysterious dignity of death, the snow-white hair and thick drooping moustache, blanched with suffering and illness rather than with age.

The long procession to the cemetery, where the grave was dug in earth sent from each of the fifty-two counties of Hungary, the streets hung with black, the weeping crowds,—these were but the natural and spontaneous tokens of the nation's heart-felt grief at losing the honoured, citizen, who, for forty years had spent his life ungrudgingly in the service of Hungary, and who had loved his country not only well but wisely.

CHAPTER XXXV.

AT the time when all Hungary had been anxiously seeking for some fitting reward to bestow on the successful champion of the constitutional liberties of the country; when the Emperor himself, fully recognising the service which his Hungarian subject had rendered to the whole monarchy, would gladly have found some way in which to do honour to the loyal citizen of Pesth, Deák had refused all recompense; desiring only, he declared, that when he died the King might say over his grave, 'Deák Ferencz was an honest man.'

No one would deny that he had full right to this modest epitaph. An honest man he had assuredly been, from the day when the young deputy, in no burst of passing enthusiasm, buoyed up with no false hopes of speedy success, but with a steady determination to serve his country, had resolved to take his share in stimulating and guiding the reforming zeal of the nation, down to the last year of his life, when, in the interests of the Liberal cause in Hungary, he generously held out the hand of good-fellowship to those who had once been his most vehement political opponents.

But not even his great statesmanlike abilities and absolute honesty of purpose could have given Deák the extraordinary hold he exercised over the minds and affections of his countrymen, had he not possessed at the same time, that fervent, deeply rooted enthusiasm for Hungary, which makes 'patriotism' the cardinal point in the political creed of every true Magyar.

A patriot he was to the backbone; but one who felt, as he once said, 'that he had it in him to love his country even more than he hated his country's enemies.' 'A white raven,' a German writer has called Deák, 'a Magyar who did not hate the Saxon.' It is this large-minded charity, in his public as well as in his private relations, which lends a special charm to the character of the keen, fearless patriot, with his masculine force of intellect and sturdy penetrating common sense.

Deák's love of his country, his absolute confidence in the all-sufficient power and ultimate triumph of law and a good cause, were so deeply grounded, that he could afford to extend some sympathy and generous consideration even to those whose national and political aspirations were sometimes supposed to be detrimental to the interests of the Magyar-

Orszag.[1]   In his private relations this natural kindliness was never allowed to warp his conduct nor make him deviate from the principles of justice; and he always sought to act in the spirit of his own maxim, 'Generosity is a good thing, but there is something better, and that is justice;' yet none the less did it pervade all that he did and said, and enabled him to refuse an unreasonable request in such a manner, as to send away the applicant resigned to the requirements of justice, if not convinced.

If we consider what the result of his work and influence has been, we shall acknowledge that the people of Hungary were justified in trusting, as they did so implicitly, in the patriotism and wisdom of Deák Ferencz, that, according as he gave the word, the most fiery and impulsive spirits in the nation would consent to remain quiescent in silent endurance, the most cautious and passive would nerve themselves to encounter the risks of a vigorous resistance.   We have seen that it was in no small measure owing to the influence of Francis Deák, that the independent, vivacious, law-loving spirit of old Hungary wisely adapted itself betimes to the altering conditions of a new age, and that the reformed Constitution, now become a treasure well worth defending not only by a privileged class but by the nation as a whole, was able to survive the

[1] The Kingdom of Hungary.

terrible disruption of 1849. When the blow fell, Hungary was already armed with a strength which enabled her to emerge from the ordeal, weak it is true, and for the time helpless, but full of the capacity for future action ; and preserving uninjured, in the charter of her lawful and constitutional rights, a weapon that, when guided by the hand of a true statesman, availed to win for her complete and lasting victory.

Deák, as has been said, was before all else a Hungarian patriot, a Magyar of the Magyars ; but he was something more than this. That which distinguishes him even amongst the most eminent of his countrymen, that which gives him his title to the name of 'statesman,' was not only his power of realising with keen perception and pursuing with unwearied zeal and courage a single political truth, but the calm far-reaching wisdom which enabled him to see this truth in relation to other truths, and to shape his actions accordingly.

During the thirty-five years that elapsed between 1833, when Deák first took his seat in the Diet at Presburg, and 1867, when, under a Hapsburg Emperor duly crowned King of Hungary, a free representative Parliament, presided over by a responsible national Ministry, assembled for the first time in Pesth,—Hungary had passed through such a period of internal change and convulsion, of outward storm and conflict, as few nations have

experienced.   But during all that time, Deák
himself never once departed from the line he had
originally adopted as the rule and motive of his
political action.   It is no exaggeration to say, that
there were certain critical times in the history of
Hungary, when Deák held in his hand the destinies of
his country, and consequently of the whole monarchy;
times when a single speech from the trusted leader
—whose long silence had only heightened his influence among his countrymen—might have made
the peaceful restoration of the former relations between Hungary and the Austrian Empire an utter
impossibility.

The very contrast between the calm reticence, the
habitual moderation of the lawyer-statesman, and
the passionate, impetuous disposition of his fellow-
citizens, with their natural promptitude to action
and quickly roused enthusiam, gave him a power
which, had he willed, he might have used in
inflaming the nation to such a pitch of patriotic
resistance to the sovereign authority, as would have
made it impossible for a Hapsburg ever again to
wear the crown of St. Stephen with the free consent
of his Hungarian subjects.

But to what end had Deák used his power?
For the assertion and defence of law.   He did
not attempt to excite the people by appeals to their
patriotism, to their love of liberty and independence, to the recollection of their past wrongs—

though none felt these more keenly than himself. He appealed throughout to that side of the Hungarian nature which few but he could have touched with such magical effect—to that innate reverence for law, which he showed by his own example to be no unworthy or insufficient motive in the conduct of public life. He perceived that in this reverence for law was to be found the true secret of Hungary's greatness in the past ; that it was this, even more than the brilliant valour, the devoted patriotism of the Magyars, which had kept their ancient Constitution in existence for eight centuries. Therefore, in spite of all perplexity, danger, and temptation, he remained steadily true to his watchword of strict fidelity to the law ; from which followed, as was natural, loyalty both to King and people.

There were times, when this staunch adherence to an abstract principle might seem to put him out of sympathy with the mass of his countrymen ; if so, Deák was prepared to see the leadership of the nation pass into other hands ; for he could not be false to himself and the tenour of his whole life, for the sake of dealing more easily with the passing exigencies, or even the imperious necessities, of the moment. He never lost sight of the fact, which it takes a nation, says M. Renan, so many lessons to comprehend, 'that it is general principles alone that have a far-reaching application ; and that without them, the most ingenious combinations are at bottom but a matter of chance and good luck.'[1]

On the whole, however, the Hungarian people responded nobly to the appeal of Francis Deák; they were worthy of such a leader; and the leader, it may well be added, was worthy of such a Sovereign as he had in the Emperor Francis Joseph.

The great champion of law could indeed have wished for no better recompense, than that he should live to see Hungary acknowledge of her own free will, the sovereignty of her lawful King, and the Emperor of Austria recognise with equal loyalty, the full right of Hungary to her lawful Constitution. It was no mere courtly compliment when the Emperor declared on the death of his great Hungarian subject, that 'by his fidelity to throne and country, Deák had earned the confidence and affection of his sovereign and his countrymen.'

The statesmen of our day have need of a certain enlightened flexibility, if they would adapt their policy to suit the varying currents of this age of change and development; but none can hope to leave a permanent mark upon his time, to influence successfully the course of events, whose work is not based upon some ruling principle, some 'ground idea.'

The ruling principle of Deák's life, the landmark which neither the darkness of national misfortune,

---

[1] Renan, *Questions Contemporaines.*

nor the dazzling gleams of returning prosperity, could make him lose sight of, was the principle of reverence for law—for that law which is sanctioned both by eternal justice and by the authority of historic tradition ; in obedience to which, kings and people, nations and individuals, alike find the truest freedom.

Surely among the countrymen of Somers, of Hampden, and of Burke, of men who in deed and word have shown how reverence for law may be combined with the staunchest patriotism, the history of Deák's work should meet with special sympathy and interest.

The new phase upon which Hungary has entered, bids fair to offer no lack of difficulties and dangers. But if the past may be taken as an augury for the future, we may well believe that the nation which has come safely through so many perils in the past, is not destined to succumb under the new dangers and perplexities of the present.

There is no better wish that Englishmen can form for the noble country which has so many links of affinity with their own, than that the spirit and the principles of Deák Ferencz may find many followers amongst the politicians whose duty it will be to influence and guide the future destinies of Hungary.

LONDON : PRINTED BY WILLIAM CLOWES AND SONS, STAMFORD STREET
AND CHARING CROSS.

Messrs. MACMILLAN & Co.'s
PUBLICATIONS.

Bismarck in the Franco - German War. An Authorised Translation from the German of Dr. MORITZ BUSCH. Two vols. Crown 8vo. 18*s*.

The *Athenæum* says :—"Their importance to historical students, and to all who care for an insight into the inner complications of one of the most marvellous periods of modern history, and for a comprehension of the wonderful man figuring in the centre of it, is of the greatest. Nobody can understand the political history of the Franco-German War, nor the man Bismarck, its chief maker, who has not read the diary of the Reichskanzler's Boswell."

The Daily News Correspondence of the War BETWEEN GERMANY AND FRANCE, 1870–1. Edited with Notes and Comments. New Edition, complete in One Volume. With Maps and Plans. Crown 8vo. 6*s*.

The Daily News Correspondence of the War BETWEEN RUSSIA AND TURKEY, TO THE FALL OF KARS. Crown 8vo. 6*s*.

—— FROM THE FALL OF KARS TO THE CONCLUSION OF PEACE. 6*s*.

COMMANDER CAMERON'S JOURNEY THROUGH SYRIA AND THE EUPHRATES VALLEY.

Our Future Highway to India. By V. L. CAMERON, Commander, R.N. Two vols. Crown 8vo. With Illustrations and Map. 21*s*.

Cyprus as I saw it in 1879. By Sir SAMUEL W. BAKER, F.R.S., &c., Author of "Ismailia," "The Albert Nyanza," &c. 8vo., with Frontispiece, 12*s*. 6*d*.

"The book may safely be pronounced to be by far the most valuable contribution that has yet appeared towards enabling us to form an impartial estimate of the present condition and future prospects of our new acquisition."—*Academy*.

Cyprus; its History, its present Resources, and FUTURE PROSPECTS. By R. HAMILTON LANG, late H.M.'s Consul for the Island of Cyprus. With Four Maps and Two Illustrations. 8vo. 14*s*.

"The fair and impartial account of her past and present to be found in these pages has an undoubted claim on the attention of all intelligent readers."—*Morning Post*.

The Annals of our Time. A Diurnal of Events, Social and Political, Home and Foreign, from the Accession of Queen Victoria to the Peace of Versailles. By JOSEPH IRVING. Fourth Edition. 8vo., half bound. 16*s*.

Supplement. From Feb. 28, 1871, to March 19, 1874. 8vo. 4*s*. 6*d*.

Second Supplement. From March 1874, to July 1878. 8vo. 4*s*. 6*d*.

"We have before us a trusty and ready guide to the events of the past thirty years, available equally for the statesman, the politician, the public writer, and the general reader."—*Times*.

MESSRS. MACMILLAN & Co.'s

PUBLICATIONS.

Life of Victor Emmanuel II., First King of Italy.
By G. S. GODKIN. Two vols. Crown 8vo. 16*s*.

" An extremely clear and interesting history of one of the most important changes of later times."—*Examiner*.

Napoleon I.—THE HISTORY OF NAPOLEON I. By P. LANFREY. A Translation with the sanction of the Author. Four vols. 8vo. Vols. I., II., and III., price 12*s*. each. Vol. IV., with Index. 6*s*.

The Seven Weeks' War ; its Antecedents and Inci-DENTS. By H. M. HOZIER. New Edition. Crown 8vo. 6*s*.

France since the First Empire. By JAMES MAC-DONELL. Edited with Preface by his Wife. Crown 8vo. 6*s*.

Memoirs of the Right Hon. William, Second VISCOUNT MELBOURNE. By W. M. TORRENS, M.P. With Portrait after Sir T. Lawrence. Second Edition. Two vols. 8vo. 32*s*.

Fifty Years of My Life. By GEORGE THOMAS, Earl of Albemarle. With Steel Portrait of the first Earl of Albemarle, engraved by JEENS. Third and Cheaper Edition. Crown 8vo. 7*s*. 6*d*.

Life of William, Earl of Shelburne, afterwards FIRST MARQUIS OF LANSDOWNE. With Extracts from his Papers and Correspondence. By Lord EDMOND FITZMAURICE. In Three vols. 8vo. Vol I. 1737–1766, 12*s*. ; Vol. II. 1766–1776, 12*s*. ; Vol. III. 1776–1805, 16*s*.

The Holy Roman Empire. By JAMES BRYCE, D.C.L. Sixth Edition, revised and enlarged. Crown 8vo. 7*s*. 6*d*.

The History of Italy. By the Rev. W. HUNT, M.A. 8vo. 3*s*.

A History of the Commonwealth of Florence from THE EARLIEST INDEPENDENCE OF THE COMMUNE TO THE FALL OF THE REPUBLIC in 1831. By T. ADOLPHUS TROLLOPE. Four vols. 8vo., half-morocco. 21*s*.

www.ingramcontent.com/pod-product-compliance
Lightning Source LLC
Chambersburg PA
CBHW021759110726
47902CB00006B/1584